A *NEW YORK TIMES* BESTSELLER

ONE OF *PEOPLE'S*
TOP 10 BOOKS OF 2016

A *WASHINGTON POST* BESTSELLER

A *LOS ANGELES TIMES* BESTSELLER

A *USA TODAY* BESTSELLER

ONE OF VULTURE'S 100 GREATEST
BEACH BOOKS EVER

"[Ephron] excels at [depicting] characters' unintended comedy, their emotional warfare and witty observations of travel and consumption ... with a deft, stinging touch. They are a wise reminder that the hungers driving these people are a ravenous, even violent, business."
—*THE NEW YORK TIMES BOOK REVIEW*

"Delia Ephron's *Siracusa* is a stunning portrait of two marriages coming unraveled during the stress of travel abroad. Insightful and engaging. A must-read!"
—SUE GRAFTON, AUTHOR OF *X*

"Delia Ephron writes like a warm-blooded Patricia Highsmith, her story's treachery matched by a deep and easy feel for the various human, imperfect ways that people find themselves bound together, and sometimes painstakingly unbind themselves. An absorbing, tense, and original novel."
—MEG WOLITZER,
AUTHOR OF *THE INTERESTINGS*

Praise for *Siracusa*

"The word 'unputdownable' is somewhat overused when describing a good book—but really, I just could not put this book down. Delia Ephron's *Siracusa* is a dark tale with incredibly well-drawn characters. It reveals the slights and secrets that can bring about chaos among friends and within families, and adds more than a spoonful of evil into the bargain. I stayed up well past my bedtime to finish."

—Jacqueline Winspear, author of the Maisie Dobbs novels

"*Siracusa* is an Italian aria, a Greek tragedy, and a modern American masterpiece written by Delia Ephron at the height of her powers. This is a story of two complicated marriages, one vulnerable child, and a trip to Italy that changes each of their lives forever. Secrets, lies, love raging, love dying, and the shame of unrealized potential are exposed in detail under the Sicilian sun. And, like the Moro blood oranges that grow there with abandon, the taste is both sour and sweet at once, but the bitterness that remains is not only haunting but unforgettable."

—Adriana Trigiani, author of *The Shoemaker's Wife*

"*Siracusa* is dazzling. Here is Delia Ephron with a stunning noir tale of marriage and morality, as two couples tangled in secret longings and betrayals travel through Italy, along with a gimlet-eyed ten-year-old daughter who could have been created by Henry James. Beware. You will be up all night to finish. I was."

—Marie Brenner, author of *Apples and Oranges*

"A seductive and edgy dissection of two imploding marriages—
and an unhinged mother-daughter alliance. . . . Each of these
toxic relationships puts the characters on course to careen head-
long into a dark place of deceit and rage in Ephron's brilliant
takedown of marital and familial pretense."

—*Publishers Weekly* (starred review)

"[*Siracusa*] starts innocuously enough, as an ironic travelogue
about American sophisticates abroad. . . . The situation begins to
resemble a Ford Madox Ford novel, with each narrator recount-
ing and interpreting the same encounters from vastly differing
perspectives. . . . As the clues pile up, the coming storm is expertly
foreshadowed—but when it arrives, it's utterly surprising."

—*Kirkus Reviews*

"A master of precise and keen character development, a virtuoso of
pacing and surprise, a wizard at skewering convention and expec-
tation, Ephron offers a bewitching take on relationships—marital,
parental, casual, and serious—in this read-in-one-sitting, escapist
escapade with a message." —*Booklist*

"[A] suspenseful, thoroughly delicious tale. You can almost taste
the gelato." —*People*

Also by Delia Ephron

SIRACUSA

DELIA EPHRON

BLUE RIDER PRESS

NEW YORK

blue
rider
press

An imprint of Penguin Random House LLC
375 Hudson Street
New York, New York 10014

LIBRARY OF CONGRESS CATALOGING-IN-PUBLICATION DATA

Names: Ephron, Delia, author.
Title: Siracusa / Delia Ephron, author.
Description: New York: Blue Rider Press, [2016].
Identifiers: LCCN 2016007679 (print) | LCCN 2016013168 (ebook) |
ISBN 9780399165214 (hardcover) | ISBN 9781101621530 (ePub)
Subjects: LCSH: Americans—Italy—Fiction. | Married people—Fiction. |
Marital conflict—Fiction. | Adultery—Fiction. | Domestic fiction. |
BISAC: FICTION / Contemporary Women. | FICTION / Literary.
Classification: LCC PS3555.P48 S565 2016 (print) | LCC PS3555.P48 (ebook) |
DDC 813/.54—dc23
LC record available at http://lccn.loc.gov/2016007679
p.   cm.

Blue Rider Press hardcover: July 2016
Blue Rider Press paperback: June 2017
Blue Rider Press paperback ISBN: 9780735212329

Printed in the United States of America
1   3   5   7   9   10   8   6   4   2

Original hardcover book design by Gretchen Achilles

Should I get married? Should I be good?
Astound the girl next door with my velvet suit and faustus hood?

—GREGORY CORSO, "Marriage"

SIRACUSA

Lizzie

I HAVE A SNAPSHOT of me standing on Finn's shoulders when I was twenty-nine, a trick we'd perfected. I would sprint toward him and work up enough steam to climb his back to his shoulders. I look triumphant and not a little surprised to have done this—it was unlikely I would ever stand on a man's shoulders, having been neither a cheerleader nor a gymnast, and I am not physically daring (a deficiency). I was unhappy that day on a Maine beach fifteen years ago, but you'd never know it from the four-by-six glossy. Finn and I broke up that afternoon.

In the photo I am looking at now, you can read my mind. I am depressed. I'm hunched on a stone bench, wearing a black quilted jacket, not flattering. There I am looking like winter on a June day. Behind me in the distance lies the little port, dotted with sailboats and small yachts, one of Siracusa's few sweet spots.

My hair, always a tumble, is messy in a way that suggests I hadn't bothered with it. My eyes are hidden behind sunglasses. This seems intentional. I was confronting the camera, my face turned toward it but flat. I had neither the inclination nor the energy to strike a pose.

Who took the picture? I can't remember. Events that day are muddy. Suppressed? It's been a year and some of us no longer speak, not the ones that you would expect or maybe you would. I didn't. Since the photo is on my cell, odds are Michael is the photographer, although possibly not, because I am centered in the photo. The subjects in Michael's shots are frequently missing the tops of their heads or their arms.

Snow should never have been on the vacation at all. It was a grown-ups' trip, but Taylor never went anywhere without her, so Finn said. Although you never know in a marriage who is responsible for what, do you? Husbands and wives collaborate, hiding even from themselves who is calling the shots and who is along for the ride.

She was ten years old and a mystery, Finn and Taylor's daughter. "She is brilliant," said Taylor, but in England the year before Snow had spoken rarely and then softly. Her mother had ordered for her. The waiter would look at Snow studying the menu, clearly intelligent, and Taylor would speak. Snow often read straight through a meal, the iPad on her lap. When I asked her a direct question, she looked to her mother. Anxious, I'd thought. For rescue. "You prefer milk chocolate, don't you?" said Taylor. "You loved that movie *Pitch Perfect*? Didn't we see it three times?"

For Michael and me Snow was wallpaper.

I've barely begun, and undoubtedly with that remark, I've turned you against me. I'm like that, unpleasantly blunt. Some people like it, some hate it. I tend not to worry. Finn would be horrified to hear that even if he were not Snow's father, but not Michael because he's a writer. Writers often forgive cruel observations. They even admire them. It makes them feel empowered, justified, off the hook for their own ruthless words. For doing that thing writers think is their right: taking a friend, swallowing him (or her) whole, and turning him into a character to suit their own fictional purposes.

The trip was my idea, a moment of spontaneity, enthusiasm, and slight inebriation. Liquor played a role right from the start.

Since our summer fling years before, Finn and I had maintained an attachment that neither of us fully understood. We were given to bursts of e-mail intimacy, intense for a few months, then lapsing for longer. The intermittent friendship was solely between us. We'd been at each other's weddings, but the four of us never got together socially. Then I discovered that by chance we'd all be in London at the same time. We had dinner. Then another and another. We had little in common (except that Finn and I had history, which is not quite the same as something in common). They weren't from our world—Michael's and mine—which turned out to be relaxing, and yet they were curious and playful. Especially Finn. Taylor was obsessed with culture, which I admired, although I wasn't. Good travelers, different travelers. "Where should we meet next year?" I'd said on our last night together. I raised my glass. "To next year."

I still wonder about that moment. What if I'd let that convivial feeling pass?

Taylor mostly planned the trip, her thing, fine by me. Michael normally scours travel books for weeks before we leave, hunting out the obscure and offbeat—on a trip to Paris he'd whisked me off to the Musée de la Vie Romantique to see a cast of George Sand's arm and her lover's too, Chopin—but he was in the home stretch on a novel and utterly preoccupied.

I'm used to this. I've done it to him. I haven't written a novel, nothing major like that, but I write too, mostly articles for magazines and websites. Writers have to allow each other a private world. Finishing is always more compelling than anything else, than anything real. A thrilling narcissism sets in. It's so much fun. I could never deprive Michael of that. I was good about tolerating it. I took pride in tolerating it. I put up with silent dinners—a "What?" two minutes after I'd said something interesting.

"It's not a good time to go anywhere," he said.

"It's too late to cancel. It's all in the works, much of it paid for. A break may help you, it really might. Please. I want it desperately."

An eight-day vacation—how could that hurt when I was adrift? Panicked. It was the most difficult time of my life.

Taylor

FROM THE START it was a conspiracy between Lizzie and Finn to be together. Michael and I were in the dark. We'd had such a lovely time the year before in London. We happened to be there when they were, and met several times for dinner. The fivesome was comfortable. Snow really enjoyed it.

Why not repeat the experience?

"That's so brave of you to travel with Lizzie, she is terrifying," my friend April told me. She remembered Lizzie from our wedding. As a toast Lizzie had recited three haikus she'd written about Finn, all about how she never thought he'd get married, and then she presented him with a book, *Toilets of the World*. The book was what it sounds like, photographs of toilets from Appalachia to Madagascar. That is Lizzie, highbrow and low, equally intimidating. Finn loved the book. He kept it on the coffee table. It was his childish notion of a shocker. At the time I found it only silly, the book a bit of foolishness. Looking back, reconsidering everything, I think it was a way for Lizzie to be there every day of our lives, reminding Finn of something, something about the two of them, a kind of *I get you and she doesn't.* Eventually I got rid of the book and Finn never noticed. If something's not in front of his face, it's not on his mind.

I spend a lot of time reconsidering what I thought, but it's nobody else's business. I'm certainly not seeing a shrink. *I* don't have the problem.

Way back when we first got married twelve years ago, Finn was starting the restaurant and we were a good team. I have class. He needed that. He became the hometown boy with something extra, me. I'm from the Upper East Side, the best private schools, Vassar, summa cum laude. My hair was long, thick, blond, and straight. I had power hair. That made me more of a catch. "If you have hair like this," my mother said, "you only need to be half as pretty." Once I'd snared a husband, I didn't need long hair and chopped it off. Now I have it cut at the local men's barbershop. Under my direction, Rudy does it short and slicked back off my face. I keep it smooth and shiny with a L'Oréal gel. No other woman in town goes to Rudy, and it's safe to say that no other Portland woman of my acquaintance has my talent with home hair products. (I'm being funny here, and the reason I point this out is that people often don't know when I'm funny and when I'm not.) Even though Finn complains about the money I spend on clothes, he likes a cutting-edge wife.

It's difficult to keep that up, to maintain originality in Portland, Maine. I find it a welcome challenge.

Finn and I met when I was twenty-six (he was three years older) and teaching English at a private school in New York, Spence, the same one I'd graduated from. I'd stopped in Portland on the way to my summer camp reunion, and he was driving a water taxi, subbing for a friend (unlicensed, he told me later, and I guess that is part of his story). He showed me his "joint," as he called his future restaurant, then just a dusty empty space with grimy leaded windows. We sat on the floor—it was actually a subfloor, the linoleum had been stripped off—and ate lobster rolls. I believed in him, believed that he would be successful, I'm not sure why. Perhaps mere instinct. As a mother I've learned that instinct is very important and some have it and some don't. I have instinct. Besides, on the way there, he'd known every single person we passed. That impressed me. Now I realize everyone knows everyone in Portland.

He wore khaki shorts with big flap pockets. When he came to New York, my mother was horrified. "Men in shorts," she shuddered. And he pronounced the *t* in *often*, one of her personal pet peeves. Out to dinner at Gerard, where jackets and slacks are the rule, he wore them, but not socks.

"You wanted to get away from your mother," said April.

I wanted to shine. It's so much easier to shine in Portland.

I had to improve Finn's wardrobe, which I did by giving him presents, always coming home with a shirt or sweater, gradually weeding out the old. Once a week I threw something of his away or gave it to our cleaning lady for her husband.

Lizzie sent me an e-mail in January. "So is it still Italy?" I was surprised. I'd expected her to forget. I said, "Snow's heart is set on it."

"Works for us," she wrote.

Wonderful, I thought. I was excited. It would be like two

adventures in one, traveling with them and in a foreign country. Besides, Lizzie and Michael could keep Finn busy because Snow and I don't like to stay out late and Finn does. These differences that don't matter at home can be a bit of a hiccup on a vacation. Also, honestly, there is such a thing as too much togetherness, and on a trip Finn and I sometimes run out of things to say. That would never happen if we were with Lizzie and Michael. Still, how stupid was I? Lizzie told me to make all the decisions. Of course she didn't mean that, I realized later, because if Lizzie can't force everyone to do what she wants, she's not happy.

When Lizzie e-mailed, Snow and I had already spent hours together at the computer Googling Venice: gondolas on shimmering water, ancient palazzos, sunburnt colors. "Streets of water?" Snow was captivated.

By nature my daughter is reserved. I always say that Snow is living proof that still waters run deep. Not only is she shy, diagnostically shy (I'll tell you about that later), but some might experience her as aloof. I live for her smiles. When she lights up, I do too.

"We should do all of Italy, not just Venice," I said.

Snow nodded.

This is a tradition, by the way, although I'm not sure it is anymore. Every June we would take a three-week vacation as a family. A blowout. Snow and I would decide where, and for months and months we prepared.

As far as I am concerned there is no point in traveling unless it's five stars. I cannot see flying across the ocean to stay in a hotel room with coarse sheets or with a worse bathroom than the one we have at home. I was figuring Rome, Ravello, Venice. Then Lizzie e-mailed, "How about going to Sicily?"

I ran it by Gloria, our travel agent, who is a treasure. She suggested Taormina. She knew a gem of a place to stay, even knew the manager. Lizzie insisted instead on Siracusa. It doesn't have a five-star hotel—that tells you something right there. A very ancient world, Lizzie assured me, off the beaten track. From Siracusa it was only an hour and a half to Taormina, which she called a tourist trap with a view. If I wanted to go I could hire a car. In fact, Taormina has an extraordinary ruin, a *teatro greco*, but to be accommodating I agreed to skip it. I'm very accommodating, although I'm not sure anyone realizes it.

Lizzie is uncultured. That's something you'd never suspect. "In London, she bragged about never having been to the Tate," I told April. "Trips to other countries should not be wasted. Who brags about missing those remarkable Turners?"

"What's really wrong with Lizzie," said April, "is that she doesn't have children. Women who don't have children are entirely different from those who do."

"She's nice to Snow," I said.

"Nice isn't what I'm talking about. This may be a terrible thing to say but women without children lack depth. Emotionally they're stunted."

Secretly I have always thought that too. Until April said it aloud, however, I had never quite admitted it.

So it was agreed. Lizzie and Michael would be with us on the southern part of the trip: Rome, Siracusa. Then we'd go alone to Ravello and Venice: Snow, Finn, and I.

Finn never asks about vacations. I tell him where we're going, when we're leaving, and pack the clothes, even his.

The day before we left, Snow and I drove to CVS to buy sunblock. "Call me Tawny," she said.

"Tawny?"

"I want to be Tawny."

"Why? I love your name. You were born in a blizzard and the next morning the world was blanketed in beauty. That's why we named you Snow." I had told her this time and again. I thought of it as a lullaby. "Where did you come up with Tawny?"

"Celebrity mug shots. On the computer. There was a woman named Tawny Nichols." Snow is very graceful, and with one movement she smoothed her hand over her head, drawing all her long sleek hair, blond like mine, to the side and over her shoulder. "I'm ready for my mug shot."

"Mug shots are taken when you are arrested."

"I know," she said.

Snow is sometimes unintentionally provocative. It comes from innocence, her naïveté. While I am careful never to react, Finn gets off on it. He laughs and she's never sure if his laughing is good or bad. She looks at me wondering. If it's appropriate I smile. Otherwise I shake my head.

I often think about that conversation with Snow and wonder if it wasn't a warning, if I should have been more protective. No, according to April. Mothers feel guilty about everything even when it's not their fault.

Michael

PROMISED K I'D GET OUT OF IT. Had every intention. Mornings I'd lean against the counter drinking coffee watching Lizzie make a smoothie. The speed with which she can do things in the kitchen used to dazzle me—tops popped on plastic containers, bits of banana, blueberries, whatever tossed into the blender. A handful of ice. The freezer kicked shut while she tipped in the soy. Masterful.

I'd drink my coffee intending to tell her. Any second now. Days went by. Weeks. Aware of my cowardice, if that explains it, I considered telling her while the blender was making that god-awful noise. Telling her when she couldn't hear—a sick amusement. Evenings mostly I wasn't around, and Lizzie provided the excuse, assuming I was at my office. Writing. "You're so involved with that novel."

"You're so involved with that novel, you haven't taken your suitcase out of the closet yet and we're leaving in two days," said my wife, sipping Pinot Noir. Lizzie was obsessed with an Oregon

Pinot Noir. She fixes on things and brags about them, in this case because the top twisted off.

"Someone should have invented this no-cork thing years ago," she said.

Why am I even mentioning this?

Spoken words are irretrievable. They can be bombs.

I don't love you anymore, the man said to his wife, telling one horrible truth, omitting others.

I don't love you anymore and haven't for some time, Elizabeth. I'm not going to Italy. Almost said it out of curiosity. For some excitement. To wake the dead.

But didn't. Couldn't face the hysteria. Her energy turned on me. I understand why men leave notes on mantels and disappear.

The night before the trip, she swabbed a piece of bread in olive oil and was about to pop it in her mouth when she looked up. Here it comes. I saw the thought flit through her head. *I'm happy here.* She was reassuring me, isn't that ridiculous? It doesn't matter that there is not a fucking thing left to say. *I'm happy here.*

There was so much familiarity in our marriage that I didn't need her to be there to be there. I could supply her lines. Her thoughts.

But then I'm a novelist. That's my job.

I recalled a comment Lizzie once made about a couple we knew. "Casting," she said, about their marriage. Probably that's what has kept our marriage going—we're whom we think we should be with, whom everyone else thinks we should be with. Everyone who matters in New York City. In our circle. Journalists. Editors. Writers. I'm being ironic. I'm not that much of an asshole.

At least we were traveling with Finn and Taylor and that child of theirs who keeps to herself. It would relieve the monotony of scraping the bottom of my brainpan to find something to say to L that isn't hostile. That was my thinking to the extent I thought about it. I couldn't be friends with Finn. He doesn't read, that I'd ever noticed. Not that I have a lot of male friends. The very idea of friends seems female. But he's a great traveler and I am not. I prefer to be home, especially preferred it then.

It's madness to travel with a woman you've lost interest in. The isolation. The sexual expectations, which I had no intention of fulfilling. At least in that manner I could be loyal.

Finn

I CAN TELL MY STORY as well as the rest of them. Although I'll mess with you now and then, I warn you. I like to do that. Until I took this trip, I didn't grasp all the angles I could play.

"Forget Michael and Taylor. Let's just us go," I told Lizzie.

I said things like that to frazz her. Lizzie's cute when she's frazzed. She pretended I hadn't said it and went all Hillary Clinton on me, super serious, like she was planning a Mideast summit. "I think we should go to Siracusa."

"I'm not kidding. Let's ditch them."

"Siracusa looks falling down and great."

"You know you'd rather travel with me than Michael."

She kept repeating it. "Siracusa." Like I knew where it was. What it was. Like anyone did. Lizzie's nuts. Wherever it was— in Sicily it turned out, western or eastern coast, whatever—I figured it was good for Tay. I said, "Get Taylor someplace real."

Taylor is a good person, she's a great mother, and she knows how to take care of things, but if she never spoke to a foreigner she'd be happy. She works up a sweat about these trips, about all the art, the architecture, the culture, then hires a guide to whisk her and Snow around and about. Nothing unexpected. Nothing left to chance. Spending money. She's genius at spending money. My money.

On the buildup to this fiasco, Lizzie and I were texting ten times a day. I started hounding her at Christmas. "Italy in June. Remind Tay, remind Tay, *grazie prego.*" Badgered Lizzie's brains out. Taylor had no idea I was feeding Lizzie, making it happen, getting a bit of control. What's that called? Passive aggressive. I was having a passive-aggressive field day pulling Lizzie's strings so she'd pull Taylor's, and getting off on it. It never crossed Tay's mind.

I swear I could come home dead drunk—I have—and as long as it didn't interfere with Snow's homework or bedtime, Tay wouldn't notice.

I was smoking again. And worried she was going to detect it and go ballistic. Smoking. It's worse than drinking in this fucked-up world. Worse than some felonies but don't quote me on that. I'm just blowing smoke. Thank God for Binaca. I used it like bug spray. Round the clock.

I was considering seeing a shrink.

That's not what you would expect. You'd expect one of the other three would have been going that direction, but I was screwed up. Cheating. It was on my mind.

I should have married Lizzie, although she wouldn't be half the mother Taylor is.

"Taylor is very organized and efficient," said Lizzie. "She's brilliant at what she does."

Taylor, who runs the Portland Visitors' Bureau, has single-handedly increased tourism by five percent, and yours truly benefits from that. But who was Lizzie kidding? She thought if she said that to me about Taylor, I'd think she liked Taylor. She tolerated Taylor because Lizzie had a thing for me. Women think men are stupid, or at any rate stupider than they are.

"Taylor will take care of me in my old age," I told Lizzie. "If I get an awful disease, I know she'll be there at the hospital, bossing the doctors."

"How do you know you'll die first?" said Lizzie. "You know what? I hope you get a horrible disease so she can take care of you. I hate to think you're staying in a marriage for something that's never going to happen."

Not that she's wrong, but over time Lizzie's personality could do you in.

But she's fun. First Siracusa night and day and then she was off and running about how Sicily invented ice cream, it's her favorite food, and we had to go there and eat it. Those tourist books are full of crap. But Siracusa sounded great, Lizzie great. She'll take a meaningless thing and spin it until we're like dogs, tongues hanging out, panting to go. Signing her e-mails Angelina Pistachio, Carmela Vanilla.

Siracusa fucked up Taylor's whole trip, which, truth be told, I loved.

Rome, Day 1

Lizzie

MICHAEL SUFFERS HORRIBLY from jet lag, and it takes a few days before he's functioning on all cylinders. Upon our arrival at Cesare Due, having left the taxi and deposited our luggage with the bellman, we collided. What I mean is, while entering the hotel we attempted to pass through the entrance at the same time and nearly became wedged there like cartoon characters. "Oh my God, you want a divorce," I said.

Michael looked startled, as if a flowerpot, dropped from above, had narrowly missed him.

I started laughing. "That's a joke, you know, because—"

"Because what?" said Michael. He's querulous when he's wiped.

"Nothing. Sorry. Forget it. I'm tired. I don't know what I'm saying."

I have learned when to back off, but here's the thing. Michael has the most perfect manners. He unfailingly helps me on with my coat, lets women exit an elevator first, crosses to the street side when we walk together, and has never once preceded me through a doorway. Before his appendectomy, when he was writhing in pain, he waited for me to enter the emergency room ahead of him. I always thought, and joked to my best friend Rachel, that if he ever walked through a door first, it would mean he was through with me. In Rome, lo and behold, he did it.

That's how jet-lagged he was.

I wasn't surprised that he wanted to sleep the day away, whereas I wanted only a short nap. After leaving a message at the front desk for Finn and Taylor, who had flown to Rome from Boston, I visited the carnival of activity at Piazza Navona, had spaghetti carbonara and a macchiato, and sat for a few lazy hours. Then I went back to the hotel, and was exploring, wandering down a labyrinthine corridor when from behind someone grabbed my hand. I swung around. Finn backed me into a corner.

"What are you doing?" I said.

"Looking for you."

"You are not."

"Looking for the bar," said Finn. "There it is." He pulled me along.

With amber sconces providing the seductive glow of twilight and narrow leather banquettes, the tiny cavelike space had the requisite romantic anonymity of a perfect hotel bar. Couples who don't want to be seen or remembered have rendezvoused here.

He peered around, saw no one serving, scooted out to wave down the hall, and scooted back. A waitress appeared a second later, slim and young in a seriously tight black skirt and a tailored white shirt buttoned to the collar, her hair slicked back in a twist.

"Do you speak French?" he asked her in English.

"No, but I speak English," she said in English.

Finn ordered every bar snack blithely in French, and I do want to explain the significance of this. Finn speaks fluent French because, while the rest of us went to college, he crewed on French yachts. As a result, when in foreign countries, he has a status and respect far beyond his occasionally goofball demeanor and working-class roots. Speaking foreign languages can make an American something more than an American, made Finn something more than Finn. "Do you speak *lingua mista*?" he then asked. She smiled, and into his French he sprinkled some Italian as well as English words like *martinis* and *olives*.

"I can't drink a martini, I'll be on the floor. I'll have a kir, *per favore*."

"*Per favore*." He mimicked my terrible accent and told the waitress that I should be locked in language jail. Now the waitress was laughing.

"Do you live with your mother?" he asked.

"Yes," she said.

In a minute he'll get her to sing the Italian national anthem. Finn can get women to do things they normally do only in front of the mirror. Not that she's singing the national anthem into her bathroom mirror, but you know what I mean. The first time we hung out together, we were wandering around the Portland harbor past ferries and cruise ships very late at night and Finn was quizzing me about everything. Did I like the Eagles (who didn't?), pretzels salted or not (salted), could I salsa? No, but I could tap. I performed my routine to "Take Five" from one end of the pier to the other. I'd studied tap when I was ten. I hadn't tapped since and I have never tapped again. Finn.

"I brought you something," he said. From his shirt pocket he handed me a shiny vacuum-sealed packet of peanuts that read *TWA*.

"TWA? That's a dead airline."

"Not to me," said Finn.

In the middle of our fling, we'd flown to Montreal on TWA and had a big fight there, and I flew back alone. Finn had mentioned he hunts. He had a freezer full of elk steaks. "You eat them, I shoot them, so what?" he said.

"I don't eat elk. I don't go around pointing guns at animals, pulling a trigger, and watching them die."

"You just ate fucking foie gras," he said.

I had. At a great restaurant, Les Amis de Pierre.

"So you own a gun?" I said.

"A thirty-ought-six," he said.

I'll never forget the name because it was so weird. Then it occurred to me. "I bet you don't believe in gun control?"

"Suppose I need to protect my family?" he said.

What was I doing with him? What? He was a Republican. Every digging deeper led to massive disagreement, even screaming, but I was having fun. Fun was Finn's specialty. I felt free around him too. Fun and free turned out to be rare enough to create lasting affection.

I knew the affair was temporary. I was on my way to New York City. Besides, speaking of foie gras, Finn was dessert. To take him seriously was to commit to an all-sugar diet.

"Seriously, TWA? Where'd you get this?"

Finn grinned. I knew I'd get nowhere.

"Where are Taylor and Snow?"

"In the room. They'll be down eventually."

I ripped open the packet expecting to see black shriveled bits, and instead found perfectly ordinary golden-brown nuts. "Eat one, I dare you."

Finn threw a few into his mouth and chewed.

Shortly I was on my second kir.

"Your eyeballs are spinning," said Finn. "Wait till Michael sees you four sheets to the wind."

"Michael might not come to dinner. He's beat. I really love these green olives. What happened with Jessa?"

"Nothing yet. What do you think? Should I?"

"I'm not telling you to have an affair."

"Are you available?"

"No, Finn, I'm not available. Will anyone do?"

"No."

Finn was incapable of not flirting. I always ignored it. "When did you start smoking again?"

"Yesterday."

"Liar."

"Want a drag?"

"No, I don't want a drag."

He wrapped his hand around mine and pried the glass from it. "What are you doing?"

"Shut up." He separated my fingers and placed the cigarette between them. At that moment I realized Michael was here.

"Lizzie smokes," said Finn.

"Finn smokes. Take it back," I told Finn. "I don't want that awful smell on my hand. I thought you were sleeping through dinner?"

"I changed my mind."

"Taylor doesn't know I smoke. Don't tell her."

"Finn, we don't want to know things about you that your wife doesn't know." I said this knowing that I knew many things about Finn that Taylor didn't know (and Michael didn't either). About Jessa, for instance. "We really don't."

"Speak for yourself. I don't mind," said Michael. "I like knowing people's secrets. Then I can write about them. Disguised, of course. Macallan, if you have it," he told the waitress. "On the rocks."

Looking back, that trip tricked me out from day one. I *was* flirting. I offered Michael nuts without telling him that they were fifteen years old. In the beginning, I'd have to admit, I was collaborating with Finn.

Michael

THE MAN PHONED AGAIN, feeling a fool. Her cell was turned off. Conclusion (obvious) he drew when unable to reach his lover, when one ring triggered her voice singing "Jingle Bells." "I love Christmas," she'd told him.

I was getting sloppy. K was not a "contact," but more dangerously a pileup of "recents." Would carelessness rescue me from ambivalence? Should I leave my cell on Lizzie's unpacked suitcase?

I enjoy concealing, lying less so. Some may claim otherwise. I did both, do both. A secret is something you can play with, to keep or give away; a gift or a poisoned dart, it can be either. Concealing may be merely letting other people draw conclusions. As for lying, in this story, which is also my life, I will make a case for the charm of it. *"You will be fooled," he said arrogantly.*

I'd stopped in at Tino's for a drink. Eight months ago. Early November. I did that occasionally when the writing wasn't happening. Ducked out of my office and around the corner to the local Italian. Coffee break but no coffee. To jump-start the process with Macallan. Writers have been doing that forever. Imagine I'm Irish. We fell into a conversation. Knew each other's names already. Lizzie and I ate there every few months, and K always gave us the table Lizzie liked in the corner. I was ruminating about Julien, his particular need to be accepted and his disdain for the good opinions he craved. "Problems with Julien," I told her when she settled onto the stool next to me.

"Is that your son?"

"I'm a writer. He's a character."

"Julien," she said. "Cool name."

I had to laugh at that. "Based on *The Red and the Black*. A modern version."

She nodded. I knew she didn't know what the hell I was talking about. Intentional on my part. Figured it would impress her. That she would be intimidated and flattered that a man as . . . what? As literate as I was sharing with her, talking to her as if she would know the book, know anything. Character matters. Hers. To seduce, a man divines a woman's insecurity and compliments it. Kath needed respect. I say this in retrospect. Conversation moves too fast to be consciously aware of all one knows.

"What's your given name?" I'd asked.

"Given?" She didn't understand that either.

"Kath is short for what?"

"Kathy."

"You're beautiful."

I didn't expect to say that. Took me by surprise.

Katarina. I rechristened her after I laid her. It's not her fault that her parents had no poetry, bestowing on their daughter a nickname for a name. I'm here to correct the wrongs of her life.

"For God's sake, Kath, turn on your phone. This is solving nothing."

I soaked in the tub (Italian tubs are too narrow, let it be noted), dead tired from the flight, Lizzie mercifully off somewhere. She hits the ground running.

Two in the afternoon in Rome, eight in the morning in NYC. On her days off, K's at the gym by nine. Spin class. Two, she's in my office, naked. Where was she today?

With a man who wants to see those breasts as much as I did?

Blame it on the breasts. Some things must be . . . must be, fuck, what, experienced. They are a siren call. A deathbed regret. She hides them. Clever woman. Attempts to—although not successfully—under big things, oversized sweaters, slinky slippery tops that drop straight from her shoulders to her hips. Technically they resemble landmasses. She's got two continents under there begging to be explored. They shift with the slightest adjustment of her body. She reaches for an olive. She takes a sip of water. She licks her lips. I swear, a movement that minute and her breasts are alive to it.

"If you want to write a woman, put in modifiers," I told her. It was quiet at Tino's at three p.m. Lunch over. Snacks only. A tasteless dip of chickpeas and pimientos, compliments of the house. She didn't know what a modifier was. Kindly I explained: "Woman: 'I'm just so crazy about you.' Man: 'I'm crazy about you.'" It was that easy to seduce her. Subtext.

She was friendly. It was her job to make diners welcome, happy, comfortable. Kath was ready with smiles. Sometimes, in uncertain situations, over her head as was often the case in conversation with me, her cheek twitched in a moment of indecision. She wanted to please. Was a smile the correct response?

I'd asked her about herself. Knowing that men rarely did. She'd been in the city ten years and was still circling, waiting to land. "There's something here for me but I don't know what." She was earnest, a quality one doesn't often encounter, genuinely puzzled by her life. "Why, at thirty-two, am I still living with a roommate rather than married with three kids in Bloomington?"

"I might be the reason," the man suggested.

"Turn on your fucking phone, Kath. Fuck it. I'm going out."

I was on my way to the bar for fortification. Dinner would be less irritating. Liquor oils the nerves. "First doorway on the right, signor." The porter directed me.

As I was about to enter, an instinct that I was intruding caused a sharpening up. Have you ever found yourself wandering aimlessly through a museum and a painting stops you? Arrests you? Penetrates the self-centered fog. Like that. Tucked into the corner banquette was a woman, a stunner, brown hair in a tangle falling into her face, dark eyes lit bright and shining. I shifted to take it all in, the man whose hands cupped hers. She was pulling away, laughing. "Stop it, Finn."

Lizzie.

A man doesn't recognize his own wife. Because she's happy.

Lizzie with Finn. Lizzie and Finn. Of course.

On the way to dinner, I detoured to the room. "Need to make a note about something," I'd explained to them all gathered in the stylish paneled lobby overwhelming the space the way Americans do.

"For his novel," said Lizzie. She waved a map. "I know where we're going."

"You start. I'll catch up."

"Of course we'll wait. You'll get lost."

"Kath, pick up. Katarina, I have a plan." I didn't say, *Trust me*. Avoid clichés. I'm not a cad. *Cad*: an old-fashioned word but a good one. Best not to remind her of the many years between us. "I'm not a dog," I said instead. "Impossibly difficult, I know, sweet Katarina, but be patient. This trip will solve everything."

It will even be a favor to Lizzie. New York is finished with her. She had a modest little run but now it's over. One day she will thank me.

Taylor

I READ AN ARTICLE about how damaging it is to find out that nothing was as you thought. I forget where I read it. The *Press Herald* or the *Maine Sunday Telegram*. It could not have been *Vogue*, the only magazine I subscribe to besides *Parents*. Usually I don't recognize the starlet on the cover of any magazine. With her baby bump. (I do think that is a cute expression.) I'm not someone who combs the Internet to waste my day or fill my brain with inconsequential data. I don't surf gossip websites. My friend Betsy sends me links to unusual animal stories, which I enjoy and show to Snow, like a dog that is friends with a gorilla or a duck that can sing.

I'm very busy. Mayor Beemer e-mails me as often as three times a day. I don't think anyone realizes how important tourism is to the Portland economy. Most people, if asked, would say lobstering is the primary source of income for the city, but would you be surprised to learn that there are twenty or so Jet-Ski rentals on Casco Bay? Twenty Jet-Ski rentals on a coastline less than twenty miles long.

Am I meandering? My mother used to draw her finger across her throat whenever I did that. "You are a long trail through the woods," she said. "And in the woods people prefer a shortcut."

Our first day in Rome. Let's start there. Thank goodness our room was ready. We all fell asleep within seconds of arriving and woke up around four. Finn went off for a stroll and was mercifully out of our hair. He is always climbing the walls in hotel rooms. The second we walk in, he turns on the television. That's a given. The only channel in English was the BBC. I don't like to hear news when I travel. I like to imagine that I am in a world where nothing happens except what happens to Snow and me. A mother-daughter adventure not cluttered up with Angola, a country no one hears about in the United States but comes up a lot on foreign television. The BBC backdrops are dreary and English news commentators don't dress with much style. I don't like their accent either. It seems put on. Have you ever wondered why Americans don't speak the way the English do? They settled America. They invented English, not us. It tells you something about Americans that we gave up that fake pompous accent.

This is an example of why travel is important. It changes perspective. It alters your eyes and ears, puts unexpected notions into your head, provides aha moments. That's what I always tell Snow.

Whenever we go on a trip, Finn, Snow, and I stay in the same room. Snow and I sleep in the double bed. Finn takes the cot because he stays out late. That way no one gets disturbed. Because of running a restaurant, Finn is an owl. Sex in this culture, its importance, is overrated, and that is the last I'm going to say on the subject.

I loved the hotel, which was not the case in Siracusa, and I do wonder how much of a role that played, as a bad hotel room is very discombobulating. At the Cesare Due our room was spacious, the furniture old and elegant, a bureau with a bow front, deep drawers, curved legs, and gilt trim in charming need of touching up. The maroon rug with a border of tiny white diamonds had been recently installed; I could tell because the color was almost too bright and the texture prickly in a new-carpet way. I didn't feel squeamish walking in bare feet as I did in Siracusa, where the floor was tile and worrisome as far as sanitation is concerned. I fell in love with the silver-and-white-striped wallpaper (I am always looking for ideas I can apply at home). The silver was shiny, the white matte. I took photos of that and of the sage drapes with swags.

From very tall windows was a lovely view onto a small piazza with a kiosk. I drew Snow's attention to that and to the pots of daisies surrounding it that were especially picturesque.

Because I always wrap each of our toiletries separately in plastic wrap, Snow and I had a lot of unpeeling to do. This was how I happened to notice the only thing I didn't like about our room, the disposable plastic bag form-fitted to the leather wastebasket and folded over the top.

At the time of the trip Snow hadn't yet had her growth spurt—as had many of her classmates—and her breasts were just beginning to bud. She was a tender sprout of a girl still, but clearly a beauty like her mom. That's a joke but, in all seriousness, we do look alike and turn heads, and occasionally people kid Finn, "Are you sure you had anything to do with her?" It makes me laugh. She is pure Seddley. I have shown her a photograph of her great-grandmother Charlotte Seddley as a child to prove it—wide-set gray eyes with a penetrating, I might even say hypnotic, gaze, a heart-shaped face with a delicate pointed chin. I had worried that her nose would be a lump like Aunt Janny's, but it has narrowed to aristocratic elegance. Her lips are thin (Finn's contribution, his Irish heritage), thank goodness not horrible and measly like a keyhole, which some of his relatives have, only a mite less plump than might be optimum. She is reserved in manner, part of her shyness, and rarely surrenders to extremes like a fit of giggles. Her smiles are modest, lips together. Most often I see her even, perfect teeth when she brushes them, a slight exaggeration. Of course I should not forget to mention the Seddley crowning glory: thick, straight twenty-four-karat-gold hair.

We are a pair.

When she was a baby, she had the softest, loopiest curls. While she slept I would lean over her crib and twirl one around my finger. I keep this in my memory bank filed under moments of pure happiness. Snow in her crib, safe and sound, her heart beating. I always checked to make certain of that.

Sometimes I think about the mother of that Lindbergh child, kidnapped, snatched at night, or the mother of Elizabeth Smart, the Mormon girl. The stark raving horror of an empty bed. The helplessness. The shriek. I imagine it went on forever. Even when that mother had stopped screaming, she was still screaming. We are different, mothers, because we understand the terror of that possibility.

The day after I gave birth to Snow—at 5:58 p.m., November 22—and Finn was bounding up and down the corridor inviting the nurses to the restaurant for a free meal, I spiked a fever of 104. They stabbed me with an IV and pumped me with antibiotics. They never did understand the cause, but I knew it was dread. The dread of realizing how vulnerable I now was, the fearsome responsibility of having a baby and keeping her safe.

In Rome that first evening, while I brushed her hair, which I love to do, I kept up a patter about what we might eat for dinner, the sights we would see tomorrow. I always do that. Preparation lessens anxiety, that's my belief. Snow bit her nails. I shouldn't mention that. It makes her sound like a little animal and not the graceful preteen she is. But, and I do hope she grows out of it, she does bite her nails to the nub. This is all part of what her pediatrician diagnosed, when she was five, as extreme shyness syndrome. Finn said, *Bullshit.* He said it right to the doctor. Brenda, who is outspoken—that's the most polite way to describe my mother-in-law—backed Finn up. She said she'd never heard anything so quacked.

"You want to wear my earrings," I said to Snow. It wasn't a question. I can often read her thoughts. I had bought the tiny platinum crosses studded with diamonds at Tiffany. I always tell people that they were an engagement present from Finn, and they were, but from myself to me. Snow was too young for them, but given the special occasion, our first night in Rome, "Stay still," I told her. An unnecessary admonishment as I've never known Snow to fidget in the least. I took out her amethyst studs and replaced them with my diamonds.

Surprisingly—I say surprisingly because I expected her to appreciate herself in the mirror—she hoisted herself onto the bureau.

She sat there surveying the realm. Of course she wasn't. I don't know why I described her that way. She perched on top of the bureau until I was dressed and ready to go.

Leaving the hotel, Snow looked both ways not once but several times. She always does that. I noticed Lizzie noticing that too before she saw me and looked away. It's not as if she hadn't seen it before, in London. Snow is always hesitant moving from inside to out. On the quietest, narrowest street my child acts as if she is crossing a busy four-lane highway.

My hand in hers gives her security.

Lizzie led the way, waving a map for all to see, calling attention to us as tourists. Has she never heard of blending in? She never "modulates," April's word when I described Lizzie shouting out turns as if we were a tour group from Pittsburgh. (She never did that in London, but we had all been there before and knew it quite well.) Finn flaked along by himself as usual. He is not what I would describe as the escorting type. In our restaurant he's very good about making sure diners are happy. He buzzes from table to table, he has a knack for it, but when the three of us are out, I hold Snow's hand and he trots alongside like a horse without a rider.

Almost immediately we turned onto the Via del Corso.

How misleading were those art books. Glorious photographs,

a feast for the eye, not only of beauty but also of ancient civilizations, and then we visited and what did we find? That world was now barbaric in a modern way, crowded and cacophonous with Vespas and cars zipping every which way.

Italians do not light their streets well. Their monuments, yes, but not their streets. While it wasn't pitch dark, people were indistinct, shadowy, and mysterious until right in front of us. It reminded me of the Portland piers on a Saturday night, tons of frat boys, most drunk.

I suppose you are speculating that I have passed my anxieties on to Snow, but I believe anyone would experience the Via del Corso that night as jarring and threatening. We were traveling against the crowd.

Someone knocked into me. I lost Snow's hand and spun in a panic. But Michael, gentleman to the rescue, tucked her arm in his as if she were quite grown up. He steered her out of the maelstrom over to a shop window. The dresses displayed, gowns I should say, were over-the-top and fairly ridiculous. One tangerine floor-length I remember in particular: its fabric too shiny to be chic, plunging neckline, and short sleeves puffed at the shoulder. The skirt fell in folds like heavy drapery and pooled at the bottom. Who would wear this, and where would they wear it? What Italian life did it reflect? Yet still, it was so over-the-top it was something out of a fairy tale. I pushed through to keep close to Snow. I didn't want to miss a word.

I stopped behind and a little to the side so they wouldn't see my reflection. I didn't want to intrude.

"Someday I'd love to see you in a dress like that," he said.

"I'd take you to a ball and we would dance all night." Then he
leaned down and whispered in her ear.

Later when she was in her pajamas sitting cross-legged on the
bed, I asked what he'd said. She gave me her blank stare.

"At the shop window, Snow. When you were looking at the
fancy dresses. What did Michael whisper?"

"He hates Lizzie."

"What? That's what he said?"

She began drawing in the journal I gave her to make
memories.

"Snow?" I said, but I knew it was fruitless.

I've given considerable thought to Snow's shutdowns. She
drifts someplace else and it's sudden and quite a powerful state-
ment, a turtle pulling into its shell. Perhaps for her, the conversation is over or simply boring. She's so bright, that's possible.
Once she withdraws, there is no reaching her. According to her
teacher, she rarely engages with other kids. "It seems to be her
preference," said Miss Halsey, which I told the pediatrician
because it fascinated me. I even admired it. I had pined for my
classmates to like me. When called upon—and Snow never
raises her hand—she responds in a whisper. Miss Halsey knows
to go to her desk, lean close to hear her answer, and then repeat
it loudly for the rest of the class. "She throws off my pacing,"
Miss Halsey said, laughing.

Could Michael have possibly said that about Lizzie?

Michael is a bull—compact, muscular, even burly. I would
guess he is about five-foot-eight. Lizzie is a bit shorter. His skin is
as white as mozzarella, a comparison that only occurred to me in

Italy, and makes me giggle. He might lose his appeal on a beach because the sun would scorch him. His neck is short and his head is large, like a boulder really, and shaved bald. When I was a teen-ager, I loved *Kojak*. It was in reruns every afternoon. I swooned over Telly Savalas. This must be why I found Michael especially attractive, although he is so charming and masculine that truly any woman would. He has style too. Every day he wore faded jeans and a blue or white shirt, solid or striped, with the sleeves rolled up to the middle of his forearms. Evenings he wore a char-coal gray, lightweight sports jacket. I checked the label: Zegna.

April and I analyzed every inch of this trip when I returned. I fell on the phone and we talked for more than two hours. We concluded, among other more significant things, that Michael is very aware of his forearms, that he knows they are sexy. He is vain. I needed to talk especially about Michael because he was charismatic and, I suspected, tortured, and was such a powerful influence on Snow.

From the first night in Rome she was under his spell. She loved being on his arm, I could tell. How kind of him to show her those floor-length extravaganzas. *Someday I'd love to see you in a dress like that.* It must have made her feel beautiful and quite grown up. And whispering a secret to her, whatever it was. Her father never made her feel like a princess.

Lizzie shouted, "Left turn here," and finally I met the Rome of my picture books: a narrow street paved with age and sooth-ing colors—saffron, a mustardy yellow, the dustiest rose. One of my guidebooks put it exactly right. "Rome is a bath for the eyes." Even the moon cooperated, a horizontal sliver low in the sky, a smile at the end of the street, so perfect it could have been photo-shopped in. "Snow," I called, but she was way ahead entering the restaurant with Michael. I had to take a picture to capture my first truly Roman moment (if you don't count ruins from a taxi, and I don't), and that is why I didn't notice at first a big black bird skimming across the cobblestones like a skiff across Casco Bay. When it was barely a nose from me, it thrust a tin cup in my face.

I screamed.

Only then did I realize that this big black bird was a nun. A nun in full regalia.

Thank God Snow was already inside the restaurant. I would have scared her.

"She probably wasn't a nun," said Lizzie at dinner. "Not if she was begging with a tin cup. She was simply dressed as one. I'm sorry she upset you."

"It was just a surprise."

"I know what you mean. Plus you're tired."

"*Un Bellini pour madame,*" said Finn. (He's ridiculous with that French.) He always orders my drinks. He loves to pair a person with a drink. He told me that on our first date.

Because of the nun I was not quite myself for a while. Still, I couldn't help but appreciate the aroma of fresh garlic that permeated Beppi's, an attractive, unpretentious restaurant with gracious and attentive service. "Garlic is as potent as pot," Lizzie whispered. "I'm getting a contact high." She inhaled in an ecstatic way.

"What's that smell? Is that you?" Finn snorted his way up Snow's arm. She batted him as if she were swatting a fly, which only made him laugh.

Are you beginning to see how he drives his daughter crazy?

An odd thing. It only registered later when my head hit the pillow. Between jet lag and the nun attack, I was discombobulated enough to wonder if I'd imagined this, but when Michael opened the door to Beppi's, he slipped something out of his pocket, unscrewed the top, and took a sip.

The man with the flask. Doesn't that have an appealing wickedness?

He really, really was especially disarming that night. At dinner he continued to enthrall Snow, entirely my doing. I'd suspected that would happen if I asked him about his play *Dealing*, his first success. I was just a kid when it opened. I remembered my parents went to see it. My mother was shocked by the language. Isn't it funny that years later, we were friends traveling together?

"Listen," Michael said to Snow. "I'll tell you this story but I was bad. I don't want you thinking, *I want to be like that when I grow up.* Do you swear? 'I, Snow Dolan, promise that I will never be like Michael.'"

Snow laughed the way she does, with her fist pressed to her lips.

Michael held up her right hand. "'I promise to forget everything Michael says right after he says it.'"

She looked at me. I nodded.

"I promise," said Snow.

Even though his story was about drugs, it was wonderful to see her hanging on his every word. She watches television, she hears the news, she goes to the movies. There is only so much screening a mother can do.

Michael had a hardscrabble childhood. He made it sound almost like a Grimms' fairy tale or Harry Potter's life before Hogwarts. He grew up in Brooklyn, in a scruffy neighborhood near Sheepshead Bay. He was mugged four times before he was ten. Play meant running up and down the aisles of the 99 cents store. "Stealing," Lizzie whispered in my ear. His dad left when he was five, and he never heard from him again. How heartbreaking. His mother taught second grade in the public school. My Manhattan privileged life and his in Brooklyn were a world apart. "I lived there before Brooklyn was Brooklyn," he said, "or when Brooklyn was Brooklyn, depending on your point of view." He is so clever. The only times he came to Manhattan were for museum field trips, and he was very funny about his teachers herding them onto subways with bullhorns. Then he got a scholarship to Yale.

"His IQ is one-forty," said Lizzie.

"That's genius," I told Snow.

"Ignore them," said Michael to Snow. "If anyone here is a genius, it's you."

Her cheeks glowed from his flattery.

His roommates—Schuylar, Dexter, and Rachlan—were all rich WASPs while Michael didn't even know that there was such a thing as two forks at a place setting until he visited Schuylar's over Christmas vacation. "I had never seen a pureed soup," he said. "Who would eat a soup so thick that it had wrinkles?"

I loved that detail and pointed it out to Snow.

They sold pot that Rachlan had grown over the summer. His roommates needed the thrill. Michael needed the money. He was trying to keep up with his friends, who regularly commandeered a choice table at Snookers, a Yale haunt for the wealthy and snotty. "I wanted to belong," he said.

"Belonging is a stupid thing." He said this especially to Snow. "Belonging is stupid. Standing out is what matters." She sucked in her cheeks so I knew it registered.

"One day," he said, "the maid came to pick up the laundry, and Rasky, who was stoned, gave her the laundry bag full of weed by mistake. He was an idiot whose parents had bought his way in. You can buy your way in and out of anything, did you know that, Snow?"

"Anything?" said Snow. That especially caught her interest. I loved how engaged she was. A rarity. She spoke so quietly, however, I wasn't certain Michael had heard.

"Snow asked, 'Anything?'" I told him.

Michael smiled at her and spoke as softly as she (how sensitive was that?). "There is a get-out-of-jail-free card for people with money and influence. If you stole all the silverware here, I bet your dad could pay the owners to make it go away, and you would get off scot-free." (I was glad Finn had managed to inveigle a tour of the kitchen and wasn't there just then. He might have something to say about that and it would have ruined the flow.) "Although"—Michael laughed now and spoke normally—"who would want to risk getting trapped in the Italian justice system? Swear you won't steal the silverware."

Snow clamped her mouth shut and refused to speak. That made us laugh.

The next thing you knew, all the dads drove up or flew in to plead for their sons' futures. Don't expel them. Isn't it sad that his roommates had fathers to fight for them and Michael didn't? They threw Michael under the bus. He was, they claimed, the ringleader.

"Why did you do it?" the dean asked him.

Michael made up his excuse on the spot. "I was doing research for a play."

"I'd like to read it."

"It's not finished."

"Leave it with Marjorie," said the dean. Marjorie was his secretary.

"This is where a lie can lead you," I told Snow, although Michael said if he hadn't been terrified, he would have burst out laughing.

Imagine, this was our first night in Italy. I thought, if all the meals are this exciting and stimulating for Snow, it will be hard to go home.

"Time to cover your ears, Snow," said Michael, doing it for her. "I got high and wrote a play in three days." He took his hands off. "Did you hear what I said?"

Snow nodded.

"I don't believe you," said Michael.

"He ate three cantaloupes while he was writing it," said Lizzie. "That's my favorite part. The only part that's true."

"She always says that," said Michael. "Ignore her."

As instructed, he left the play with the dean's secretary. For weeks he awaited his fate. His roommates had been transferred to other rooms to save them from further contamination. I can only imagine the terror and isolation. "It was a wickedly harsh March. I'll never forget how barren the campus looked," he said. Finally he got a summons.

It was sleeting that day and he slid and skidded his way, nearly falling, and then dripped all over the dean's Chinese carpet. The dean said, "I sent the play to Martin Loomis, and he wants to produce it."

"Who's Martin Loomis?" said Michael.

"Look him up," said the dean. "You're done at Yale but you have a future."

"A year later his play opened on Broadway and won the Pulitzer Prize. You're dining with a very famous playwright, Snow."

I had Googled Michael before we took this trip to be better prepared to talk to him than I had been in London and had read the reviews of *Dealing*. "The reviews compared you to David Mamet," I said.

"He's better than Mamet," said Lizzie, so quickly I worried I had said something wrong. "And he's a novelist too."

"Mamet's play *Glengarry Glen Ross* was also about salesmen," I said.

"The men in my play sold pot, not real estate," said Michael. "Out of their Yale dorm."

"Michael's play has broader themes," said Lizzie.

"I'm sure," I said.

"About how the rich close ranks against the poor, and WASPs against Jews. And he gave himself a girlfriend in the play who wanted him and not the snotty guys with the pretentious names," said Lizzie.

"I wasn't in the play," said Michael.

"Excuuuusssse me." Lizzie threw her napkin over her face. "The character of Peter was entirely fictional." She lifted up her napkin to speak, which made Snow and me laugh. Then Michael clapped his hands over Snow's ears again. "Once the play came out, all I had to do was show up and I got laid. There's nothing like a hit."

The most fascinating part to me was that, at the time it was produced, Michael could never talk about the inspiration for the play, its origins, getting kicked out of Yale, because he had to protect the dean. He was sly about it. All he ever admitted to was being a college dropout because the dean knew they were dealing other drugs too (Michael didn't say what), and the police should have been notified. If anyone had really looked into the scandal, like a reporter, Yale would look bad. Instead the entire incident was swept under the Yale Chinese carpet.

"Several years after the play closed, he started telling people," said Lizzie. "Informally. At dinners. It wasn't news but it was a great story. We love stories. I'll drink to stories."

She raised her glass, and Michael remembered to include Snow, clinking her glass of Orangina first.

Then Lizzie said, and this was sweet, "Let's drink to your wives and how well they dress."

Finn wasn't happy with the wine, it was tannic and too robust, a lot to be wrong with a red, and he insisted we get another before that toast, and then Michael said, "It might be interesting to be married to a woman who wears baggy clothes because then you're the only one who knows the body underneath."

"That's the thinking behind the burka," said Lizzie.

I did envy their repartee.

Lizzie

MICHAEL ENCHANTED AT DINNER, regaling Taylor and Snow with his boot out of Yale and into theater and fame, which became the monkey on his back. He left that part out. He left out the curse of early success. He never acknowledges what he has in common with Bret Easton Ellis. "Who is that?" my friend Geralyn said when I compared them. Geralyn is a therapist who lives in Berkeley and who helped scrape me off the pavement after this trip. She reads everything from *The Jew in the Lotus* to Donna Tartt and she listens religiously to *Fresh Air*, but she doesn't know who Bret Easton Ellis is. Writers like Ellis never leave New York City (well, in his case, unless they move to Los Angeles to further their disintegration) because the only people who know who they are live in Manhattan.

Oh, the cynicism. The spite. Mine, I mean. The world in which Michael and I lived. I was jealous of Michael. That was new, and hard to admit, the result of my own shelf life expiring earlier than expected.

That first night, with Michael at his most disarming, I had the happiest sense of feeling free. Carefree. Finn was relentlessly naughty. I came out of the *bagno delle donne* and he was waiting. "Let's take off."

"We can't."

He blocked the way with his arm. I ducked under. "You are bad," I said. "Bad. First of all, you're playing with me."

"What's second of all?"

"You are full of shit. And you know I never cheat."

Even that felt good. The flirting was a way to reclaim something I'd lost, a sense of possibility, I think. It was harmless, just the ridiculous way we relate or don't. (Although I do vacillate on that—what it was, what it became, and my own guilt.) I was happily adrift in a sea of other, surrounded by chatter I didn't understand, menus I couldn't read, unfamiliar streets wending past destinations unknown. I was severed from hope and despair. From e-mail and texting. I'd sworn it off. Tweeting too and Instagram, not that it mattered. I had only four hundred followers. I felt pretty, all in black, an off-the-shoulder Donna Karan sweater, and for the first time in a long while I felt competent because I was the one with the maps. I am good at maps. Maps and where to eat are things I excel at. I had purpose.

Michael is a terrific raconteur, a skill he'd honed over the years. In his retellings, he plays with the facts, and I loved that. I found his stories as much fun the twentieth time as the first. He was dealing not simply pot but cocaine, he sometimes admits, and in other retellings, it wasn't sleeting, it was spring, and he had only two roommates, and when he answered that second summons from the dean, he borrowed a jacket that Rachlan had left behind. Thanks to Rasky being a world-class cokehead, the navy blazer had a smattering of snow on the shoulders.

How perfect that Michael was telling this to a girl named Snow, but he gracefully slid over this detail, a concession to her age and innocence, and perhaps concerned that she did not know that her name was slang for cocaine. He was very dear with Snow. I never knew him to be interested in children, but I wasn't surprised that she clearly adored him because he was good at everything he set his mind to.

Like stories.

This one was unbelievable and yet no one doubts it because, I suppose, his becoming a playwright encapsulates what we want to believe about life: that good comes of bad and all the absurdities play out in your favor.

In any event, the kicker: As he was leaving the dean's, Marjorie the secretary followed him to the elevator and suggested sotto voce that before meeting Mr. Loomis he buy some Head & Shoulders.

The crowds were off-putting, no question about it. Siracusa would be easier, better, more authentic, I thought that first night, as we battled our way through. How sad that Rome, and Paris too, are no longer evolving, pulsing entities, but preserved as if in aspic to satisfy the fantasies of tourists. "Don't knock tourism," said Taylor when I compared Rome to Disneyland. I don't know why I did. It wasn't a particularly original thought, God knows. I was trying to find something to write about, some little notion that would jump-start my career. I floated stuff, anything. She took the remark personally. She's Portland's queen of tourism and I suppose it made her defensive.

Taylor was nearly run over by a nun. That night in the hotel room I started laughing, thinking about it, and couldn't stop.

Snow appeared as fearful as she was the year before, the last time we saw her. I was curious to see if she'd outgrown her anxieties but apparently not. She did her frantic eye dance, darting looks this way and that before venturing out of the hotel into the streets. When she laughed, she covered her mouth, as if she were stuffing the laughter back in. Her laughter was soundless too. Was that a new development? I wasn't sure. As usual, her mother ordered for her. They had matching food, linguini with clams. I noticed something else about Snow, perhaps because she was maturing, but she had beautiful posture. She sat straight up in her chair, her back like a board. She was efficient. She ate all the clams first and then dealt expertly with the linguini, twirling it on the fork and polishing off every morsel. Taylor almost never took her eyes off her daughter, which must have been exhausting for them both, but what did I know? At the same time, it's my impression that Taylor was well aware of her own impact, and that, when we were waited on, the waiter attended to her especially. She's striking. All the men clocked her as she passed, tall and waifish in her stylish edgy clothes, one sleeve shredded, the other not, a slice of skin visible from a slash in the back, sleek, short unisex hair, eyes kohled, and of course her magnificent accessory, a beautiful blond daughter, herself in miniature.

I don't think she's sexy. I'm sorry, I never did. It was all too controlled, too bloodless.

The restaurant managed to do that thing they do so well in Rome, combine casual and elegant: the space, a series of cave-like rooms with stone floors and dark lacquered wainscoting, the tables dressed in white cloths, and the waiters both welcoming and formal in their white shirts, white jackets, black bow ties, and white cloths folded and draped over an arm. The food was glorious. Of course we can get branzino baked in a salt crust at some New York City fish restaurants, but it wouldn't taste as fresh and sweet. Finn said the preparation was beyond the capabilities of his joint. I started with *cacio e pepe*. The burrata we all shared was sublimely creamy, and I figured I would be eating a lot of figs on this trip, as I tasted Michael's served with prosciutto. Finn took care of the wine. He made a production of it—which the Italians loved—asking questions about fruitiness and balance, rolling the sample around on his tongue, and waiting a dramatic moment before pronouncing his approval. He told them he was on the lookout for cheap Sicilian wines. They seemed to admire that, think it wise. When he dropped the name of Angelo Gaja, the sommelier, or whatever that person is called in Italy, went wild. Finn was invited to the kitchen for a tour. "Angelo Gaja is a famous winemaker from the Piemonte region, chiefly producing a number of Barbaresco and Barolo wines." I just Googled him and that's what came up.

The cost of a single glass of wine in a restaurant is generally the price of the bottle, according to Finn. I had no idea.

Finn started his meal with grilled fresh anchovies followed by spaghetti with sea urchin, a briny dish that Taylor said Snow would not like when he offered her a taste. Finn was far and away the most adventurous of us. He insisted we finish the meal with limoncello. From the travel and all the drinking, I was loopy.

"If you could return to any age, what would it be?" I asked.

Michael shoved back from the table to signal he wasn't participating. "I know your answer. Twenty-one. That's when *Dealing* opened."

Finn answered fifteen, and I fell on him in protest. Who picks the most awkward, insecure time of life, but he said he'd gotten laid for the first time at fifteen. Actually he said he had his first girlfriend, a concession to Snow's presence, but the meaning was clear. Taylor's favorite was thirty. Snow was a year old. Taylor had stopped being exhausted and was now content. "I understood my destiny," she said.

Why do I think her remarks about the satisfactions of motherhood were barbs directed at me?

I picked thirty-two. Michael and I had been together a year. My career was blooming. I was getting plum assignments, did a profile of Nancy Pelosi before she was speaker, covered food as the organic movement grew and food became a national obsession. My favorite was one I did on Emeril Lagasse, the telegenic chef of the Food Network. My dad would have been proud, not only of my writing but for snaring Michael, a great literary talent. His second play had been admired but a disappointment, running only six months, but his memoir, *Bastard*, about his missing father, was about to be published and we had big dreams. *Bastard*, I should explain, has a double meaning, himself as a fatherless child and his father for abandoning him. It got fine reviews, "respectable" is the word, although it didn't sell as well as hoped. That's what gave him the fear, although he never admitted it, that the novel he was working on was his last chance to secure or reclaim his literary reputation.

My dreams were more humble and equally elusive.

We met at a book party. I had tagged along with Rachel, who used to freelance like me. These days she's what the newspapers refer to as a stay-at-home mom. Over lemon-berry smoothies at Crush, we often lamented being sidelined too young, too soon, like athletes. She'd cycle. I'd do yoga. One week she switched to green tea and, while we talked, she did some origami, folding a napkin into a swan.

Michael had been the center of attention as he often is, even though it was not his book being published. As I passed behind him, he caught my hand and pulled me into the conversation. "Does everyone here know—?"

"Lizzie Ross," I said. "And they don't."

"Elizabeth," he called me for some time, the only one besides my dad who ever did, but eventually Michael conceded that I am essentially earthy. Not without a New York style, but too ethnic for a name as genteel and cool as Elizabeth.

Michael loves the female body. I'd never been with a man who enjoyed mine quite as much as he did, and, when I met him, I'd slept around. He loved knowing how to play me. An impatient man in life, but he took his time in bed. He was generous, curious, for me an addiction—that was another reason I picked thirty-two. Our sex was rollicking. Edgy sometimes—quickies in elevators, games played in bars. It had been hard to be disconnected while he rode this novel home. I had been looking forward to the erotic anonymity of hotel rooms. I had hopes. Our vacations had always been sexy.

Taylor and Finn parted ways at the hotel. Without a discussion or a good night—it must have been routine—or even a kiss for Snow, Finn took off down the street, his lopsided gait familiar and dear like an animal with a limp.

"Finn, wait up. Lizzie is going with you," called Michael.

"I'm not." I waved Finn on. "I'm exhausted. I could sleep standing up."

In the elevator I fell against him. "Kiss me." It was one of those small, beautiful old elevators, its polished wood the color of almond. I like to kiss in them.

"Lizzie, behave."

"Seriously?"

"You're into Finn."

"What are you talking about? Oh my God, you're jealous. I love it that you're jealous."

I trailed him to the room, thinking, *Do I want to get into this? No. He's cranky. I'm cranky. We're jet-lagged.* Over the years— eight married, thirteen altogether—I've gotten smarter about when to fight. Never at night.

Besides, Michael's not into kissing, never has been.

He was asleep before I was out of the bathroom. I think he took an Ambien. I woke him up. Not to be coy but I know how to do that, who doesn't? And before he was fully awake, I had come.

"Jesus, Lizzie," was the last thing I heard before I dropped off.

I woke him the next morning the same way, straddling him before he was fully awake.

Rome, Day 2

Finn

"HE'S FULL OF SHIT," I told Taylor the next morning, and she blew up at me. Blowing up for Taylor is a silent-treatment thing. Her lips pinch, sometimes she sniffs as if there's a bad smell and I caused it, and she stiffens like she's got a stick up her ass. I dropped the subject, but what the hell, something was wrong there. And why was he paying attention to Snow? He'd looked right through her in London.

"Michael's nice, isn't he, Snow?" said Tay. "We're going to the Forum now. We'll see him later."

Snow's a smart girl. Smart the way I am. She keeps stuff hidden, but she's got those sneaky glances that tell you she knows more than she's saying, and she slid one of those my way. "He could go, not you," she said.

"You're kicking out your dad?"

"You don't want to go," she said so softly I had to ask her to repeat it.

"All that crap about the miracle of his first play," I said, "getting tossed from—"

"Yale," said Taylor.

"A three a.m. fairy tale." That's what we call the ramblings of drunks at the bar before closing.

"Snow, your dad's ridiculous. I remember his play. I remember my parents talking about it. It's not a secret. He won the Pulitzer." Tay pushed me into the bathroom and shut the door. "I want this to be great for Snow. I want this to be a vacation she'll never forget. Michael is such an opportunity for her."

"Want to fuck in the shower?" I said.

"Snow would hear."

"You would otherwise?"

I got a smile out of her, tight-lipped sure, but I wasn't shooting for the moon.

"Forget it," I said. "I like the guy. I do. He's smart. Just not as smart as he thinks."

What had bugged me at dinner (and was bugging me already that morning) was where could I smoke? How could I find a way to get outside and scratch the itch? Taylor had been gaga, listening to his stories, Snow wishing he were her dad for all I knew, and I was all, *God give me nicotine.*

Michael's right for Lizzie. At any rate, Lizzie wanted me to think so, wanted me to think she was happy. Was he right for Lizzie, not my Lizzie, but they're both Democrats, and the truth about Democrats, no surprises there. Gun control, abortion. (Personally I don't get that sales pitch about a fetus not being a person until it's twelve weeks old.) They should try being a bleeding-heart liberal and owning a restaurant. They'd go broke, the endless fucking laws, every friggin' one protecting the employees. I've got to write chapter and verse on folks to fire them. By that measure I've written more than Michael. And you've got to let the bartender steal from the till, acknowledge it up front, make some rules about it. And deal with your waitresses' STDs, seriously you can't believe the shit they tell you, the sobbing about the losers they're involved with. Sometimes you have to fuck them to cheer them up.

Just playing you. I don't do that but I could.

If I said that to Lizzie, she'd start screaming about how I'm a pig.

I'd never been to Rome. That afternoon I had a glass of Chianti and a smoke near the tomb of Marcus Nonius Macrinus. It got to me, how insignificant each life is basically, all the stuff we go crazy over. I'm in Rome. There a guy next to me texting, and down the *via* is the tomb of a Roman general who died in the second century.

I tease Taylor, but she's right. Travel rocks your perspective.

Beppi's was excellent. I had fresh anchovies. They aren't salty, a bit tangy, and if you're into that part of the female anatomy, I'm not, fresh anchovies are in that ballpark but milder. I could never get my diners to order them. Anchovies and capers are not popular in Portland either with the natives or the tourists. They like chowder, the lobster roll of the day, the fresh fish I get off the day boats. I wish I had a dollar for every time a diner ordered a Caesar salad, hold the anchovies. I can get fancy with the lettuce, serve sockeye salmon crudo, spike a tartar sauce with jalapeños, but tourists tend to be conservative. They come for a Maine experience and we've got to give it to them.

I appreciated how elegantly the Romans prepared their food without turning it into something pompous. I try for that too. These waiters were lifers and proud of it. That's something I have respect for. I wasn't happy to spend the entire meal with my hand in my pocket rolling a Camel Light between my fingers. I never carried a pack. Taylor could spot the bulge in my pocket. I knew that because, way back when, she had. I engineered a tour of the kitchen to duck outside and take a couple of drags.

Why didn't I tell her?

It's never good to be honest with Taylor. It's an invitation for her to fix me.

Smoking is a reason to get up every morning. If I pass a smoker, I breathe deeply and for a second, life is better. I could spend all day scarfing other people's nicotine, and this obsession gets in the way of, no question, in the way of just about everything. I quit cold turkey when I met Taylor thirteen years ago, which does not feel like yesterday, it feels like thirteen years. It's dumb when people say it feels like yesterday, at least it's not a feeling I'm familiar with. When we got engaged, she called it "a pledge of love." I would have promised her anything. I felt clean when I was with her. Clean, classy, and kind of powerful. Smokes had no place in that scenario.

Right after we got married, I started up again. One a night. Stashed the pack under the bar and extracted a cigarette at precisely one a.m. I capped every night with a beer and a fag, and finished it off with a Tic Tac.

That was when I was into beer. Taylor said I was getting fat.

I had to agree. I'd been downing a six-pack a day since I was eighteen, no side effects, and suddenly I've got a pouch you can pet. My face was getting puffy. I caught a glimpse of myself walking by the bar one night—there's a long mirror, Tay's idea, hung across the back, that cost me two thousand dollars—and didn't recognize myself. I switched to wine. I know a hell of a lot about wines now. They're interesting. They're kind of like customers with their quirks and ins and outs.

After a while, one smoke wasn't cutting it, and I added another with my morning coffee in my car, holding the damn thing out the window so it wouldn't smell up the vinyl, and then, boom, I was back up to a pack. Tay's fault. She got sick when Snow was born. Sick enough to die, the nurses were white-faced, and it scared me. What would I do without her, what would I do with a baby? I spent the whole night outside, smoking, freezing, and praying. I called my mom and asked her to hustle her ass to church, light some candles, and pray to Saint Jude.

I was a rube about marriage. I believed all that shit about sharing. I believed in honesty, and this is when it started changing for me. "I'm smoking again," I told Taylor.

It began as a trickle, pretty little tears, then Tay was bawling that I was going to get lung cancer and leave Snow without a dad. Taylor, sitting up in bed, in her white frilly nightie her bitch mom sent, had got Snow sucking her tit while the tears flowed.

"Whoa, stop," I said. "The baby's not getting your milk, she's getting your feelings."

I wonder. It crossed my mind and continues to—Tay was wacko those first few months. Wailing like that wasn't like her.

Did her mood swings affect Snow? Did they cause the shyness thing? They say, if you breast-feed, the baby gets all your good stuff, antibodies and shit. If they get that, can't they get other stuff too? It doesn't make sense that breast milk when you're happy tastes the same as breast milk when you're bawling. Besides, all Tay's wailing was a lot for a baby to handle. Did it make her bashful? She didn't get it from me.

I tried to comfort Tay, but the baby was in the way. She used the baby's blanket to wipe her eyes, which was cute.

"Cheer up, I've got an insurance policy." I'd signed it the week after Snow was born. "You've got a reason to murder me."

She laughed.

That was when she laughed. All my dumb was funny then.

I like to look at Tay. She's a babe. I like it that other men look at her and she's married to me.

After dinner everyone went to bed and I was free. I'm a night guy. Like a vampire or a werewolf, I come alive when it's dark and when I'm on the prowl. I lit up and walked. There were people out everywhere, teenagers in huddles, guys straddling their Vespas, groups of tourists, lots of fat ones, I noticed. Rolls stretching out their tees, fanny packs sitting on big round butts. Some real beauties—Romans, I'm guessing. The women seemed to know where they were going and they had that southern Italian flavor—black hair, dark eyes, skin the sun loves, smooth and silky, shiny lipstick. Noisy with laughter and brio. Brio—where did that come from? I told you I could tell this as well as the next. Did I use it correctly? I passed a piazza, jammed—which one I was clueless—music screaming from boom boxes, nuts

shooting red flares, other nuts sticking carnations in my face. I
gave a beggar with a scrawny Pekingese a couple euros and got
out of there.

Speaking French—alone, I'm French—I picked up a couple
of tall Swedes, Brigitta and Karin, and walked across the river to
a bar. The bridge, one more magnificent relic, spooked me the
way I was getting spooked all over Rome, but more so because
it was night. Every twenty feet or so a stone angel ten feet tall
reminded me of how I never go to church and how puny I am,
in the scheme of things, worthless. Vowed to give up smoking
somewhere in the middle of the bridge but lit up as soon as I hit
the bar. Karin said it was a hanging bridge. Not possible, it had
to be sacred, not a place of execution, but Catholics are twisted,
I know, I'm one of them. Ever heard of Saint Agnes? You could
jerk off to Saint Agnes, stripped nude and dragged through the
streets for refusing to have sex with a pagan.

At the bar full of locals we were crammed in jostling for
drinks, then squeezed outside into a pen fenced off with a rope.
I had the house red, downed three glasses quickly trying to get
someplace else, to a dull sweet spot. Bought a couple for the
Swedes and left them to head back. The river was still and black
as tar and the lights along the bank reflected in fiery bursts of
gold like there were bonfires in the water. I thought about calling Jessa, but the call involved too many numbers. Couldn't wrap
my brain around dialing. Wasn't into articulation besides. In no
hurry to resume the suffocation of my happy family, I stopped for
another smoke by a harp-playing angel alongside a vendor whose
wallets were placed in rows on a blanket in this ancient city that

never stops bilking tourists. Enjoying his thrust and parry, lulled by it since I couldn't understand a word, I leaned back against the iron grating and dozed.

The ash woke me, burning my finger. Looking around, reminding myself where the hell I was, the bridge now nearly deserted, I saw a young girl all in white. She twirled, and her dress, a gauzy thing, fanned and fluttered. Then she twirled again faster, spinning herself silly.

I believe in God and the afterlife, which makes me a sucker for ghostly visions. I know Snow was in the hotel room with Tay, but she was on that bridge too, beyond reach, the way she is always beyond reach, keeping her secrets, teasing us all.

Michael

I WAS UNFAITHFUL.

My loyalties were compromised not once but twice. I enjoyed it. I won't lie. It was a nice nightcap, an even better wake-up. Lizzie climbed on top of me.

A hostage situation. I had no choice in the matter.

If you don't answer the phone, Katarina, what do you expect?

My mind courted madness. Spun. Fantasy. Plot. Subplot. K picked up a man at the gym. Someone sweaty. Younger, buff, taller, with the physique (a formal word) of an Olympic swimmer, no, of Michelangelo's *David*, how ironic and deliciously vengeful. With half the IQ. No wit. Less technique. More stamina. Less compelling.

Had a vision of K riding me the way Lizzie did. While Lizzie showered, I jerked off.

Then it crossed my mind that Kath—princess, slut, garden of unearthly delights—now had the upper hand.

Breakfast. Lizzie was excited about the buffet. "I'll meet you there," she said. From the bed I watched her dress. Critically. Her breasts, sloping now, bottom-heavy. She wiggled as she adjusted them in the cups of her bra, and threw me a look, a half smile, enjoying my watching. Her waist was a memory, hidden in a crease in her sides, and her stomach, once flat, now pillowy. The lace thong she pulled on left her fleshy butt cheerfully exposed. She shook it at me. Pulled a T-shirt over her head and swore with frustration as she tugged on tight jeans. Her once gorgeous legs were getting meatier in the thighs.

She'll order my cappuccino, she said, or do I prefer a latte? Hurry up, Michael, get up already. She'll do a plate for me too. She was looking forward to mango. She was certain there would be fresh mango. She was happy. Solicitous. She looked out the window. "Not a cloud in sight," she said.

As soon as she left, tried K. Again her phone kicked to voice mail. Fuck her.

Last night while Lizzie slept, I went into the hall. Called Tino's. The woman said, "It's not her night. Is this Mr. Shapner?"

"Yes."

"I thought I recognized your voice. It's Tessa, Tino's wife. May I help you with a reservation?"

I made one. A random date a month ahead. For three. Why three? What three? I hung up. Then I thought, *K's going to go to work tomorrow. She'll see my reservation and think I'm never leaving Lizzie. I am full of shit.* I called back and canceled. *You have done your cruelest, Katarina. You have made me second-guess. Grovel. You have turned me into a girl.*

I can bend the will of a woman, always could ever since the

first play. Since I was anointed. Success was an aphrodisiac. Only the novel won't be seduced. Only the writing betrays me. A woman never yet. *I will win, K. You will see.*

With Lizzie it was a sexual attraction. That's always first for me. During a forced march through a publication party, a book about the Gulf War, I spied her casing the buffet, stretching her body like a cat as she did, plucking this and that from here and there, stacking the plate high. "Did I miss anything?" I heard her say, and liked her low, throaty laugh, amusement at her own greediness. Sometime later she passed by behind me while I was in conversation, and I caught her hand. I knew she was available, have an unerring instinct about that. She'd written something interesting, about five investment bankers, what they wore, what they ate and where, favorite books, heroes, the last six things they'd done for entertainment. Just the facts. It was smart, a bit of fluff to some, but she knew the facts would tell you more than a conventional interview. *New York* magazine does pieces like that all the time now. So does *Vanity Fair.* Lizzie did it first. Without knowing her I had saved it to steal from for my next book or play. That I had clipped one of her articles Lizzie found more seductive than champagne and roses. She'd never been told her writing was substantive.

Divine the insecurity and compliment it. That's always been my way.

In Rome, after dinner that first night, Lizzie was, for her, subdued. She loved to chew over an evening, reconsider, despair, crow, dissect, but mercifully she was groggy with wine and jet lag. It occurred to me that if I wanted to leave her . . . correction, when I left her, I had to be firm. A waffle would be an invitation to a conversation. I'd be trapped for eternity.

She should never have had two glasses of wine, she said, and isn't limoncello awful? "You were darling to Snow," she said. "What do you make of her?"

I didn't respond to see if it mattered.

"She's odd. Well, Taylor smothers her. I mean, don't you think? Am I being too critical? That's what happens when you feel shitty about yourself. You turn into a bitch. Where was I? Taylor smothers her. God, mothers."

I was right. For a conversation I wasn't necessary.

She disappeared into the bathroom and left the door open. She has no modesty. Never has.

Lizzie

"THE BRITISH FLAG, that's what you want." Michael was at the Bancomat with me peering over his shoulder. To get prompts in English, I reached in to press the button.

He knocked my hand away.

"You hit me?"

"Did I ask for help?"

"Sorry."

"I didn't hit you, I flicked you." He pushed cancel by mistake and had to start over. "Damn you."

He got his cash and strode off.

"Michael, I'm sorry." I hurried after. "I want this vacation to be . . . It means so much to me that we made love last night. And this morning too."

He stopped and studied me.

"We're together in Italy," I said. "Let go of the book, please try."

Two Germans walked between us. Germans for sure, they always wore the most intimidating sunglasses.

I expected Michael to appreciate the ridiculousness of tourists parading through our tiff, but he pressed his fist into his forehead as if I'd given him a massive headache.

"You're blaming me," I said. "The book's like a lover, and it's all my fault for taking you away from that lover."

A flicker of recognition—what a relief because Michael intimidates me when he's steely. Then he laughed.

"What's funny?"

He only shook his head.

"What?"

"Nothing."

He reminds me of a boxer, big head, strong jaw, nose with a jog as if it's been broken. He shaves his head, well, the barber does, a point of vanity as partial baldness projects weakness, makes a man a potential target, the butt of jokes. He'd confided that very late one night, I guess we'd been together about a year. He was optimistic that his memoir would be a success, more than that, a hit, so he was cocky, more able to reveal insecurities, feeling, I think, that they no longer applied. We had taken to walking around naked—our naked phase, we were so hot then—it led not only to great sex but to confessions. I worried that he might leave after he told me. A morning-after regret. He would feel too exposed, vulnerable. The subject never came up again, but it was a marker— we did cross into something deeper and more dependent that night.

By the way, at the time I didn't even think it true. The fear that he might be a goat came from something inside, I believed, and had nothing to do with his hair or lack of it and everything to do with the father who had walked out.

I liked to imagine Michael in the ring, sparring, contemplating his next punch, an exciting fantasy about a man of words. His physicality made him more compelling than the other male journalists and writers we hung out with whose only weapons were wit and sarcasm.

"In your screwed-up heart, you really do blame me for this trip," I told him. "And I apologize."

"My heart is screwed up," he said.

"We agree on something."

Since we weren't traveling by ourselves, I had to eat crow. It wouldn't be fair to our friends if Michael and I spent the day angry. I'm not a great defuser. Normally I take the bait as easily as the next, but I always tried to give Michael the benefit of the doubt. *He is different*, I thought. Highly strung because he's creative, wary and distrusting because of that disappearing dad. As writers, both Michael and I—although I'm not on his level—liked being alone with our thoughts six hours a day. Living in our heads, we called it. My problem: I wasn't living in my head anymore. Nothing much was going on there. That was why I loved traveling. I didn't expect to get anywhere except the next restaurant. I didn't feel a failure at the end of the day for not writing, the way I did these days at home. If I was present, that was enough.

I wanted to enjoy being married.

"You should draw the Pantheon," Taylor was telling Snow when we found them drinking *frullati di frutta* at a café opposite. She had snuggled their chairs so they could share the guidebook. "It says here that the Pantheon, built in 125 B.C., is like a children's drawing of a house. Elementary. A triangle on top of a square. You should draw that, Snow."

She often suggested activities to her daughter as if her budding teenager were a toddler.

"I love your shoes," said Taylor.

"Oh, thank you. I love them too. They're Nikes. But not heavy-duty like most Nikes. Isn't the checkered fabric inside cute?" I folded back the high top. "What do you think, Snow?"

"I love your shoes," she said. Taylor's words. She captured her mother's inflection perfectly. It might have been an impression. Was it an impression? Was that a comic move? Was it ridicule? I studied Snow's poker face. She shifted her attention to the Pantheon. "Did someone shoot it?" she asked.

"It looks that way," said Michael. "Like it's been machine-gunned. I think it's simply pockmarked with age. Where's Finn?"

"Lingering at the Campo de' Fiori," said Taylor.

I got a pang. I was missing something wonderful, prowling through a Roman market with Finn while he flirted with the marinated peppers.

I have to confess, sightseeing makes me feel inadequate. I expect to have an emotional experience—swoon, feel my heart swell, be awed in the face of, in this case, such a monumental architectural achievement. But it never happens.

"No one will criticize you for abandoning the Pantheon." Michael tipped down his sunglasses to let me see his eyes and that he meant what he said. He didn't mind being alone with Taylor and Snow. "Snow, come on," he said. "Let's check this masterpiece out."

Snow looked to her mother, who must have assented, although communication between them was too subtle for me. He pulled back her chair with a flourish and took her hand. They squeezed between tables and out of the café into the crowd.

Taylor arched sideways to keep Snow in her sights. She has beautiful slender arms and impossibly small wrists. Tall and tiny, she is both. I did feel lumpy around her. That day, as always, she was terminally chic in something geometric: a pleated top, front black, back white, the neckline and armholes slits in a perfect square.

"Michael's so sweet with Snow. Finn could learn from him." From one of six compartments of her efficient purse, she extracted a mini bottle of Purell and offered me a squirt.

I didn't know about the Purell. I don't think I would have wanted to vacation with someone who brought Purell along. I even fantasized later that if I'd known about the Purell, maybe the vacation wouldn't have happened. I didn't remember Purell in London, perhaps it was a new fetish. Purell *is* a fetish. Once one carries it—I have noticed from those who do—it seems necessary throughout the day to cleanse. It reflects a constant awareness that the world is awash with bacteria and you, going about your innocent carefree way, are all the while collecting microbes that can murder you or at least give you the twenty-four-hour flu. It's awkward to turn down Purell, so I didn't. That struck almost as powerfully as the Pantheon, I'm ashamed to admit. It's as if one is saying, *I prefer germs, I prefer to eat with dirty hands, I have poor hygiene. I am a pig.*

While I was playing with the possibility of spinning Purell into something, into some puny article to sell, Taylor shot up out of her chair and stared. Snow and Michael had stopped to talk to some husky Italians dressed as gladiators.

"Would you mind paying?" she said, and sped toward Snow.

It took me a minute to figure out the euros, which were mixed up in my wallet with American money, and to guess the tip. I finished off Taylor's smoothie and left in search of Finn.

The market—open-air stalls shaded by umbrellas—is what makes my heart pitter-pat: stacks of prickly-looking vegetables (or fruits) I don't recognize, baskets of peppers, fresh berries (the prettiest marble-sized cerise-colored ones that turned out to be slightly sour), mixtures of spices named after the pasta sauce they season (arrabbiata, puttanesca), a dizzying assortment of cheese, some in giant farm-sized hunks. I wanted to get stoned on their smoggy dense aroma.

Finn was eating a slice of *pizza bianca*, chatting with a signora at a checkered cloth–covered table where several large pieces were available by the slice.

"Close your eyes."

I did, and took a bite. "God, it's even good cold. Why is it better to eat with your eyes closed?"

"It concentrates you," he said. "You can't feel pain in two places at once." He wiped my mouth with a paper napkin. "Same thing."

"That makes no sense. I'm sure I could feel pain simultaneously in twenty places."

"That's because you don't respect me. Whatever I say, you disagree. It's a problem, Lizzie, your loss. You felt that, didn't you?"

"Felt what?"

"Us. A *frisson*." He gave the word the full impact of his French accent. "Just now."

"No, I didn't feel a *frisson*," I said, although I did. "Have you been sneaking calls to Jessa?"

"Her kids are trying to murder each other. Also she's a volunteer firefighter. She's got a lot happening. It makes it hard for her to focus. Don't mention Jessa. It disrespects Taylor."

"You are bad."

"Look," he said, "if your eyes are open, whatever you see distracts you from the taste, dilutes intensity. You're employing two senses at once, and not only that, instead of smelling what you eat, which will enhance the flavor, you might be smelling what you see or something else entirely. Never eat while you're having sex either. Are you following, Lizzie?"

Almost every encounter we had alone featured a moment from our past—a flash of a flirt or a fight or a joke. In this case he'd fed me fried clams in the middle of—well, some things are better left mysterious. And here he was telling me not to be distracted when he was the king of distraction. During our short life as a couple, his attraction to anyone or anything other than me was constant and indiscriminate. He'd stop to chat up a passing dog, jump in a truck driven by someone he'd gone to high school with. Something as insignificant as a bobbing balloon might intrigue him. With Finn, the time between when we fell for each other and drove each other crazy was no time at all.

"Try it again," he said.

I closed my eyes and took another bite. "It might be the greatest pizza I've ever tasted. It's like—"

He put his hand over my mouth. "Never describe taste. You can only desecrate it. *Merci bien, Violetta*," he said to the pizza lady. "*Ici, Lizzie. Elle l'aime aussi.*"

"*Desecrate* is not what you mean."

"Hold out your hand."

I did. He put the balled-up dirty napkin into it and closed my hand around it. "When are you dumping Michael?"

"Don't project your escape fantasies onto me, Finn." Just like him to do that. My marriage made sense and his didn't. His marriage was a stagnant pond. He and Taylor hadn't had sex since, I had no idea really but they never touched. Never. His attraction to Jessa—she had to be Taylor's opposite. I imagined her in huge rubber boots wading into the Maine surf, dragging a dinghy, climbing in deftly as if it were easy, barely a splash, definitely no squeal, no near capsizing, then with muscled arms she would power the oars, plunging the boat through high waves before switching on the motor. "How do they start motors on dinghies?" I asked him. "That string they pull—what is that?"

"The starter," said Finn. "You're an idiot."

His hands on my shoulders, he steered me through the market, pausing to admire vats of olives and *pomodori secchi*, moon over vinegars, curse airport security because he couldn't bring home exotic olive oils. "Tay had us up at seven," said Finn. "By nine we were at the top of the Capitoline Hill." He ranted on about his chic cultured wife the way husbands do when they secretly admire them, at least that was my take. By eleven they'd toured the Forum, imagined Caesar holding forth with the help of their guide, Signor Sixty-Euros-an-Hour Giorgio.

A tour group swarmed in and swallowed us up. We found ourselves being lectured in a Scandinavian language.

"Is Siracusa a rat fuck of tourists?" said Finn.

"I know. It's insane here, isn't it? And yet who wouldn't want to come to Rome?"

Finn pulled me to another stall. Off a tray of samples he picked up a thimble of wine. "To Siracusa," he said. He gave me a sip before finishing it off, getting into a discussion of Sicilian reds, and dropping the name of Angelo Gaja.

Michael

NO WAY TO TAMP DOWN CHARISMA, the man shrugged, reconsidering events, deflecting responsibility. He patted his face with a napkin. It was suffocating in Siracusa. No breeze, no flow. He decided against dissecting his own behavior and motives in favor of burying his head in the Herald Tribune *while sipping an excellent espresso. The café at least was hidden. It even had armchairs.*

Did he have a role? Was he collateral damage or an instigator? Stop here. He was getting ahead of the story. He wasn't yet in Siracusa.

Rome, day two.

Gravitated to Snow by default. Preferred the child. She was a way to avoid Lizzie. Inadvertently, it turned out, to charm Taylor and show up Finn. Taylor was a nervous woman. I liked to study her contrived style. Made a mental note to someday write a woman who masks her insecurity and at the same time parades it in fashion she doesn't understand.

Plan in motion: Sending Lizzie off to Finn was easy. I felt a wizard. How natural it would be for them to fall into bed. They'd been there before. That, by the way, didn't bother me.

"No one is going to criticize you for abandoning the Pantheon. If you'd rather hit the market," I told her.

All she needed was permission to be lowbrow.

The Pantheon is humbling. Built in 125 B.C. I'd already been, came to Rome years before with another woman, an art historian. (I received a liberal arts education from the women I dated.) She had known to come in wet weather, and for a long time we had stood inside that solemn cavernous space hypnotized by a perfect cylinder of rain falling through the oculus, its splash and tap on the marble floor.

Being a tourist destination, the Pantheon was surrounded by opportunities to experience comic-book versions of ancient Roman life. Two gladiators waylaid us, drawn for sure by Snow's beauty and because children are a mark. A correction: Snow wasn't a child. I have not yet lit on the word for what she was at that particular moment in time. Not childlike if she ever was. Too silent, too composed—cunning, did I think that in Rome? On the brink of a spectacular blossoming, which made her, don't misunderstand, erotic. Forbidden fruit, but erotic.

"I'm Brutus," said one.

"Titus," said the other.

Their absurdity was irresistible. Two middle-aged men in short skirts, plastic brown chest plates festooned with plastic gold medallions, flimsy capes that would billow behind them should they ever find themselves in a chariot, sandals with leather straps winding up their hairy legs. Every day they tumbled out of bed and dressed in gladiator outfits. Did they have wives, children they kissed good-bye before donning plastic helmets with earflaps and stiff combs of feathers—one bright red, the other bright blue—sprouting from the top?

They were pros, trapping us in a drama before we could protest, and obviously good-natured, who could resist? "Fair maiden, please kneel." Their English was perfect.

I expected Snow to cower or make a frantic dash for her mother, but astonishingly she knelt.

"How many gladiators have you slain?" I asked.

"Hundreds," said Brutus or Titus, waving his plastic sword.

"How many lions?"

"Twenty. For four euros, we behead you, and you can take a picture."

"A deal."

Brutus and Titus struck poses on either side of Snow, lunging and thrusting. I stepped back to take a photograph and bumped into Taylor. Hadn't noticed she was at my elbow. Realized then we were surrounded.

"Snow's upstaged the Pantheon," I told her.

A crowd pressed in, arms raised, phones held high for an unobstructed shot. They snapped the beautiful blond princess about to lose her head to the Halloween gladiators.

Snow wore her stone face, her preternatural composure betrayed only by her eyes shifting this way and that. Was she scared, I wondered, but then she adjusted her position to give tourists on the right a better view.

Taylor would record every inch of Snow's life as she trekked her around. My conversations with Snow at dinner were at some point snapped. "Snow," she would call, and Snow's mouth would stretch into a facsimile of a smile. Here, however, Taylor gaped at all the people treating Snow as a tourist attraction. She rushed in to shoo away Brutus and Titus, and, as Lizzie said later, to get Snow's knee off the dirty ground.

I might like a child, I realized. That thought surprised and ambushed.

I liked Snow's hand in mine, her trust. Her intelligence and curiosity, visible and masked. She was intriguing, this girl who kept her cards close to her chest. I had never imagined a child like that, although children had not figured in my imaginings up to that time.

Kath was young. She could have children. We could have kids together.

Lizzie

AFTER DINNER I DECODED our way to Via della Panetteria and the sliver of a shop, Il Gelato di San Crispino, which is around the corner from the Trevi Fountain. "Don't go to the fountain without me. Promise?" I called to Michael, who couldn't care less about ice cream. He lagged behind, preoccupied with his cell, scrolling for e-mail. "Fuck," I heard him say. He'd hit the wrong key. I knew the source of his rage with no actual knowledge, the way a wife assembles a catalog of her husband's moods and the causes. His fingers are thick. Managing his phone triggers irritation.

According to my friend Rachel, who is very reliable, San Crispino makes the best ice cream in Rome. The other gelato bars seemed to have waltzed off a boardwalk. Their flavors, in garish colors, sculpted and swirled, goopy with sprinkles and zigzags of chocolate syrup, lay side by side in long trays looking cheap and overexposed. San Crispino was sleek. The gelatos in hues so alluring they might be shades of chiffon were hidden under shiny aluminum tops and dispensed by a man more lab technician than counterman, spotless in a white collarless shirt, white pants, white apron, and a white skullcap.

Taylor and Snow consulted briefly and confidentially, and Taylor related their decision, identical doubles in cups—caramel with meringue and coconut. Finn placed their order and paid. How could anyone decide quickly? How could anyone not want to taste everything? "I envy you," I told her. "I envy your decision-making abilities."

She laughed. "Snow knows what she likes." She herded her out, a sheepdog with only one sheep in her flock, leaving Finn and me to frolic.

We shared dabs off miniature plastic spoons—ginger, cinnamon, pistachio, walnut. The bright light inside tricked the world outside into near darkness. People meandering down the street or mingling as they finished their cones or cups, visible through the plate glass, were mere silhouettes. Out of the corner of my eye, as Finn was offering a taste of *melone*, I spied Michael, not by the shape of his head, which I might have because it's big like a pineapple, but by movement. A hand up to his mouth, a quick jerk back.

Oh, no, he's having fun without me. That was my thought.

Michael carried a sterling silver flask in his right front pocket. Occasionally he might spike our coffees with brandy or his favorite Scotch, enlivening some otherwise quotidian moment, having BLTs at BJ's on Lexington Avenue. At dinner parties while guests were dissecting the drama of the moment like Bernie Madoff, Michael would tap my knee under the table. If we weren't sitting together, he might simply reference the door with his eyes, and we would meet someplace private like the powder room or the hall and take a slug. A quickie juice-up. Afterward, he would pocket the flask and slide his hand up my thigh or cup my breast. This was a promise: more later at home.

Since liquor was served, why did we do it? Because it was our secret society inside a society—New York's literary world—that wasn't secret but it was exclusive. Our saucing up—the flask—was infrequent. Michael, in charge, was unpredictable. We weren't going around tipsy. I know couples who traded looks at dinner and it always bugged me, these silent opinions they were exchanging that might be about me. When it was our game, I loved it. We made wagers too. *I bet you Sam will mention Harvard. Or Miranda will serve pasta. Will it take Ray under a half hour or over to mention that print is dead and to drop six digital terms that no one understands?* The payout was usually a sexual favor. Michael participated in all things social. People wanted to know what he thought, and he told them, and made fun of them later (like Julien, Michael's alter ego, the hero of his work in progress).

When Michael was introducing me to his world, he pointed out that in so many "smart" conversations, the subtext was the superiority of our way of life. Not only that, he said, it's true, our life is superior, confirmed in every aspect, not simply because we're not dependent on cars like the rest of America or can get anything delivered, or boast the best museums, theaters, can dine in a restaurant after ten at night, blah, blah, blah, but because of our conversations. They are wittier, more brilliant. I know my dad agreed. That's why I made my way here.

How my dad would have loved him.

Finn is an extrovert. His gift is the moment. In the end, that may be the greater gift or the one that wears better—better than thinking deeply. How did it reflect on Taylor to have married a man whose gift is to be present but never to consider the implications of his actions?

Marriage. With whom do you want to take the journey? The thinker, Michael? The confabulator, Michael? Or the free spirit, Finn? Do you want to take it with someone who knows you, even intuits your secrets, or from whom you can remain hidden? By that last standard, which choice did I make? I'm still unsure. And why do most of us want marriage? Crave it for status or for stability that is an illusion. Marriage can't protect you from heartbreak or the random cruelties and unfairnesses life deals out. It's as if we're chicks pecking our way out of our shells, growing into big birds splendid with feathers, and then piece by piece, we put the shells back together, reencasing ourselves, leaving perhaps an eyehole, minimal exposure. Having pecked our way out to live, we work our way back to survive. Deluded, of course. Shells crack easily.

Do you realize what I'm doing? I'm delaying, my need to tell wavering. As long as I can drag it out, it's not over.

In Siracusa I saw three women standing at a steel railing. There is no shore, only rocky cliffs where they were, in Ortigia, the ancient preserved stone island contained within that falling-down place, connected to it by a short, also very ancient, stone bridge. Ortigia is the jewel of Siracusa, dating back to 700 B.C., and of course where we stayed, where all tourists stay. What passes for a beach there is a huge boulder rising out of the sea.

Lo Scoglio, it's called. In Italian, the rock. To reach it, sunbathers walk along a narrow metal grating bolted to a cliff, then negotiate the uneven surface of a lesser boulder and cross a short metal bridge over a drop, at least fifteen feet I'm guessing, into shallow water spiked with bleached rocks.

These women, whom I saw only from the back, were standing on this metal bridge, lime-colored towels at their feet, one in a white bikini, one in pale pink shorts—she's leaning forward, her elbows on the railing—one in loose khaki pants and a light blue pullover. Their bodies were real in that this is what women look like who have let nature take its course, who have accepted that at some point in our middle years we become pudding. The woman in the bikini was tanned to a dark copper, either ignorant of the evils of the sun or too in love with it to care. They faced the Ionian Sea, a choppy blue-gray. The sky above and behind was a blindingly bright blue but in the distance, in the direction they were facing, an enormous black creature of a cloud hovered, thick like mattress stuffing. Was it moving their way? Was it moving too slowly to discern its progress but advancing nonetheless like some plot development everyone expects but no one can predict either its time of arrival, force, or ultimate consequences?

Dinner had been an adventure. See, I am rewinding to Rome once again. Finn ordered anything anyone voiced the least curiosity about—grilled artichokes, *fritti* of all sorts to share, forks colliding in the excitement, zucchini flowers voted best. The setting was a candlelit patio cloistered between crumbling architectural survivors in a humbler part of Rome.

"Writing seems so hard," said Taylor to Michael.

He puffed up. His voice, a seductive bass, waxed more mel-
lifluous than usual. "After my first play, which I wrote stoned
without sleep, eating only fruit cocktail for nourishment—"

"Fruit cocktail?" said Taylor.

News to me. I remembered cantaloupe.

Michael smiled, delighted with his memories. "Del Monte in
those miniature cans. But after that, after the first success, I
blocked. I expected writing to come easily. I waited for the magic,
for pixie dust, for the great god inspiration. Ha. Nothing. After
months of feeling like a fraud." There are words that Michael
gives living, breathing life to. His voice is rich, his storytelling so
gifted that some of his words arrive with legs and walk around the
room. "Fraud—" He christened that one, sat it down to dinner,
and poured it some wine. He slid his arm along the back of Snow's
chair and leaned toward her to deliver his wisdom. "Writing is
sheer willpower. Discipline. That's what made me a writer."

I laughed.

"What?" he said.

"Nothing," I said, disbelief evident.

The guy was a stoner. He couldn't write without weed.
(Look, it's no big deal. I read a book, *Daily Rituals*, that docu-
mented the routines of famous creatives of all sorts. Auden took
amphetamines daily. Thomas Wolfe fondled himself. Everyone
relied on something.)

"With writing, first comes habit, then comes love," said
Michael. "With marriage, it's the opposite. First love, then habit."

It was a slap. I'd mocked him. He's sensitive to disloyalty.

"Habit is my favorite thing about marriage. What about you?" I asked Taylor.

"Our marriage works because—" She came around the table and planted a kiss on Snow's forehead and then fussed with her bangs, which she'd disturbed.

Finn set down his wine and waited. I knew he was wondering, genuinely wondering why in the world she thought their marriage worked. "Because we're parents," said Taylor. "Because we both know this beautiful girl comes first."

This is something she's selling to Finn. I remember thinking that. The car's bought. It's nearly eleven, and she's still delivering the sales pitch.

"Marriage is like nicotine," said Finn. "Nicotine is the most addictive drug in the world because it's an upper and a downer."

"Why is marriage a downer?" said Taylor.

"I'm kidding," said Finn.

"No, he's not, he's backing off," said Michael.

"Shut the fuck up," said Finn in a friendly sort of way.

"It's a downer because of habit. That's why we're in Italy." I raised my glass. "Here's to the unexpected."

Did I clink with Snow? Michael must have, but the odd thing was, she had this way of being present and not, as if she'd perfected the art of invisibility. As I said, and maybe it doesn't sound so hateful now, in the beginning she was wallpaper.

In the gelato place, that's where I left us, didn't I? With Michael outside fortifying himself. I knew I should be with him, but Finn had fallen in love with *stracciatella*, the word not the flavor.

"*Stracciatella.*" Finn spit it like a swear word. "*Stracciatella,*" he purred as if it were an endearment. "*Stracciatella,*" he whispered, the code in a spy film. "*Stracciatella.*" He brushed my shoulder to knock the pesky thing off, whatever it was, dust, a very small Italian bug. *I will be so dumb, you cannot resist me.*

Snow turned up, sliding between us without touching.

"*Stracciatella.*" He greeted her with great enthusiasm as if she had just returned from a long voyage—Carthage, perhaps—and dabbed a bit of gelato on her nose.

She swiped it off with the back of her hand. "Mom and Michael want to leave." Bowing her head, she spoke into Finn's chest, muffling her words.

"See you later, Finn." I took Snow's hand. She did not return my grip, nor did she resist. "Let's catch up with Michael."

He was ambling in the direction of the Trevi Fountain, weaving a bit. Thanks to the wine, his body had gone slightly beyond the reach of his mind. "We're catching Michael," I told Taylor too, who was looking past me to Finn, her face pinched in irritation. I wondered what he'd done.

"Call Michael," I told Snow. "So he waits for us."

She knelt to refasten the straps on her pink jellies.

In retrospect it's impossible for me to see anything Snow did as innocent, even the passive way her hand lay in mine, kneeling when I urged *Hurry.* Was she experimenting with control? What was the game here? The gain here? Did I not understand that children simply have their own way of engaging? The world interests them differently. A moment to speed up might seem the exact time to slow down. An uncomfortable shoe may matter more than a person. I still ponder and dissect events endlessly. I barely sleep now and drift to them, falling into a stupor of reflection. Like narcolepsy, memories overtake me suddenly and randomly.

The fountain. For this I need to summon my energy.

To experience the Trevi Fountain in all its glory, watch *La Dolce Vita*. Perhaps I feel this way because the film is special to me, personal above all others. Perhaps because, in *La Dolce Vita*, the Trevi Fountain is romantic. No, romance is something anyone might experience who got lucky one night. Rather, an enchantment: a turbulent crazy fantasy of a fountain in a deserted piazza, exquisite naked marble men frolicking with winged horses, the god of the sea, Oceanus, presiding over the festivities, naked too except for a swirling cloak, his body muscled perfection. The waterfalls obliterating all sound, and Anita Ekberg drifting through.

In reality, same fountain yet not. The lights were so bright, night was banished. Tourists milled about posing for pictures and tossing in coins. Shouting, loud laughter, teenagers screeching. Everyone clomping in big fat sneakers.

We couldn't see the fountain in its entirety from the stone bench where Michael had parked himself. We joined him, Snow between us. I asked her if she wanted to throw in a coin—it meant she would return to Rome, I explained—but got that mini head shake, no. Did she want to get closer? She shook her head to that too.

For me, visiting the fountain was a pilgrimage. My dad and

the Trevi Fountain were all wrapped up with falling in love with Michael.

"When I was your age," I told Snow, "my dad took me to see a famous Italian movie called *La Dolce Vita*. It was his favorite film." Snow smoothed the creases in her skirt, giving no indication of interest. It didn't matter. I was really telling Michael. I was reminding him. Our first weekend together, the only time we left bed was to go to the Film Forum to see this movie. My dad had died the year before. Taking Michael to *La Dolce Vita* was my way of introducing him to my dad.

"A famous scene takes place here. An American movie star, Anita Ekberg, has come to Rome. She was—oh God, she was as remarkable in the flesh as those gods are in marble. Tall and impossibly beautiful with long sleek blond hair like yours, and miraculous bosoms." When I talked about Anita Ekberg, all I wanted to do was use overinflated words like *miraculous* and *bosoms*. "There was something about the giganticness of her breasts. . . ."

Here's the thing about Snow's wallpaperishness. I didn't always consider the appropriateness, the effect of my words. She gave so little back, but I pulled Michael's attention with that comment. His head swiveled my way, and, since he was drunk—he doesn't jolt easily when drunk—I felt a rush of pride in my ability to engage him. Having won the prize of his attention, I talked faster to keep it.

"Marcello, a meltingly handsome Italian, is following Anita through the deserted streets of Rome, and when he arrives at the piazza, she is in the fountain. Imagine this goddess, her mountainous breasts threatening to fall out of her black strapless dress, wafting toward the falls. 'Marcello, come here,' she calls." This had become a refrain in our relationship. When I took a shower, I would shout, *Marcello, come here*, and Michael would join me.

I was wishing Snow gone. This was Michael's and my love story.

"You look like a little angel from an Umbrian church," said Michael.

"What?"

"La Dolce Vita."

"I don't remember that line."

He smiled at Snow.

"Oh," she said in her breathless whisper.

"Oh?"

"He told me," she said, "when we looked in the window."

When they looked in the window? They? Whose romantic memories was I summoning? What window? To this day I don't know.

Snow tucked a leg under her and shifted toward Michael, turning her back to me.

"Marcello's soul was up for grabs, like mine," said Michael.

Oh please. Did I say that or did I only think it? He could be so affected. So full of shit.

"Marcello visits a friend who seems to understand what life is about. Life is about family." Michael kept on, at first in a worn drunken ramble, then more lucidly, probably warming to the

sound of his own voice. "He meets the man's two beautiful children, and his wife, who is gracious and welcoming. Later in
the movie—"

I reached around Snow and rapped his back. "Don't get
into that."

He said it anyway. "Later Marcello learns that this man has
killed his children and himself."

No flinch from Snow. No gasp.

"He was a sad, sick man," I say.

Obviously he was if he did that, but the whole thing is left
an uncertain mystery. Why would a seemingly contented man
with everything to live for do that? It makes no sense except
that the world is so soulless he can't bear for his children to live
in it, which is pretentious (like Michael) and utter garbage.

He continued to spin the tale for Snow in that wicked way
he could intoxicate. What happens when Marcello accompanies
the police and reporters to find the man's wife and break the
horrific news? "The perfect wife," said Michael, "with the
seemingly perfect life. She gets off a bus and along the street she
ambles. The reporters, these vermin, swarm around her. 'Do
you think I am an actress?' she says, puzzled to find herself an
object of interest. 'Do you think I am an actress?' she says, confused yet flattered as she is about to learn the worst: Her husband has killed their children and himself."

"What the fuck?" said Finn.

I hadn't realized he was here.

He knocked Michael's shoulder. "What the fuck are you
talking about?"

"It's my fault," I said. "I brought it up."

Michael bent his head down and curled around in the laziest way to see what the fuss was.

"What's with that story?" Finn asked him again.

Taylor pushed in from behind, "Isn't it beautiful? It's designed by Nicola Salvi. I hope no one threw in a coin without me. Snow, that's no place to sit, it's filthy, who knows who sat here or has done what here?"

"Who gives a shit about that," said Finn. "What's with that story?"

"What story?" Taylor waved Snow up off the bench.

"It's really my fault," I said again.

While Snow slipped behind her, Taylor addressed Finn with the certainty of a mother: In this crowd she knew who the trouble-maker was. "What is the problem?"

"Why the fuck does it matter if she's dirty?" said Finn.

"Oh lord," said Taylor. Oh lord what I didn't know. Oh lord, watch your language, oh lord, not in front of our friends, or oh lord, don't be rude to Michael, who could not have been ruder himself, like the great god Oceanus at the fountain, present but above it all.

"My husband is drunk," I said. "I'm taking him back to the hotel."

I couldn't read his face, the bastard, and getting him up was like lifting a couch. Finn didn't offer to help and I avoided his eye, avoided everyone's, actually. "Seriously drunk," I said. "We'll see you tomorrow."

"We have the guide," said Taylor.

"Oh, right. Dinner, then. We'll make a plan."

I tugged Michael along, propped him up as well as I could, my hand locked on his biceps. I didn't hear a splash. Perhaps there wasn't one. The falls were noisy, as was the crowd. We'd turned onto a high road, the fountain now below us on the left. Were we walking the right direction? I couldn't manage Michael and the map. A boy wobbled by on a bicycle. I was about to stop him and ask but got sidetracked by two skinny guys in front of a souvenir shop. They had that slap-dash suave of young Italian men whose clothes are cool and hang just right, sunglasses at night. Babe-men. Who could resist staring? One straightened and strained the way you do when you are trying to get an eye-ful. I turned to see what interested him.

The crowd around the fountain pressed against the railing. Pointing, shouting, catching whatever it was on their phones and cameras. Two officers on Vespas drove into the piazza. From our vantage I couldn't see the falls, only one end of the still pond. A man sloshed into view, trudging through the water, carrying someone. All I could see were her bare legs and pink jellies.

"Let's get out of here," said Michael. "It's better if we don't know them."

Taylor

Before I continue, I want to tell you about Track It Back, a game I play. You take an incident and work backward to the cause. For example, I wouldn't have had Snow if my mother hadn't sent me to Camp Windward in Camden, Maine, every August. A sailing camp. I loved boats. I loved getting them ship-shape. I loved memorizing the parts—jib, bow, prow, keel. When I have insomnia I put myself to sleep reciting boat parts. At this camp everyone said *ahoy* instead of *hello*. Isn't that cute? Every so often I still do that. I'm a fair sailor but I don't like receding shorelines—watching land diminish, details evaporate. I never sail now and have put my foot down about Snow. Even with a life preserver it's risky.

On my way to my camp reunion I stopped for the night in Portland and met Finn. Hence Snow. Hence it tracks back to Camp Windward.

As for what happened on our second night in Rome, I track it back to the tiff. Because of the tiff, I arrived late to the Trevi Fountain and Snow ended up under Lizzie's influence.

"Why did you put ice cream on her nose?" I said to Finn. He is such a frustration. "That is no way to relate to your daughter."

"How did you know?"

"How did I know? I saw." Why did that matter?

Snow hated his teasing, I could tell. Once when he tugged her hair and pretended he hadn't, I had considered whether we should all go to a therapist to fix Finn, to make him more aware of his actions, but on reflection I realized we might have to discuss other things. You can't control what happens in a therapist's office if more than one family member is allowed to speak. When Snow was five, at the suggestion of our pediatrician, we'd all visited a child psychologist for advice on how to handle Snow's extreme shyness syndrome. I had to force Finn. The therapist asked questions about breast-feeding, implying it was odd that I did it until Snow was three and a half. Why was that odd? She sent Snow out of the room and inquired about our sex life. "How would you characterize it?" she asked. "I wouldn't," I told her. I refused to return.

Teasing is unacknowledged hostility. One Google turns that up but when I pointed that out to Finn, he said, "I'm not teasing. I'm kidding around."

I've discussed his teasing at length with April. April has fraternal twins, boys, who are not IVF. Everyone assumes they are, which is irritating. Her boys are both hyperactive, and I don't use that word carelessly. I'll take shy over hyperactive any day. April is exhausted and her living room looks like a battlefield with plastic dinosaurs and Legos strewn from one end to the other. She's given up on it. I suppose family counseling might work for us if I insist that Snow always be present. Then we could stick to Finn and steer clear of intimate things that are irrelevant and inappropriate. Still, suppose the therapist asked to see us separately? As you can tell, I consider all possibilities.

Because of that tiff over his teasing, I missed an opportunity not for me but for Snow. All the preparation I had done before we left, all the magical moments I'd envisioned for her, and then Finn—he's such a rug rat—scrambled me.

I had wanted Snow to hear the fountain before she saw the fountain. At the corner, she would stop, shut her eyes, and tune out everything except the rushing of the falls. Only then would I have led her into the piazza. Only then would she have beheld the magnificent Baroque fountain, the grandest in Rome.

After exchanging words with Finn, however, I couldn't bear to walk with him. I let him hustle ahead in that quirky limping way I used to find endearing. He would never have that limp if he had a brain in his head, playing a fourth quarter with a torn ligament. It wasn't even a championship game. With a throb I realized, because Snow had walked ahead with Lizzie, she would miss the moment I'd dreamed of. By the time I caught up, Finn was badgering Michael, who was dulled to stiff from drinking. Snow hadn't even thrown in a coin, I don't believe, and, with the kerfuffle, she knew to hide behind me, take a bit of refuge.

Michael is troubled the way I imagine geniuses are. He needs more caretaking than Lizzie can provide. Still, when Lizzie helped him up, I was struck by how tender she was with him, firm but calm, and very kind, and a little bit embarrassed, of course. I watched them for a minute negotiating the steps, thinking, *How sweet*. How misled was I?

It's hard to write about what happened next; my hands are shaking, my breath shortening, the memory cruel. The last thing I remember clearly was Finn saying "Yoo-hoo" to me. Yoo-hoo? Why would he say something that silly? I turned back to Snow and she was gone.

Here I draw a complete blank. I think I screamed, "My daughter, where's my daughter?" Perhaps I screamed, "Snow?" I must have screamed. I'm sure I screamed. I scanned the crowd for a glimpse of her towhead, her pink top, the ruffled one I'd bought at this store I love called Little Pink Lady. It has the cutest tween clothes. How long was this eternity? Less than a minute.

"The fountain," said Finn.

I swear, my first thought was, *What fountain?* Finn pointed, and I saw Snow in the Trevi Fountain, meandering through. Meandering is the only way I can think to describe what she was doing although I am well aware that a person cannot meander through water, even shallow water. Her route was leisurely, tacking this way and that—a dreamy fairy-tale girl in a world of her own.

"Get her," I said.

Finn pushed through the crowd. By the time he'd leapt the railing and splashed into the fountain Snow had ventured under the falls. There she stood, her face raised as if to the heavens, her eyes closed, her arms held straight and stiffly, palms facing forward. Perhaps something sorrowful in a church had inspired her to create this angelic vision. We had visited two that day.

Finn carried her out in his arms. People cheered. He set her, wet as a fish, down on the pavement, and climbed out himself. I was sorry I didn't have my phone at the ready and on video, but I looked around to appreciate the crowd's enthusiasm, and thank goodness I did because two security guards were bumping their way through.

"Finn, run," I shouted.

He grabbed Snow's hand and obeyed.

Finn has a funny gait, a hitch because of his high school football injury, but he can still move fast. That I didn't break an ankle on the cobblestones trying to catch them was a miracle. The streets are dreadfully uneven, being ancient. They must be brutal on one's back. I can only imagine how many Romans have compressed discs. My mother broke her ankle in March slipping on an icy sidewalk when she came out of Gourmet Garage on 86th Street. This surprised me for many reasons. My mother usually orders her food from Butterman's Specialty Gourmet. She has an account. They take phone orders and deliver. Perhaps since my dad left—"escaped" is the word Finn uses, and I have told him never to use it in front of Snow, who adores her grandmother . . . since my dad left, my mother must be expanding, trying all kinds of new things. However, I can't imagine her pushing a grocery cart or carrying one of those baskets up and down aisles or toting her purchases home in a plastic sack. Heaven forfend, to use her expression. I can't imagine her sorting through onions or selecting apples. That's difficult, by the way, figuring out which apples are crisp and not mealy. That's something I could help her with. Perhaps she compared yogurts for fat content. Whenever she sees me she pinches my waist. Sometimes Snow's too. Luggage, she calls it. "Are you carrying any luggage?" While we were in Italy, she was stuck on a couch with her leg elevated. Her ankle hadn't healed properly and she had to have surgery. I might be on a verbal detour but that makes me laugh because, talk about a detour, Finn ducked into a gift from heaven, a stone archway where we were quite hidden. I had to hug Finn; he was a hero. I completely forgot how wet he was, and I got soaked too. That made me laugh so hard it was painful.

"Snow, for goodness' sakes, the Trevi Fountain is a national monument. What were you thinking?"

She was back in a dream world, a glazed expression. That pretty pink top and her pleated polka dot skirt stuck to her skin; water trickled down her face. Her hair was matted, a snarly mess. She appeared neither to know nor care.

"Do you think I am an actress?" she said in her whispery voice.

"I think you're wet."

"Do you think I am an actress?" she said again.

I turned because she didn't appear to be speaking to me. I thought perhaps someone was behind me, someone just over my left shoulder, but no one was there.

"You can be an actress, Snow. When you grow up, you can be whatever you want."

We hustled her into a taxi. I felt guilty because I knew we

would soak the vinyl seats. Leaving something the way you found it has always seemed to me a rule to live by, but we had to take a taxi because we had no idea where we were. "Are you cold?" I asked Snow, patting her face with a tissue.

Sometimes Snow responds with a click of her tongue. She did that now. I used to think it signaled contentment, but truly I don't know. My daughter is mysterious, and one of the remarkable things about Snow is how inventively she relates. Finn calls it "the cluck."

We dripped through the lobby. Finn and I tried not to crack up, and Snow kept right by my side, her hand in mine. In spite of her shyness, I could see that she didn't care about being judged. As a mother, that meant I'd done something right.

"*Buonanotte,*" said Finn to everyone we passed.

I was brushing my teeth when he came in and closed the door. I'm smiling as I write this but that's all I'm saying because what happened next was private and the mirror wasn't steamed from the heat we generated but it should have been.

Afterward, when Finn was sitting on the tub, he said, "That was a line from *La Dolce Vita.*"

"What was?"

"That actress thing Snowy said."

"'Do you think I am an actress?'"

"Yep," he said.

"She was quoting?"

"The wife of the man who killed himself."

"Good grief. Lizzie's fault, I suppose. She must have told Snow."

"Michael's."

"Honestly, Finn, you can't imagine that Lizzie is responsible for anything. At dinner she said quite clearly how her father raised her on Chinese food, foreign films, and Gregory some-one. Her dad's favorite movie, she told me, was *La Dolce Vita*."

I went to bed irritated and Finn went out.

Finn

TAY MAY HAVE DRESSED HER like a doll, talked for Snow like she was a ventriloquist's dummy, but you can't keep a Dolan down. What a crazy-assed thing to do. That's my girl. That's a Dolan in action. No Seddley's popping herself in the Trevi Fountain, strutting around, striking poses.

Excuse my bragging. I don't experience the thrill of fatherhood often. Even when I think I've got my daughter to myself, a chance to have some fun, tweak her funny bone, Tay turns out to be lurking. Here's a fact. When we go places, I drive and Tay and Snow ride in back. It started when Snow was a baby. Tay would buckle Snow in the car seat and stay there to "keep her company." Why not, we weren't going far. Snowy cried when Tay rode up front. Sad for the kid to cry, I agreed. It got to be habit or whatever you call it when a bad idea becomes status quo. If I'm in a good mood, I call myself the chauffeur. If not, I shut up and drive. My mom shakes her head every time we cruise over to her place. "This doesn't make sense to me, Finn."

The cigarettes. It boils down to that. If Tay rides in back, she's less likely to smell them or detect stray bits of tobacco. So hey, I live with it.

Snow put on a show the tourists won't forget.

What did those folks think if, say, they weren't looking at the fountain and then glanced over and spied this innocent under the falls? Was it a miracle, a visitation, a mirage? An angel? A saint? I'm kidding. Kind of. I'm Catholic. I might have already mentioned that 'cause if you're Catholic, is it ever fucking not on your mind? I eat guilt for breakfast. I'll take life with a side of guilt—that's a joke we cracked like once a month. What's on the menu? Life with a side of guilt? I didn't go to college but I did go to Sunday school. I know Oceanus wasn't a Christian, and he is the dude presiding over the homoerotic festivities at the Trevi Fountain.

Naked men frolicking with horses. Who are we kidding? I don't care, mind you, I'm only pointing out something that might not be in the guidebooks but anyone with half a brain could see.

"The grandest fountain in Rome," said Tay.

Grander now that a Dolan's been in it. Two Dolans.

Here's how it happened in case you're confused. You might be used to reading in order: first this, then this, then this. No problem. Michael was telling Snowy about a man who kills his kids and commits suicide. Why would anyone tell a child that story? Drunk doesn't explain it. More like twisted. Sick. You take the measure of a man not when he's sober but when he's drunk. That's when the uglies come out. He didn't mean it, he was drunk. Bullshit, he meant it. I'm an expert on drinking.

That makes me an expert on human nature. Later I'll tell you my theories. I've got categories. Drinking's a national pastime. It's bigger than football and its culture is as fucked up, and that's about as smart as I get. I can give you the lowdown on all the year-rounders who come to my joint just from clocking their booze consumption.

As I was saying, Michael was filling Snow's head with nightmares. I was pissed but I wasn't going to punch him. Maybe I should have. He'd crossed a line. A fight sometimes solves a dispute cleaner and quicker than words. You fight, it's over. Take it outside. I say that now and then. A guy's nose bleeds, he gets a shiner, big deal. A Dolan protects his own, but Lizzie looked miserable. When Lizzie's upset, she's like a cartoon character with zigzags in her eyes.

I couldn't do it to Lizzie. Or to Taylor's vacation.

Still, what's a vacation if it doesn't get crazy? All this civility, after you, shall we share, this relic or that, let's toast. Let's fight. It's as good a route as any to magic memories.

This night was unforgettable. Snow snuck into the fountain, filling my heart with pride.

The second we were out, I heard Tay shout, "Run."

I grabbed Snow's hand. "Hold on, baby." The crowd parted like the Red Sea. No one wanted to get wet and we were soaked. Nuts too, they figured. Tay caught up and we barreled down this *via* and that. Were the police on our asses? I kind of hoped so but not, if you know what I mean. Ducked under a relic of some sort, didn't know what the hell it was. Half expected Tay to whip out her guidebook and give us the lowdown—when it was built, note the trickle of water from a nearby sewer—but she was bent over, gasping like she'd run the marathon. Snow was one bedraggled devil, hair plastered, that top with ruffles slapped to her skin. She should have looked miserable but my daughter was blissed out.

As soon as Tay caught her breath, she was dancing around Snow. I hadn't seen Tay so hyped up in years. She even forgot she has reservations about that thing called touch and hugged me. All three of us looked like we'd been fished out of a well.

"She's a Dolan," I told Tay. I whispered it in the elevator. I had a boner and was pressing against her. Maybe my imagination was running wild but I thought she was pressing back.

"She's a Dolan." I said it again later in the bathroom. Tay all dried off, prim and perfect in that thin silky robe of hers. She wears it wrapped tight as if the north wind were going to show up and try to blow it off her. Still I was putting the moves on, nuzzling her neck.

"Snow," she said.

Code. "Snow" means no sex, not happening, kid alert. The kid might hear. What? What can she hear? I've never known Taylor to even squeak. She's a silent fuck. I shouldn't call my wife a fuck, it's disrespectful. I'm not taking it back, just letting you know that I know that I shouldn't but fuck it I am. Thought a lot about why I wanted Tay. Talked to Dorothy the shrink about it. Started going to Dorothy after we got back. Part of Tay's power is, "I'll let you." The grant-a-favor thing she's got going is powerful.

Most men aren't fucking their wives. I should say most wives aren't fucking their husbands. I know that from the business I'm in.

Tay, genius at buzzkill, started in with the face cream: a dab on each cheek, one on her forehead. She got up close and personal with the mirror while she rubbed in circles, using two fingers, middle and ring. Same go every night. She and the mirror have a good relationship. She and the mirror are tight.

She saw me watching. "What?"

"Nothing."

"Giorgio's coming at nine tomorrow. We're going to the Vatican." She turned on her electric toothbrush. *We're done here.*

"Snow's a Dolan," I said again. There's more than one way to fuck my wife.

I met the Swedes later, spent an hour sandwiched between them at a rave, everything strobe-streaked an inky sick yellow-green, violent music. They were slithery, could do things with each other while their hands and legs got tangled up with me. Thought about opening a restaurant in Sweden.

Rome, Day 3

Michael

ONLY DRINK WAS SAVING MY SANITY. Brought home by
my wife, I was told. Behaved badly, she said, although I had no
memory and seriously doubted that assessment. No memory of
the Trevi Fountain. No memory at all of the previous night
except for clicking, phoning, ranting, raging. My hand itchy for
the phone. Lagging behind, plowing ahead, jockeying for privacy. Deluging K with texts and messages. Clicking, phoning,
ranting, raging. No answer, no indication whatsoever that
she was anything but a figment. The fish at dinner, the waiter
extracting a perfectly intact spine. After that, nothing (remembered) till morning.

Although earlier:

I'd called the restaurant. Again. Six p.m. Roman time. Noon
in New York. Made the calculation repeatedly, compulsively.
Here this, there that. K arrived at eleven. Her job to answer.
She will answer. Magical thinking. *She will answer,* I told myself as the phone rang. God, I felt ordinary. Ordinary. I whipped

myself with it. The phone rang and rang. Eventually Tino answered. Tino, oily with charm, silky manners. "Mr. Shapner, hello. Wonderful." *Wonderful* was Tino's word. He used it willy-nilly. "Will you honor us with a reservation? No?" Of what assistance could he be?

"I had offered Kath some help, a connection, is she there?" Polite. Impersonal. Vague about details.

"Kath did not come in today," said Tino with a sigh, implying that she had let us both down. Was he lying? He was lying. She was standing right there, dabbing at tears with a cocktail napkin. She'd probably confided all. "Tino and Tessa are my second family," she'd said. Hell, she babysat their grandchildren.

"I hate you. I hope you die," K had said months before, lying on her back in the sun.

She'd spoken the words, then turned her head toward me.

I'm not a sun guy, by the way. Brought the *Times*, was sitting up, Yankees cap, sunglasses, reading about yet another *Hamlet* coming next fall, wondering why I didn't like Shakespeare more, the dramas not the comedies, and if I would ever admit it, glancing over often to appreciate how juicy she was. Sunbathing in Central Park was against my religion, creed, or whatever affiliations to which I belonged. But she loved to lie in the sun, loved the park, bounced and jiggled all the way there, her body barely contained in the briefest of light summer dresses. The fabric adhered to her thighs, getting stuck between. She tugged at it now and then. What miracle of science caused a young woman's skirt to cling like that on an unseasonably warm and windless spring day? I was certain I wouldn't be seen, L safely distant, downtown at some event. Still, I adhered to the rules of the road, the road rules of philandering husbands. Leave enough space for a person between us. A man and woman cannot be faulted for occupying the same sidewalk. "Central Park, fresh air. Yippee." She'd clapped, her hands upright, a happy baby clap. I acquiesced, feeling generous, gracious, letting her life be mine, a favor I occasionally granted.

She'd lain on the grass, spoken the words, and turned toward me. "I hate you. I hope you die." How refreshing. She could still summon the spite of a teenager.

It was, I knew, the first time K had admitted she loved me. But then.

On our third day in Rome:

"Is this a Prius?" Lizzie asked.

"My first wife was a Prius."

The spell broke. It was as if the hypnotist snapped his fingers.

Why did Lizzie ask the cabdriver the question? She wasn't interested in cars. We didn't own one. What would make her ask that? How unexpected she was. I'd forgotten that (and everything else). She'd crawled into the taxi like a cat. Lizzie did that sometimes. Even at a restaurant. Everyone else slid into the booth. She might prowl across the seat, then settle, slipping her legs down, unfolding upright. Some leftover thing from child-hood, I'd always assumed. Was it charming? I'd never been able to decide. It was unself-conscious. Lizzie probably had never noticed that other women didn't do it. In the class photo, there she was: the third-grader in the front row who forgot to keep her ankles crossed.

The seduction had begun that morning in the hotel room. She'd plunked into my lap.

"Jesus, Lizzie, you're crushing my balls."

"Oops." She adjusted. No, she wouldn't say where we were going, only that she'd done a Taylor's worth of research. "You will love it. I promise you." She felt terrible for me, awful, her face crumpled thinking about it. On all our trips I'd searched out the thing that would enchant us and I'd been too immersed in work. "Struggling with your creative demons. Poor Michael. Come on." She pulled me along. "You were awful last night and now you must make up for it. Don't ask where we're going." She held up a small waxy bag and shook it. "Italian gumdrops. Never too early for sugar. You are going to love this surprise."

No resisting. Trundled down to the lobby and out, a stop at the kiosk where Lizzie anguished, the white daisies versus the tipped. "Dunked in dye," she called them.

The doorman hailed a cab. In she crawled, sat, and leaned forward to hand the driver the address. "No problem," he said.

"Do you speak English?" she said.

"Yes."

She proffered the candies. *"Delicioso,"* she insisted. Close enough: Spanish.

"Thank you," he said.

Naturally she was emboldened, his *Thank you* was flawless, and desperate to connect with a native, "Is this a Prius?" she asked.

"My first wife was a Prius," the driver said.

We fell apart.

Like that I remembered I loved her.

Our destination: Cimitero Acattolico. Final resting place for non-Catholics, mostly eighteenth- and nineteenth-century British and Americans who had visited Rome and died there. Whose lives had ended far from home. Lizzie showered euros on Paolo the driver, with whom conversation had continued to confuse and entrance.

"Does Italy have national health care?" Lizzie asked.

"Only on Saturdays and Sundays," said Paolo.

I had been possessed. I had had an illness: K. Now the fever had passed, broken by laughter.

Surrounded by parking spaces and spotty grass, enclosed by a wall built of large crumbling blocks (of concrete or no? sand? stone?), the site from outside was more suggestive of Third World than antiquity, of an end, which it was, being full of the dead, than a beginning, which it was for us, an improbable land of rebirth.

Adding to the confusion or simply misleading, the top of a pyramid loomed in the distance. "The Romans had a crush on the Egyptians after they conquered them," said Lizzie. "That's the tomb of Cestius."

"A man with a large ego."

"The earliest known narcissist."

Our connection was heady. Banter flirtatious.

"We're visiting the poets," she announced, and paused before entering. A significant pause. Touched me to see it. Her eyes closed, she took a calming breath. She was making a wish. I knew what it was: *Please let this deliver.*

Inside she directed me left into chaos. Divine chaos. Tombstones, marble slabs, carvings and sculptures vied for attention like children in a classroom, all waving their hands, *me first me first*. A park where life, death, and art jockeyed for space and love.

Its palette was cool, not sun-baked like the rest of Rome, we agreed, and now we agreed on everything, but the deep primal green of a forest owing mainly to the cypress trees, erect and severe, and the density of other foliage—box-cut hedges, a tumble of snarly low growth creeping over and around tributes and remembrances, the myriad ways grief had inspired the living. By turns modest, whimsical, poetic, emotional, grandiose—it was instantly an overwhelming experience. I could not remember when I had been so smitten.

Above all it was a peaceful park with gravel paths, a sense of refuge, but Italians are failures at order.

"They can't help themselves," said Lizzie. "They are essentially mad, no, comical. Everything reflects it, even this cemetery, except perhaps churches, although . . ." She unclipped her hair, shook it out, and pinned it back again, an action she performed so frequently in a day it could be described as a tic, yet I found it just then inexplicably sexy. . . . "In those churches with Christ bleeding on all those crosses—he was nailed, he bled, see the red paint, here it is as clear as day not implied or suggested, this man suffered big-time although worshipping pain runs counter to comedy, still there is humor in the excess." She babbled on, doubled back, reconsidered, her usual dance. All of it captivating once again.

She had a map. Of course Lizzie had a map, grinning, knowing it was silly to navigate this cemetery like a city, left at the angel, right at the cross.

While the man followed along—stepping carefully, taking detours in and around the graves, trying not to tread on anything sacred—his attention wandered, sidetracked by the sudden appearance of his conscience.

I felt ill, sick to my stomach, not worthy of this woman who wanted only for me to have an enchanted day. She knew I was back, not why I'd been absent. As we traipsed around, her voice grew gayer. She didn't peek at me nervously when she thought I wasn't looking, and her smile, no longer beseeching or needy, relaxed into a genuine expression of pleasure.

She has a beautiful smile, the man remembered. She surrenders to feeling.

Should I confess?

The notion took me by surprise. Confess? Knew I shouldn't. Not under any circumstances. Ignore the inclination. Why confess a fever anyway?

Although:

I was responsible. Truth was never my friend, an overrated virtue I'd always thought, but for the first time I had to admit I wasn't entitled to K. Wasn't forced into the affair by Lizzie's deadly personality. I'd betrayed Lizzie.

What does a man do with an ugly truth? Will it fester? Will it fade?

We sighed over Keats. The romantic poet John Keats, dead at twenty-five of tuberculosis, insisted on anonymity—no name on his stone, which was rough, plain, and altogether unassuming.

This Grave / contains all that was Mortal, / of a / Young English Poet, / Who, / on his Death Bed, / in the Bitterness of his Heart, / at the Malicious Power of his Enemies, / Desired / these Words to be engraven on his Tomb Stone. / Here lies One / Whose Name was writ in Water. Feb 24th 1821.

"'The malicious power of his enemies.' Who were they?" said Lizzie.

"Fate. His publisher. The riffraff aka public that didn't buy his books."

"Maybe Keats didn't know who his enemies were. Do you always know who's out to get you?" said Lizzie.

That remark skipped by, unremarked on, noted only in retrospect.

In life one rarely knows which remarks of the hundreds uttered in the course of a day will turn out to be auspicious. In fiction, foreshadowing is planted and flagged in some (hopefully or desperately) subtle way, drama demands it.

As we sat on the grass and lay back, propped up on our elbows, I confessed that my book was a bear, that I wasn't at the end, as I'd led her to believe, but blocked in the middle.

Lizzie listened, making cooing sounds of comfort. "Don't worry, you'll get there. I have a good feeling about this one, Michael."

"How did this day become about me?" I said, laughing.

"It's hard to be in a cemetery and not have it be about you," said Lizzie. "Not you specifically. I'm not criticizing you. I mean every feeling comes up here."

Manipulating. That I'll confess. By confiding my pain, I was paving the way for sympathy, making the case for extenuating circumstances, for mental illness. Like Julien, my alter ego, my fictional hero, I was incapable of not playing the angles. *Men do this*, I thought. *I don't want to lose her.*

Knew too that I would steal every moment of this adventure for my novel, every feeling, even the way the gravestone looked as I lay on the ground, as if it were my own. Like me, Julien would confide his crisis of confidence. He would muse about foreshadowing. Like Keats, Julien would rage at the fates. Nothing would be wasted.

Shelley's stone, a flat white marble slab, was bland in comparison to Keats's. "Read it in your gravitas voice," said Lizzie.

"Nothing of him that doth fade, / But doth suffer a sea-change / Into something rich and strange."

"Optimistic, philosophical," she said. "He died unexpectedly, drowned in 1822 at the age of twenty-nine. He was a cheater. Poor Mary Shelley." Lizzie took a blade of grass and, with her hands together and pressing it between her thumbs, she blew, making horrible honking sounds, a childhood trick, before going on to mourn Mary's choice of a husband. "And what do you make of this?" she said. "After Shelley drowned, his friends cremated him on the beach, and one of the friends noticed that his heart wasn't going up in flames as speedily as the rest of him. The man snatched it out and somehow returned it to Mary in England, and in some reports she kept it wrapped in a sheet, in others a silk purse in her desk drawer where it was discovered by her son after she died and buried with him sixty-seven years later."

"His heart was in a desk drawer for sixty-seven years?"

"Oh, no. Around for sixty-seven in total but in a drawer for only thirty-nine."

"Bullshit."

Lizzie threw up her hands. "I knew you would think so."

"Who believes this?"

"It's been reported in *The New York Times*, on the BBC, a doctor in a medical journal even speculated that Shelley must have had a calcified heart. I asked Dr. Curtis. He thinks maybe it burned slower 'cause it was protected by the rib cage. Although no mention in reports of a rib cage. How does a heart get back to England? No one mentions embalming. There were no coolers then; picnics were carried in baskets. The refrigerator wasn't in anybody's house until the twentieth century. Can you imagine the smell coming from that desk drawer?"

"A literary lie?"

"Yes. Just a great big lie. How perfect that Mary Shelley, author of *Frankenstein*, ends up with her husband's heart. How ironic that this romantic poet's heart doesn't burn? Like he's heartless, like her freaky creation. Why is success not enough? Why does a writer need myth?"

Was she trying to zing me? Was she talking about my first play? No indication. She was kneeling, brushing twigs off the marble, tidying. She looked up, grinning. "I have uncovered a literary fraud of less than momentous proportions. Do you think I could get it published? We can deduct the trip and I'll cause a sensation and get my career back.

"I need a story," she sighed. "This seems like a good place to pray, doesn't it? 'Please, an idea, please come to me.'"

"You'll think of something," I said, although doubtful.

She left daisies on the stone, placing them carefully crossing the stems. "*Ius iurandum accipiens tibi fidem spondeo officia omnia sodalitatis praestare, quantum in me sit,*" she said.

"What is that?"

"'I pledge to you that I will execute all the duties of the club, insofar as I am able,'" said Lizzie. "In high school I was elected an *aedile* in the Latin Club. The SPQR. *Senatus Populusque Romanus*—the Senate and the People of Rome. That was the oath of office. And the only Latin I know."

"I love you."

God, it was awful. I could see she was grateful.

Having sex in a cemetery didn't seem right, but it seemed right to want to have sex with Lizzie in this cemetery. Lizzie today, lush enough to be Elizabeth, earthy enough for a roll in the grass, hoisting her skirt to scratch a bare thigh. How could I resist the most irrepressible version of my wife? Besides, if we made love, the urge to confess would be subsumed under the need to come. For as long as it lasted. For only as long as it lasted, but God, already I needed a respite from guilt and shame. It was sex or tell.

Considered making a pass, then realized she was crying.

A moment of confusion. Had I confessed and didn't realize it?

Crying that way Lizzie did, sweet Lizzie who hated to cry.

Her face reddening, her cheeks plumping as her lips tightened, refusing to give in, tears squeezing out nonetheless. She burst out crying. I wrapped her in my arms.

She pushed me away and pointed.

The monument by the stone wall was so poignant, so sad, Lizzie brilliantly said later—now she was even brilliant—that it seemed to be grieving for everyone.

An angel lay prostrate over a stone tomb. Not a cuddly sort of angel generally located in proximity to puffy white clouds, this angel was lean and limber, life-sized and human save for its graceful and elegant wings protectively draping the tomb's sides. The angel's head was buried in its arms, except one forearm hung limply over the front. This was the tell: The angel had cried itself into exhaustion.

"Emlyn was the sculptor's wife," said Lizzie, regarding the sole engraving. "The wife of William Wetmore Story."

"Imagine loving your wife that much," I said. Only when Lizzie didn't respond did I hear the implication. "That's not what I meant."

"Yes it is, Michael. *Ius iurandum accipiens* et cetera. I will execute the duties insofar as I am able."

She was cheerful about it. Understood my limitations, was under no illusions. Now I was primed to confess. Upside, lose guilt, banish shame. Downside, there appeared barely to be one. Lizzie knew whom she'd married. Could not shock her. Besides, we were in a cemetery. In the face of death, all things fall into perspective. Even betrayal is a minor offense.

"Finn is thinking of cheating," said Lizzie.

I waited. What was next?

"With a lobsterwoman. A woman with muscles." She giggled at that. "I thought, why not, Taylor will never notice, he deserves to be appreciated, but we're all on vacation together and if I know something about them that you don't, it feels wrong. Out of balance. Not betrayal but like betrayal. I've felt lonely, really frightened about my work, my writing, and now that I know how much you've been struggling, I feel guilty. I think I let Finn confide because I felt so distant from you. It's not right of me or even fair to Taylor. It was sneaky of me."

"I forgive you." For effect I uttered a short bark of amusement. "Finn cheating—" I considered it. "Hardly sneaky not to have told."

"I tell you everything. I don't have secrets from you, so when I do it's a big deal." She traced my lips with her finger.

"I've been a rotten husband."

"You're right. You've been a horrible crank."

I slid my hand up her skirt.

"Later." She wiggled away. "Don't you wish you could live here?"

"It would keep life in perspective, perhaps too much."

She dug the map out of her satchel, turned it this way and that. "Where are we? Aha, come on, now the finale."

She brought it to a close with drums and cymbals. Gregory Corso, beat poet, counterculture hero of the angry 1960s and '70s, decades now sugarcoated—peace signs and free love, what was that war? Vietnam? There's a great Vietnamese on 88th and 2nd, prefer it to Chinese, less greasy. Corso, king of irony, soul mate of her father's. She was raised on his poetry. It was read to her as bedtime stories. His photo was on her father's desk. "A large soft man with a big square face, oversized sunglasses, shirt untucked, wiry gray hair, possibly never combed ever, unkempt." She brought him to life as we stood over his small clean white marble plaque, the ivy neat around it. "Corso's ashes are buried here along with the remains of a joint. He had an entire manuscript of poetry stolen, and he survived the trauma to publish more."

She was pleading with me to identify with this survivor. Then, to prove that no one understood me better, she quoted a poem of his.

I ran up six flights of stairs
to my small furnished room
opened the window
and began throwing out
those things most important in life

First to go, Truth, squealing like a fink:
"Don't! I'll tell awful things about you!"
"Oh yeah? Well, I've got nothing to hide . . . OUT!"

She continued reciting until Corso threw out everything—beauty, death, love, the kitchen sink—until finally he realized, "Humor was all that was left."

Humor, the last man standing. Laughter, the cement in our fragile edifice. Laughter, when all else fails, this is why we belong together.

Lizzie passed a test she didn't know she was taking. K was gone. Three days of suffering, obsession, and rage, and now I was rushing her into oblivion. Soon, in memory, K would be the predator and me her prey.

I knew how these things worked.

We left a message for Finn and Taylor passing on dinner. Lizzie slipped off her thong in the elevator. Made love as soon as the room door closed behind us. I hiked her onto the bureau. "Oh." I heard her surprise and then the sigh as we began the rhythm of connection and self-absorption, the miracle of sex.

"Do you think people with children make love like us?" Lizzie said later in the afterglow when the bottle was almost empty, the toy flares sparking the air seemed as magical as shooting stars, and our togetherness was intense and apparent, even waiters kept their distance and the pushiest Italian respected it.

I watched her sleep that night, feeling a misery. She surrenders to sleep wholeheartedly as she does to everything, on her back, legs splayed, one arm flung out, expecting me to lift it out of the way and, after I do, only then will she turn on her side, tug the pillow lower, and curl up. If she'd awakened, I'd have confessed. But she didn't, and in the morning, everything was bright and foreign, New York City seemed as far away as childhood, and we flew to Siracusa.

Siracusa, Day 1

Lizzie

How do I want you to meet Siracusa?

On a bone-white china plate, spaghetti—ropy, its color a light tan—tousled with tiny clams, baby tomatoes, parsley, and showered with toasted bread crumbs.

Finn, swirling red wine in the bowl of his crystal glass, whispering its name, Amarone, as if he were enticing a mermaid to enchant him.

Snow breaking open a fig, gnawing the insides, discarding a shred of skin, and starting in on another. It was something to behold. Primal.

"She's staring," said Snow in that flat affectless voice. We were at a narrow small rectangular table, Snow next to Michael, me opposite, Finn and Taylor at either end.

Michael sweating. It was unseasonably hot, we were told, and might change in an instant, that was June here. The wind had died and the air eerily still. He patted his forehead often with his large white napkin.

Taylor worn-out from her tussle with the hotel receptionist, nursing a grudge, looking sour.

We had dined outdoors that first night on Piazza Minerva, in front of a pink palazzo with filigreed balconies and impossibly tall windows. Outdoor spotlights artfully placed made us and history look our most glowing. How beautiful we were. How beautiful everyone was—starched white tablecloths, black lacquered chairs, the silverware substantial, the china plain and regal, the pasta sublime, as was a Sicilian dish—potato, octopus, orange, and olive. The waiters, handsome and charmingly inattentive, stood in a cluster talking as if they were at a party of their own.

Finn flicked an olive at Snow. "They eat horse in Sicily, did you know that, Snowy?"

"Finn," said Taylor, a warning.

Snow plucked the olive off the cloth and popped it in her mouth.

Maybe Siracusa begins there, seeing her closed mouth working as she separated the pit from the flesh and then pushed the naked pit out with her tongue.

"*Cavallo,*" he said. "That means 'horse.' Watch out for *cavallo* on the menus. They put orange in everything too."

Or should I begin this way. Snow's hand in Michael's as we came off the plane in Catania. "Michael, she wants to ride with you." Taylor, sitting behind, had leaned in between our seats.

The hotel sent two taxis, whose drivers greeted us silently with creased, stained (the blotches looked like olive oil) cardboard signs. *Hotel Rondine,* they said, the *R* with a fancy curlicue bottom.

Our driver—sullen, bony, and baked to a very dark shade of tobacco—could have been anywhere from forty to seventy. The tacky signs must have signaled danger for Taylor, a premonition of disappointment that Finn had been looking forward to—the shock of her sudden emersion into something genuinely other—not taking account of the fact that when it happened, he would have to deal with it. Finn didn't always think things through.

I was relieved that I wasn't squished into a car with Taylor to experience her dismay as we entered Siracusa and trolled along empty streets—people do add something, don't they? I think it's called life—passing dilapidated low-rise apartment buildings, glimpses now and then of a practical seaport with tugs and small freighters.

Snow, in her new bloodred goggle sunglasses, sat squeezed between Michael and me in the tiny Fiat. Italians are wild for sunglasses—extreme sunglasses—and on their last night in Rome, the Dolans had lost their marbles in an eyeglass store. Finn's black frames decorated with a slim line of silver circled his head and wrapped his ears in one sleek piece as if it were fiberglass. His lenses, large and square, were tinted rose, or as he said grinning, rosé. Taylor's tortoiseshell frames with *PRADA* stamped along the side had oval lenses way too big for her. With her blimp eyes and skinny body, she could have been a character in *Frozen*. The sunglasses transformed them all into a cartoon family. Falling for native fashion and not realizing until you're home that a fever had overtaken you is a hazard of travel.

How happy I was. Deliriously so. I could begin that way, the saddest. On the plane I had started a Sicilian murder mystery, *To Each His Own* by Leonardo Sciascia, finally relaxed and peaceful enough to experience the privacy and contentment of reading. The ability to concentrate, that's something I miss now. I think of concentration as a friend who has moved away and I will never ever hear from again.

But not that day.

When, in Rome, in the cemetery . . . when exactly as I had written it in my head . . . when every inch of what I'd painstakingly researched and plotted unfolded as I'd hoped, I'd lost it. I blamed my tears on my encounter with the angel of grief, and that sculpture was achingly sad, but it wasn't that. It was relief. I must have understood more than I realized, how fragile things between us were. Now I do nothing but look at things other ways, flipping them up and around, examining them, trying to understand at the very least my own obtuseness. I think, I really do torture myself with this: Surprises don't come from people we know well, certainly not people we love. We call them surprises but they are inevitabilities. I must have been playing a role, a starring role, in an inevitability.

Sometimes I remind myself of my mother—not often, she was content and I am restless—but she was obtuse too. When I was twelve, we were robbed. There was hardly anything to take, but a certain amount of ransacking had happened. She came home from the library where she worked, and, noticing the house was messy, cleaned up, humming all the while. She was cheerful, a big hummer. It drove my sister and me crazy.

She was always humming Joni Mitchell. Then Dad walked in and said, "What the hell?" and she realized the TV stand was empty. Our miserably small TV was missing.

Siracusa would be a honeymoon. I was that euphoric. Michael was back. Present. Finally. With me. I opened the car window and let in a hot wind.

On arrival by car, Ortigia, the ancient enclave in Siracusa, is hidden. Only a few streets in this maze are wide enough for a normal-sized automobile. Most everyone parks along the perimeter. Our modest hotel on the east side of this finger of an island faced a parking lot. Or, put more positively, it looked out across a lot and street to an iron balustrade and, beyond that, to the bright blue-green Ionian Sea.

We walked in to find Taylor at the reception desk, rapping her knuckles on the counter, her steely posture intimidating even from behind. Without looking back at us, without as far as I could tell knowing of our arrival—did she hear the door open?—she lifted an arm and Snow slid into place by her side. "We can't call Gloria to straighten this out because Lizzie made the reservation."

"What's wrong?" I said.

"The room."

She had already seen it. It was not acceptable.

"It's small. It looks out the back into nothing. Nothing."

"You can have our room."

"They are the same," said the receptionist, a fresh, neat-looking young woman well trained to be pleasant.

Finn, silent, stood back and at an angle, his attitude obscured by his absurd glasses, although conveying an air of distraction in his sideways stance. He always managed a certain with-them-but-not.

"'Dr. Ashley felt that color has a great deal to do with the well-being of the emotionally disturbed,'" I said.

"What?" Taylor swiveled around.

Truly I don't know why that line popped to mind. Why, at that moment, did I seek to crack Finn up?

"Nothing. I don't know why I said that. It's a quote from the movie *High Anxiety*. Mel Brooks." I didn't mention it was a movie Finn and I had seen together. "I was just trying to break the . . . seriousness."

"Lizzie," said Michael in his tired tone.

I didn't dare look Finn's way.

"We don't want to stay," said Taylor.

"Oh."

"The bathrooms are tiny."

I did marvel at the receptionist—oh, the poise in someone so young who didn't even have a uniform to bolster her authority. She betrayed not a hint of irritation.

"We can't get a refund," Taylor went on. "The rooms are prepaid and there is a seven-day cancellation policy. Did you know this wasn't refundable? When we gave our credit cards, did you know?"

"No. Not sure. I don't remember. How much will you be out if you leave?"

"Seven hundred fifty euros."

While Taylor looked to Finn for the go-ahead to forfeit the dough or his refusal to stop her, Michael gave his name.

"There is something here for you." The receptionist unclipped a folded piece of stationery from our reservation card and slid it across the desk. Michael opened it, read it, closed it, and slid it back. "This isn't for me."

"You are Signor Shapner?"

"Yes, and yet not for me."

"What is it?" I asked.

Michael shrugged.

"Do you have a suite?" said Taylor, now looking to upgrade.

The young woman spent a while consulting the computer, hitting keys, searching the screen, banging them some more, you'd think she was booking an around-the-world tour. The hotel, a dilapidated stone palazzo, could not have had more than twenty rooms. How could it take this long? "Yes," she said finally.

"With a view of the water?"

The receptionist nodded, and as they began to wrestle with price, Michael interrupted, "Would you mind if we registered first, Taylor? I'm dead. I need to sleep. Is that all right?"

"Of course," said Taylor. "Please go ahead."

"What was that note?" I asked as we squashed ourselves and our luggage into the elevator.

"An invitation to scuba dive. Made no sense."

"To scuba dive? What a riot. That is the last thing you would do."

Michael gave me a look.

"Get real. It is. The hotel must supply or sell the names of its guests to local businesses. Welcome to Siracusa." I leaned in for a kiss.

I suppose that's where Siracusa began. With me supplying the cover for his lie.

Taylor

SIRACUSA WAS TACKY. I'm sorry to be blunt. While it has a historic section called Ortigia, where we stayed, as well as a Caravaggio, the rest of it appeared recently built, or rebuilt, of the most inexpensive materials in a nondescript manner and time like 1970. I imagined meetings in Siracusa like ones we had in Portland with Mayor Beemer, but in a much dustier room with cracking plaster and linoleum floors where the agenda is, "How can we attract more tourists?" But Portland, Maine (I include *Maine* because most people think of Oregon when a person says Portland, and this has always been a problem for our visitors' bureau), has much more to work with. Don't think I'm a snob, but Siracusa seemed like a tourist destination for people who were lower middle class. The Jersey Shore as opposed to Long Island Sound.

In regard to the name Siracusa, if you want my opinion, Lizzie put that *a* on the end to entice us into going, to give it romance. She liked to make more of things. That first night when we were walking to dinner in the old section down sad streets lined with decrepit buildings, many shuttered with rusted steel doors, all of them discolored, blotchy, and peeling like a person's very old skin, I told her, "It's not called Siracusa. It's Syracuse."

"Syracuse is a city in upstate New York," she said. In fact, she is right insofar as Syracuse is the Anglicized version, and on the autostrada all the signs did say Siracusa, but honestly do we call Rome *Roma*? No, we do not.

When we got to the small hotel—a glorified B&B where the good views were of a parking lot—I was upset. "This is your fault," I told Finn. "All the money spent for our big trip and it turns out to be this, here." So what that it was Lizzie's idea. Finn should have intervened, not that he ever does. I got even angrier when I saw the room. "This room is a broom closet. You expect us to stay in a broom closet? Lizzie ruined our trip."

To be sure, by this time I was already halfway to fury. In the car Finn was wondering if he served a spicy calamari at our restaurant, would anyone order it, when I burst out, "Snow is coming into her own, thanks to Michael."

Finn merely picked his teeth. That drives me crazy. It's disgusting. He does it with the nail of his pinkie. I think he lets it grow precisely for that purpose.

"Would you ever think Michael could bring her out of her shell? He doesn't have children."

While packing the night before, I had found three pieces of silverware, one fork and two spoons, tucked in Snow's T-shirts. What in the world? Then I remembered what Michael told Snow that first night at Beppi's about stealing the silverware.

She'd done it. It made me laugh. I left it behind in the room and didn't mention it. No point in making a fuss. No harm done.

"She's feeling her oats," I told Finn.

"Nothing wrong with Snowy," said Finn. "Never has been."

"You're jealous."

Finn poked his tongue around inside his cheek.

The cab reeked of cigarettes. Our driver should have hung an air freshener on the rearview mirror instead of a plastic Jesus. Within a short while I was nauseous. I dabbed Purell around my nose. "I am cursed with an ability to detect tobacco," I said. "I should be a police dog."

"Smoking's not illegal," said Finn.

"It should be."

I stared out the window at the unexciting landscape, scrubby dry underbrush, sagging power lines, an occasional dusty orchard, and here and there along the highway a lonely oleander or bougainvillea. Suppose Snow smoked? One thought led to another and the next thing I knew I was thinking about all the ways being a normal foolish teenager might lead her into degrading her perfection. Cigarettes. Tattoos on that flawless skin. "Don't futurize," April always says when my anxieties run away with me.

Suppose she pierced her nose? Whenever I see Jessa Partridge, I wince. Jessa, a local lobsterwoman, has a stud in each nostril and five tiny silver hoops in each ear, the top ones so high the piercing must be through cartilage. Otherwise she's nice, if a bit boisterous, also attractive, if weathered. Whenever I see her, I want to whisper, *moisturizer.* In a coastal town subject to nor'easters, you see what happens to the houses each year, all the rusting and shredding. Why doesn't she make the connection—house-skin? My mother-in-law believes in Noxzema and witch hazel, and, for bee stings, toothpaste. Often women tell me, *You have such a beautiful complexion*, but no one thinks to ask what my skin regimen is. I've urged Finn to use moisturizer too, and bought him some for presents, to no avail.

I could smell fuel oil from the tankers in Siracusa bay. What an assault. "You should be grateful to Michael, Finn. You don't know what it means to be a father. Being a parent hasn't changed you one bit."

"It's changed you," he said.

That's the last thing we said to each other on the autostrada.

Thank goodness I was able to move us to a suite and negotiate a lower rate.

Lizzie

THE ROOM WAS SMALL, or I should say big enough. I loved the ridiculousness of having to pass each other sideways. The style was familiar in a good way, like a hotel in Sonoma or Monterey. Piney, cheery, stripy. A queen-sized bed with a wooden headboard, a fluffy comforter, and a rickety armoire painted a sunflower yellow. The floor was tile, cool under the feet. The window looked out into a dim inner courtyard where there was room only for a statue of a centaur. It was all fine. Now I was committed to liking whatever Taylor didn't. Mostly I was too happy to care.

Michael sat on the bed, slapped the pillow (foam—that had surely bugged Taylor), and said he planned to stay there for the afternoon. When I suggested staying with him, he said, "Sleep, Lizzie. I need sleep."

I was craving a blow-dry anyway, my hair dirty enough to crawl off my scalp. I had Dani the receptionist book an appointment, left, looped back behind the hotel away from the water, and fell down a rabbit hole into antiquity. It was like opening an old book with beautiful illuminated illustrations. The tattered buildings, many with bow-shaped delicate wrought-iron balconies, were cared for in touching ways: a spiky miniature palm in a terra-cotta pot by a door, flower boxes, plastic windmills on sticks—cheery cheap carnival prizes—stuck between balcony spokes or shutter slats. Everything was sweet and innocent, and proof of how small people were before hormones in milk. No earth, no grass, only stone. It made voices echo, bounced the light, gave everything back. Perhaps that was why the few people I passed spoke softly. Perhaps, like me, they were in awe. That this world still existed, inhabited, joyful, seemed miraculous.

I fell in love with Siracusa, but like my romance with Finn years before, the time between falling in love and being driven crazy was no time at all.

"There's a Caravaggio here," said Taylor at dinner. "Tomorrow we're going to see the Caravaggio, Snow."

As dinner progressed she rejuvenated, operating once again at full throttle in a skinny long sheath with peek-a-boo slits around the middle. She came armed with guidebooks and plans. Tomorrow could they fit in the Greek theater as well as the Caravaggio and a walking tour? What about the Papyrus Museum? She'd discuss it all with Gina. Gloria, the travel agent, had found Gina through a connection who knew the mayor of a nearby town. Taylor carried on about Gina the way people in New York City brag about their doctors, how they found them, who else goes to them, how hard it was to get an appointment but this other amazing doctor had pulled strings. Snow, across from me, sat next to Michael, eating with her customary efficiency but sliding her eyes around as if she were Michael's bodyguard.

I clinked my glass with a spoon. "Attention, please, question for the night. Would you give an alibi to someone you loved for a crime they committed? If yes, who?"

"What crime?" said Taylor.

"Whatever. Embezzlement, stock fraud, armed robbery."

"My mother. I'm helpless around Penelope and feel sorry for her. Also"—she made the tiniest tip of her head in the direction of Snow.

"You would alibi your mother?" said Finn. "You should go for any opportunity to lock her up."

"Your dad's joking," she said to Snow. "There's always a reason why someone does something." She scraped a bit of apricot and pine nuts off a sardine before tasting it.

"So you're saying that no matter what the crime, in your head you would twist it around to justify it?" I said.

"Not twist it around. There is simply always a reason."

"At least there would be with anyone at this table," I said. "A good reason. Because no one here is a psychopath."

"You wouldn't alibi me?" said Finn.

"No," said Taylor.

"Wow, that was quick," I said.

"Why not?" said Finn.

She dusted more nuts to the side of her plate. "I don't know, but I wouldn't."

"I don't blame you," said Finn.

"I would never lie to the police," I said. "Not for anyone or for any reason. I would march to the station and turn the person in. I ratted out Brandon Phillips in the sixth grade. I told the teacher that I saw him cheat."

"Snitch," said Finn.

"Yes, I'm a snitch. No, I would say I have a conscience. I would never even say Michael was home when he wasn't."

Michael emptied the last of the bottle into his glass, filling it to the brim.

"Oh God, Michael, hold back. I don't want to have to carry you back to the hotel. Providing a false alibi for a crime is a crime, but obviously all lies aren't crimes."

"Like yours?" said Finn to Michael.

"Mine?" said Michael as his wine sloshed onto his hand.

"What?" said Taylor, trying to catch up.

Finn took an uncomfortably long time to answer. I remember wondering if he would, or if he would tip the table over. Finn could upend a table.

"That BS about Yale. If you went to Yale, it was to deliver pizza."

Michael laughed.

"Snow, see if you can figure out where we are." Taylor passed her the street map, but Snow wasn't interested. Her mouth had thinned to a mean line. She scowled at Finn.

"Yale," said Finn. "That whole Yale story is bullshit."

"Bullshit," said Michael. Impossible to tell from his tone or smirk if he was agreeing or disagreeing.

"It is not," said Taylor.

How strange that it was Finn of all people, Finn so infantile that he still threw popcorn at movie screens, who would smell the rot.

I was the stupidest person at the table, by the way. Just by the way.

Snow tugged Michael's arm. He leaned down. She whispered.

"Snow wants to know what I think," said Michael.

"About what?" I said.

"Murder," said Snow.

You never did know when that girl was going to decide to speak in a normal tone. Murder. She said it as if it were as ordinary as orange, pistachio, or cream, just to mention a few of the ingredients in the dessert.

Michael cocked his head down to speak to Snow personally. "I would give you an alibi for anything. I would swear to the police, 'No way, she did not do it, she was with me the whole time. Release this beauty.'"

Taylor glowed as if he had bestowed an honor upon her child by swearing to alibi her for murder.

"That's sweet, Michael," I said, "but would you alibi me?"

"As long as it wasn't me you murdered. As I recall, the Italians don't believe that children commit crimes. You can't be charged with a crime in Italy unless you are over fourteen years old. They believe children are essentially innocent and can't understand the consequences of their actions."

"So do I," said Taylor.

"Although they might try the parents if they think they are responsible, directly or indirectly."

"How do you know that?" I asked Michael.

"It's a lie," said Finn.

"Everything I know, I know from someone I dated."

"That's a lie," I said. "He reads voraciously."

"Voraciously?" Finn mocked.

"You would give me an alibi?" said Snow.

"For anything," said Michael.

She sat back, composed and content, her nail-bitten hands clasped.

Later, when we left the restaurant and walked across the piazza in what we hoped was the general direction of the hotel, Michael strode ahead. Snow hurried—she never ran, I noticed that, she never betrayed that much desire—to catch up and take his hand. Taylor sped to join them.

I could see Michael leaning down to chat with Snow, to hear her breathy words, Taylor straining to hear their conversation, not wanting to be left out. Then Michael swung Snow's arm in a loop, once and again. He might have been a good dad, I thought. Too late for that.

It would be one of those nights we wouldn't remember in the morning. The unpleasant part anyway. Kind of invigorating. Finn pugnacious. Michael deflecting.

"Hold back," said Finn softly.

We waited until the others disappeared around a corner and we could no longer hear their voices or the tap of Taylor's heels on stone.

"Lay off Michael," I said.

"You should leave him, Lizzie. He's a liar."

"And you don't know Angelo Gaja."

"Light this for me." He handed me a matchbook, pulled a cigarette from his trouser pocket, and waited for me to strike, his face close to mine. "You helpless woman," he said as I struck out again and again and the matches bent.

He kissed me. It was a chaste kiss, only our lips brushed. I managed to light the next one and we walked on as if nothing had happened.

Taylor

HAVE I EVER DESCRIBED FINN? I don't think so, and that is probably Finn's fault. Let me explain. His hair, for instance. It's that shade known as dirty blond, but on his driver's license he put *brown*. Why would anyone put *brown* when they could legitimately claim *blond*? He's unconscious even of his own attributes, of putting his best foot forward. Perhaps that is why I neglected to present him fully. He fades in comparison to, say, Michael, who has such a strong presence and sophistication. Finn takes a backseat to his own life.

The other day Lizzie said to him, "You look like an aging rocker." That is true. His face is worn like he's partied a lot, a hazard of running a restaurant and having to keep up with the diners. He doesn't have to keep up, of course, but he's a people pleaser. Also, before he met me he spent way too much time on a boat in the sun without sufficient protection. I'm glad Snow didn't inherit his lank hair. I'm only being honest. It's shaggy and almost to his chin. The first time I saw him, I was on the dock and he was fiddling with some gear on the water taxi. He looked up, saw me, and grinned. His grin was wicked. It gave me a shiver as if we had a secret even though we'd never met. I felt like someone else—a woman who might inspire a man to wicked thoughts. He wanted to know everything about me; no one else ever did. I was writing poetry then, mostly about loneliness, seems silly in retrospect. "Recite one," he said. There was a wooden crate behind the empty store he was turning into his restaurant. "Stand on this box and recite one." I wouldn't. I liked his friendly face with a dimple in his chin, high cheekbones, and pale green eyes that slant upward, as do his brows.

I was very attracted to him, but once you have a child things change in that department. April and I joke that sex is rhubarb—something I forget I like and then I taste it and remember, I like this, but then I forget all over again.

"Boy, not man," my mother said of Finn. She doesn't appreciate how well he runs The Catch, his "joint" as he calls it. I never should have told her that he keeps several shoeboxes full of money in our closet because when people pay cash for their meals, he doesn't report it. If the IRS shows up at my door, my mother will be the reason. This is SOP in the restaurant business, Finn explained. All the money doesn't get banked. I believe him. Finn is immature in some ways but he is not a liar.

I love to go into the closet and put my hand in a shoebox and take out a fistful of dollars. It makes me feel like the real housewives of New Jersey, a secret vice.

That first day in Siracusa, Snow and I needed to crash and regroup. At least the air-conditioning worked, although it went off and on every ten minutes and the activating gasp was very irritating. The hotel—it's a compliment to call it that—turned out not to have Wi-Fi or cell reception, and the only English-speaking channel was once again the BBC. I wondered if the BBC had had cutbacks or if Sicily was simply second-class, because I was seeing news stories in Siracusa that I had already seen in Rome. Once we got settled I had to traipse down and outside to phone my mother.

The balustrade along a narrow sidewalk seemed like a good spot for cell reception. It turned out to be atop a giant seawall that appeared to extend up and down the coast. I hadn't realized we were way above sea level. I was about to phone when I fell into a conversation with a young American woman, a bottle-blond buxom type in a loose, salmon pink cover-up. I asked her where she got it, not because I wanted it but because there was something screaming about it. Zara, she said. She was from Jersey City, she told me, and she was carrying *The Red and the Black* by Stendhal. Brainy, obviously, although she didn't look it. You never do know what someone is going to read on a vacation. Her hair was wet and she carried a towel. "Where's the beach?" I asked her, and she said there wasn't one, just an enormous boulder where you can sun and swim. "Close," she said. She offered to walk me over but I declined. I made a mental note to ask the receptionist about undertows and dangerous fish.

While we were chatting, Michael came out of the hotel. I waved. He put his hand up to block the ferocious sun, I suppose trying to figure out who it was waving to him.

"Are you Michael Shapner?" said the woman, all wide-eyed.

He went crimson. It shocked me. He's such a sophisticated

man and pale as a stone besides, which made it especially notice-able. So many times that must have happened to him, that some admirer greeted him; perhaps he is secretly shy.

"I am."

"You don't recognize me, do you?" The woman laughed.

"Should I?"

"I work at Tino's. The restaurant. I've seen you there some-times. I love your writing."

"I'm sorry, of course. Hello."

"I thought you were taking a nap," I said.

"I need a sandwich or something, some time to myself." He spoke conspiratorially—or do I imagine that looking back?—because I had been about to ask if he wanted company. Snow would be fine without me, and besides, who doesn't need a break from Lizzie?

"The artistic temperament," I said. "You must need more peace and quiet than us other mere mortals."

"I'm going to take a walk. Excuse me."

In spite of blushing, he was curt, which surprised me. Nor-mally he has gracious manners. "Lizzie went that way," I told him in case, as I suspected rightly, he wanted to go another.

That night at dinner I saw the woman again. I remember so clearly because on the plane home I reviewed every sighting compulsively for the entire nine-hour trip. She was eating alone and the waiters were all hanging about bringing her special dishes to taste, flourishing the wine, generally making a fuss. Seeing her in a short gauzy white tent dress with a simple scooped neckline, her hair natural in a ponytail, and bright pink lipstick, I realized she was younger than I thought. About thirty.

"Why did that woman stare at you?" Snow asked Michael as we were walking back after dinner.

"She's a fan," I said.

"She's a pest," he said, swinging Snow's arm around again and again. "I promise, Snow, no one will come between us."

That afternoon I had wanted to tell my mother all about Snow's transformation. I couldn't wait to crow about the effect of a famous writer showering her with attention, but when I finally reached Penelope after being disconnected twice, she seemed tired, impatient, and irritated. Jeanette, her housekeeper, had spilled bleach on the dining room table and damaged the finish. How odd. I almost questioned the likelihood but thought better of it. My mother is in a very negative place. Her cast was coming off the day we returned, I learned, but then of course it turned out we didn't get back when we expected.

My mother isn't interested in my life, that was what occurred to me. I made a mental note to ask April if she agreed, but that evening on the way to dinner, walking in high heels on those dreadfully uneven stones, my ankle twisted. Lizzie caught my arm. My near fall must have reminded her of Penelope immobilized on a couch because she said, "How's your mother?"

"I'm a disappointment to her." I laughed.

Lizzie nodded.

Was she agreeing, I am a great big nothing? I guess not, because, after a moment, she said, "Why?"

Finn, I thought but would never say. I didn't marry well, that occurred to me, which sounded like something out of *Downton Abbey*. Portland. I wouldn't say that either. Me. Something about me. I'm not enough. "She loves Snow," I said.

"Who doesn't?" said Lizzie. She knelt to smell a flower on an unattractive cactus plant in a chipped terra-cotta planter. Then she gazed around as if she were walking on a rainbow and couldn't get over the magic or the colors. "Michael is—" She never finished the sentence but lost that gleeful ironic look (the other expression she favors is *judgmental*, and I'm not being judgmental when I say that, simply honest). Her face softened. I envied her. I envied her adoration.

"He's changing Snow's life," I said.

"I'm glad."

"Do you want children?"

"I'm old. Forty-four. I mean, no."

"What a depressing place this is."

"I'm sorry," said Lizzie.

"I'm not blaming you."

Lizzie peered up at a wrought-iron balcony as if it were of architectural or historical fascination and mindless of the likelihood it might at any second crash on our heads. "Have you hired a guide for tomorrow?"

"Yes. Gloria arranged it. We're walking all over the place, there are a few special exhibits, one on da Vinci, and of course, we're going to see the Caravaggio."

"How much fun," said Lizzie as if she meant it.

After dinner I was tired, sick of eating out, funny because I never cook at home. Finn sends food from the restaurant or Snow and I go there and eat in the front booth. I was about to give Finn a look, signal the waiter for a check, when Lizzie said, "Question for the night. Would you give someone an alibi if they committed a crime? If so, who?"

"My mother," I said instantly. No one questioned it. (I'm never sure if everyone is as interested in what I say as they are in what everyone else says.) The reason is my mother knows about the shoeboxes. If I didn't give her an alibi, she could retaliate, trade her sentence for a lesser one by ratting on Finn for tax evasion when he is only doing something every restaurant owner does.

Besides, I feel sorry for her. I could never send her to jail if she killed my father, for instance, the only murder I could imagine her committing, with arsenic I think. My father left her for a woman who is younger than me by three years. Amanda Hugley. "The kid," Finn calls her.

I haven't spoken to my father since we met him and Amanda for dinner right after the separation. They were staying at the Ritz-Carlton in Boston. Where we ate was the noisiest, most rackety place. My father would have hated it before. I really did have to choose. My poor mother. She looked so crisp when she told me, all starched and upright, sitting on her chintz couch. "Your father has decided to be a fool," she said.

Of course I would alibi Snow. Any mother understands that. Although Snow is too timid and respectful to break the law (silverware aside!), and honest too, that goes without saying. Her caper in the Trevi Fountain was a frolic, high spirits and imagination at play. As I always say, she has big feelings. If anything she would be a victim. Because of her beauty and innocence, I discussed perverts with her when she was five years old. I told her, "If any man says, 'Do not tell your mother what I did to you or I will kill her,' ignore it and tell me." I almost said aloud at dinner that Snow was more likely to be a victim, but then pushed the thought out of my mind. Suppose it gave her a negative self-image? Lizzie's hypotheticals can lead you down the most upsetting paths.

I was freshening my lipstick when I heard Finn say, "That bullshit about Yale."

He was challenging Michael. I wanted to punch him. Finn has spent years thinking that if he tickles his daughter he's a parent, and a man comes along who treats her gallantly, talks to her as if she is quite grown up, and Finn can't take it.

Michael deflected. Finn is a flea to brush off, that's how Michael reacted.

Later in the room—thank God Finn had gone for his night crawl—I found myself cross-legged on the bed with my head bowed, unable to move. *I have to get out of here. Away from Finn.* I wished Michael might run off with me and Snow. That fleeting fantasy took me by surprise. *How can I escape this vacation?* Trapped with Lizzie and her clever questions. *How can I escape?* And the trouble had barely begun.

"Are you praying?" said Snow.

"No, resting."

"You're in the way," she said.

I was. I didn't realize it. I was sitting on her side of the bed.

Michael

THE RECEPTIONIST SLID A PAPER across the desk. "For you."

I read it. "Not for me." I slid it back.

"But you are Signor Shapner?"

"Yes, and yet this is not for me."

She was in Siracusa. Not possible. Not here. A joke. Clever. Cleverer than K. Beyond her capabilities. Not taking my calls, teenage revenge, that would be Kath. Someone had helped her plan this joke. It was a joke. Had to be.

"What was that?" Lizzie asked, taking advantage of the elevator to grope and nuzzle. Mirrored. Four sides mirrored. From every angle I saw myself entangled with Lizzie, my face scrubbed clean of panic, fear, worry, guilt. From every angle I saw myself, innocence in close-up. Couldn't help but admire how well I concealed. She could not be here and yet she was. *surprise!!!!!! meet me at the café in piazza duomo. 4 o'clock. katarina.* Her handwriting. It was her handwriting. Babyish. No capitals. Hearts too. Tilting this way and that.

"An invitation to scuba dive," I'd said, and somehow Lizzie found that plausible.

She investigated the room, what there was of it, laughed at a statue out the window. Insisted I look too. *I fucked us up, Lizzie. Can you ever forgive me?*

"Sleep. I need sleep," I said instead. "Do your usual scout, darling, and report back."

It took her forever to leave, or so it seemed, calling the desk, getting a hair appointment, dallying at the mirror, changing her shoes, despairing over her misshapen toes. Women are ridiculous.

Finally she left, blowing a kiss. "I love you."

Waited ten minutes.

Had the receptionist read the note? A sheet of paper folded in half, not even stationery, not even sealed. Did it matter? This is Italy. In Italy men cheat. Everywhere men cheat. In hotels—albeit this was slightly less than a hotel, something unfortunately more intimate—it had to be common.

Was K staying here? If so, God help me. It would be as if she were in my home. Still, the receptionist had seen it all. At twenty-three—she could not be older than that—she had surely seen this. Reading the note, did she mark me for a shit? Or perhaps she found it romantic.

"Where is Piazza Duomo, Dani?" A conscious choice to use her name, conveniently on a tag. In the world of cheating there always seemed a less or more guilty way to behave.

She flourished a map. Drew a star where we were and a path. A big X. Spun the map my way to see the route and destination. "Not far," she said. "Nothing is far. Out the door." She gestured right.

I tipped her ten euros, a bribe in case, in case of what? Banking goodwill for whatever trouble might be coming. Folded the map small, crammed it in a back pocket. Carrying a map. That alone would make Lizzie suspicious. Wondering still. Was there some sick joke awaiting me or K herself?

Across the parking lot a woman waved. I held up my arm to block the sun. Taylor. She was chatting with Kath. Did she know Kath? I suddenly couldn't remember who knew who. Although sober I did what a drunk does. I walked into danger.

"Are you Michael Shapner?" said K. Feigning awestruck. Full of shit. Foolish enough to think authors are recognized. I'm not Stephen King. She carried a copy of *The Red and the Black*. My copy. Recognized the cover's shredding edge. There were many translations with different jackets and this was the one I preferred and it had been damned hard to come by, and this twit had thought it funny to bring my marked-up copy, crucial to my novel. To my art. I'd made notes in the margins.

She must have scarfed it from my office. She had a key. Part of a game, a sex game, she would arrive before and arrange herself. I had to admire her balls while I felt a curdling fear that I wouldn't get my book back. My book with my notes. I'd risked my novel along with my marriage. Seemed almost worse. The book suddenly seemed everything.

Even if it weren't a precious object she'd stolen and carted across an ocean to amuse and taunt me, left it on a towel while she swam, held it in wet hands . . . aside from all that betrayal, the book was an advertisement of our affair. A neon sign. Taylor, in my thrall, would never smell a rat. Her sophistication was delusional, as was her sense of my fame. If Lizzie turned up, however, she would know. She would recognize K. She would see the book. She would put two and two together.

How had I gambled Lizzie?

Siracusa? I hated it instantly. Strode off, got lost, doubled back, had to make sense of a fucking map.

Siracusa. Already destabilized, I was further unmoored by the chaos of its narrow streets. A place that refused to adapt to its conquerors, whose ancient footprint still ruled, wasn't going to bend to my will. Every time I turned a corner I thought I was someplace I'd just been. I needed Lizzie.

Hurrying to greet his lover, the man needed his wife to guide him.

Eventually I found Duomo, the grand piazza, swan among the ducklings, swarms of tourists bumbling around in awe of the marble palazzos and churches, dining at the splendid outdoor cafés that K had chosen for our private rendezvous. I entered with caution, admittedly even terror, worried about being spotted while scouring the tables, and finally, there she was, perched forward, her face taut with excitement. She grinned and then doubled it—her mouth stretching into exaggeration, anticipating my shock and pleasure at her naughtiness.

"Give me my book."

"Michael," she said coyly.

"My book." I put out my hand.

She hoisted a beach bag onto the table, pulled it out, and held it out of reach.

"Are you crazy?" Not the way to begin.

Backtracked. Smiled, which made her relent and release it. I sat down and set the book on the table. Kept my hand on top.

She hunched up, chastened. "Are you surprised to see me?"

"Yes."

I checked out the area. Habit. No way I wasn't exposed, a sitting duck, still, Lizzie was safely occupied with her hair. Besides, according to Taylor, she had walked another direction. To my right, two women slouched, smoking and drinking coffee. One had a motorcycle helmet on the chair next to her and useful equipment lined up on the table: lighter, lipstick, phone. A man reading a small book, a guidebook I guessed, breathed loudly to my left.

"What do you want to drink?"

"Prosecco." She smiled at my reaction, oh something different. "I was talking to these women on the rock. German women from Germany. They said everyone here drinks Prosecco."

"Don't go anywhere," I said, knowing she'd like that. I ordered inside at the bar, was sent back to the table, and a waiter showed up with one Prosecco and one espresso.

She took a big gulp. She always drank wine like water. Wrinkled her nose. "Bubbles."

I tipped the last of my flask into my coffee. Stirred it with the tiny spoon. How best to go about this?

"I want you to tell her," she said.

I nodded.

"It's not fair." Her voice quivered.

"How did you get here?"

"Your miles," she said, as if how else.

"You used my mileage?"

"One way. You only had 52,500 miles on your Visa. Bree loaned me the money for the way back. That was so, so nice of her. But you know what, because I got the way back at the last minute, it was a great deal. I found it on CheapOair. Three hundred forty-five dollars. With a stop in Lisbon, Portugal."

"My credit card?"

"Your passwords are on your desktop. Under 'password.' If you hadn't wanted me to see it, it wouldn't have been out there, that's what Casey said."

"Casey?" People were turning up I knew nothing about. Her life was turning up.

"She runs the gym."

"Bree?"

"My friend." She shrugged.

Felt her toes tucking into the fold under my knee. She switched to a baby voice. "If she used your miles it would be okay. Why can't I? I want you to tell her. You promised. 'It's over, I promise you.' Mikey, you said that."

Didn't want to get technical. Promising it's over and promising to tell Lizzie, not the same.

"Katarina sweetheart, I can't do it here. Not in Sicily. Away from home. Give me your hands, come on." I reached across the table. "You have to leave. If we're going to be together, you have to give me room to get out. I can't be cruel to Lizzie. I can't humiliate her."

"You humiliate me."

"How?"

"You know, when you ask me to—"

"That's not humiliation, that's sex. Being free."

"Does she lie on the floor—?"

"Hey, stop it." I kissed her fingers.

"I'm telling her," she said.

I threw money on the table, took Stendhal in one hand, and, with the other, yanked her up and out.

"My Prosecco," she wailed, as if leaving a child.

With my book at her back, I propelled her out of the piazza and into a (seedy) side street, all the while speaking reasonably, cajoling. "If we have a future, we have to do this right. Lizzie's neurotic. On the edge. I don't want to push her over. This is dangerous for our future. You have to go home."

Kath stopped. Wrinkled her face.

"What?"

"She's not neurotic, I don't think. You're just saying that."

"No."

"I don't think so."

"How would you know?"

"Except for wanting that table in the corner, she never sends food back or complains that the white wine isn't cold enough. She never wants ice in a separate glass. She never even says the vegetables are cold, the ones that come with the branzino. Lots of customers say that. We have a list of difficult diners and she's not on it."

"I'm going to break her heart and I'm not going to break it here."

"You promised."

I looked into her eyes. Spoke in my most soothing, convincing voice. "I love you, Kath. I love you, and for the sake of our future, I want you to leave tomorrow."

"The ticket is the kind you can't change."

"I'll buy you a new one."

"I told my parents."

"What?"

"That I'm in love. That we're getting married. They're always saying, especially Mom, come home, you're wasting your time in New York, Kathy, so I told them I'm in love and they know I'm not wasting my time."

"It's wonderful you told your parents. I can't wait to meet them." *Agree*, I was thinking, *agree to anything. Get her the hell gone.*

She kissed me, deep-throated kisses, melding her body to mine. She was gifted at surrender. "I got a bikini wax yesterday. Dani told me where to go. The lady there asked, '*Tutto?*'" She giggled.

A woman arrives in Sicily and the first thing she does is get a bikini wax? I snaked my hand under her skirt and felt how smooth she was. She wiggled, allowing more access.

Over her shoulder I saw rickety wooden stairs to a second floor, garbage cans beneath. I pushed her under the stairs and hiked her skirt. "Ouch," she said. "It's jabbing me."

The book. I adjusted and so did she, squirming sideways. "What are you wearing under this?" I knew already. Liked to hear her say it. "Nothing," she whispered. Christ, I came so quickly I was embarrassed. She pressed me to continue. I teased her there—it took her only seconds too. Other senses reactivated after she shivered against me. Became aware of the garbage, of rotting cheese, did I detect pineapple?

Which way to go, where was the hotel? I needed to be alone. Once the sex was over I was ice.

"Where are you staying?"

"Same as you."

"Kath, no."

"I'm not leaving, Mikey. I like it here. I've never been anyplace and look where I am."

She was saucy, feeling her power, and I was in a deep hole.

We came to a corner and looked in all directions. The end of one long street was blue. Water, sky? Oblivion. *Walk the plank*, I thought.

"Keep away from Lizzie. If you value our future." That didn't sound kind, but I spoke it kindly while wanting to kick her. While wanting to stomp her, beat the shit out of her. I felt a cold fucking fury, the rage of impotence. "If you love me," I said. An afterthought.

I pulled out the map and unfolded it flat on the book. Together we pondered. "Not far," I said, "Down that road. When you reach the sea, go left."

I waited five minutes, then followed.

Later:

"Lizzie, look what I found at a bookstore." I waved it.

"You went out?"

"I couldn't sleep."

"Don't you love it here? The streets are magical. Beguiling. Do you like my hair? Vincente didn't speak a word of English. I had to mime. How remarkable that you found that book."

"I asked, 'Anything in English?' The bookseller pointed to a pile in the back."

"Not that you needed another copy, but good luck to find it here in Sicily. What are the odds? See, Michael, it's a sign. You will finish the novel."

No trace of K when we left for dinner. Expected her in the elevator. Expected her to be chatting up the receptionist, now a genial man with a mustache. Snow stuck to my side as I strolled ahead of the group. Appreciated in Rome. Here the child's usefulness was over. A burr now. An irritation. (Later, of all that I was blamed for, I pondered that as much as anything.) Perhaps, even if Lizzie saw K, she wouldn't recognize her. Insignificant K—a woman who occasionally greeted and escorted us to a table at Tino's. Sometimes people aren't recognized out of context, and God knows K here was out of context. I relaxed, drank enough to ensure it, and while reaching for the bottle, realized she was there. The waiters who ignored us hovered over her: a pretty, young American woman eating alone. She sat off to the side, at a tiny table near the wall, but if she held up a rifle, I would be between the sights.

"She's staring," said Snow.

"Do you believe that girl?" Lizzie said later. "Imagine talking about me that way. Imagine, when you were a child, saying bluntly 'She's staring' about your mother's friend. About someone sitting right there. I'm not a *she*. How rude. Snow's in love with you, by the way."

"Don't be ridiculous."

"Actually I *was* staring at Snow." Lizzie barked a laugh. "She's a ferocious eater. Did you see her demolish that fig? 'She's staring.'" Lizzie imitated Snow's flat delivery. "Doesn't Taylor teach her manners? She's too busy worshipping her."

"Why did that woman stare at you?" Snow had asked on the way back to the hotel. Spooky kid. Shook me up, she'd noticed. Lizzie opposite me at dinner, her back to K, had no idea.

Finn attacked that night by the way, which meant nothing. Called me a liar. God knows it was the first time I was impressed by him. Snarly and righteous. Got a mite feral. Bared his teeth. Perhaps I could use some of Finn for Julien. The class issues, the excitement he gets when he unmasks a superior, proving himself equal.

Finn

SIRACUSA. Where everything went in the shitter. My kind of town. Easy to hide in, no airs. Any direction seemed worth going and not worth going. I liked the creaky look in Ortigia, the old section. Buildings shabby and shredding but still standing shoulder to shoulder like some straggly army that refused to surrender. On some streets I could walk in the middle and touch both sides. That's a stretch but you get the idea. The houses shared walls. That sidetracked me. Sidetracked because who gives a shit, and not that I hadn't seen it before, but it seemed friendly. If one went down, they all did. Camaraderie. Yeah. Each building only needed, of its own, a front and back. Efficient and frugal, that's what my dad would have said if he'd come here, although he never left Portland except for a few miles out to sea in a dinghy. He built houses. Always admiring a joint or the eaves of a roof. Taught me about business. *Put everything back into it, Finn, don't borrow.* It served me well.

The nothing-much hotel put Taylor over the edge. In the elevator when I was toting up our luggage, I gagged at myself in the mirror, squeezed between the roller bags, Tay's purse hanging off my arm. *You're a pussy*, I thought.

Over a bridge and isolated, Ortigia was Siracusa's hangnail. An island paved with stone. Suppose a dog wants to dig a hole? No way, no dirt. On the flight from Rome, Taylor entertained me with its history. The Romans conquered Siracusa in 2 A.D. Hey, let's build some ships, they decided, and every tree got sacrificed. It kind of made me sick to my stomach. Mass slaughter of the innocents. Imagine waking up one morning and finding all the beauties gone. No trunks to hug—it's not as dumb as it sounds, I've done it. No tree to lean against, take cover, find shade. No rustling leaves or boughs bending and swaying. Imagine wind with no trees to blow through. Desert, right? They paved the place. Ortigia is a stone desert.

There had to be less oxygen. Doesn't it come from plants? Photosynthesis? I might have overheard that in high school. Funny what sticks.

Bees and pollination too. Where the hell did that happen here? This was one freaky world.

I grew up around water. I'm who I am around water. Been in boats since I was two. Water is home.

So, on balance, I liked Siracusa. Especially Ortigia, as Lizzie knew I would. I still like it even if Dorothy the shrink says I got PTSD there. Therapists love a label. The afternoon we arrived, I went out to escape Tay's accusing eyes. Dorothy blames her mother. She's never met Penelope, or Tay for that matter, but tries to make me understand Tay's fucked-upness. I should cut her some slack, is the idea. Weird, since the one not getting the slack is me. When Tay hated the hotel room, said Dorothy, it was because she was imagining what her mother would think of the hotel room. Bullshit, I told her. Tay's a snob. Then I got it in a way I hadn't before. I'm the hotel room. To my wife, I'm the hotel room in Siracusa. Second rate.

Snow was sitting in a chair by the window when I left, entranced with the sea. Princess Snow. Not quite sure how this kid turned out to be mine. That stillness of hers unnerved me. I remember feeling that and noticing, as opposed to most of my feelings, which Dorothy says I'm not in touch with. Snow at the window, Tay swearing because there was no cell reception, trying her phone from every corner of the suite. I'm a stranger here.

"Where's the action, Dani?" I asked the receptionist.

"Piazza Duomo," she said, map ready, brandishing a marker.

"Just point me in the general direction. Want me to bring you anything? A cupcake? Some raisins?"

"No, thank you." Firm and proper. Tay had obviously terrified her. "When you come to a corner where there is a little virgin, go right and then—" She gestured straight on.

A little virgin. I liked the idea of a little virgin as the landmark to tell tourists to look for. There it was, a miniature shrine built into a wall, chipped columns, triangle top, and inside a marble Mary, plump and pious. "Right at the little virgin" turned out to be good luck. I fell upon a sundry store, pondered the selection of cigarettes as if they were wines, and settled on loose tobacco and rolling paper. A practical decision—the tobacco came in a small soft roll that would flatten in a pocket—but I was also thinking, when in Sicily. On the way out, a local tossed me matches, then took a deep breath and held it. "Ten euros." He held up ten fingers as if he hadn't spoken in English.

Soon I was heading into Piazza Duomo with a bag of weed too.

Got to say, the Piazza Duomo was the most beautiful place I've ever been stoned. I pondered it while I sat dumb and happy in one of the sprawling cafés. Harmony. Everything in harmony. Sunlight sparkled off pink marble. Was it pink or is that the grass talking? These edifices—get that, edifices—were gleaming and polished like the pope was about to arrive in the popemobile and take a spin from one end to the other. Long trip, by the way. Duomo was epic. For the first time I wondered what Tay's guidebook had to say. Wall-to-wall tourists and still it blew my mind.

I rolled a couple of cigarettes, laced them with pot, while I asked the waiter to recommend a Nero d'Avola, the most famous Sicilian grape. The wine was as red as royal blood, the expensive glass was sexy to cradle. After the weed kicked in, I was in spicy-wine heaven. All wine talk is boring. Lizzie said if I ever said the word *terroir* again she'd kick me, but let me tell you, my tongue was singing and the tangy aftertaste seemed to linger into the next century.

Got a case of the munchies and ordered an antipasto. By that point I was dopey enough to be fascinated by the pattern on a slice of salami. Was considering chatting up a biker chick pierced every which way when I spotted a ripe blonde. I guessed Polish. Too soft and round to be German or Scandinavian, no sunglasses, which meant not Italian. Big blue eyes brimming with feeling. Couldn't see who she was with, would have had to move my chair, too much trouble, but I didn't need to 'cause I knew the story. I'd seen it at my joint, some girl getting twisted into a pretzel by some guy. Watched it play out—the pout, the plead, the tears, and then, boom, up she sat, gave her shoulders a twitch, and jutted out her chin in defiance. Way to go, I thought, give him hell, when the man grabbed her hand, yanked her up and out.

Michael.

I tugged the waiter's arm. "Water. Very cold. *Très froid.*" Even stoned I'm French. Quickly. *Vite.* Stuffed my face with the rest of the food trying to sober up. Slopped water on my eyes, rubbed and tried to blink my way into coherence. Drank the rest of the water. They're lovers. I got that far. Ordered a double espresso and gulped it. What was she doing here? I replayed what I'd seen for more information, but it was fuzzy. A hazy stoned dream. Shit, he'd invited his lover here. What kind of cruel game was that?

Not Polish, American. Maybe Polish American. That made me laugh, which gives you a sense of how far I was gone. The brain was on a long leash.

Poor Lizzie.

I sat there not knowing what the fuck to do. Ordered another wine. This time, white, a Carricante.

That night, all through dinner, I watched the asshole. My daughter was goofy for him. Shy little Snow. *Snow's coming into her own, thanks to Michael.* Fuck you, Tay. She was all dressed up for him, Tay was, looking more art than human. For years I'd wondered, who the hell is she dressing for? Now she knows. If he was nice to Snow, Tay would puff up. She doesn't have a clue where she ends and the kid begins. "Fusion," Dorothy called it. Said Tay might benefit from some therapy—good luck with that.

Michael, present, was elsewhere. Even my badgering didn't arouse him. No, he was plotting his moves. His after-dinner moves. I know about those. I ordered an Amarone to finish the meal, swooned over it (a big rich wine with flavors of rain, licorice, tobacco, and fig), forced everyone else to partake to mess with him, to screw up whatever rendezvous he'd planned. There was Lizzie, buoyant, adoring, tossing out bonko questions about murder, and I'm thinking, I'd alibi Lizzie as long as Michael was the dead man.

On the way home I wavered in the world of doing Lizzie the favor of telling her and breaking her heart. She lit my cigarette and I thought, that's how fast I could destroy her, the time it took to strike the match. How the hell did we end up in love with the wrong people?

I finished my nightly prowl in a packed dive painted a devil's red. Sitting bombed in a corner, I watched some jerks play pool. Every time one signaled a hole, he gave it the finger. Every time it amused them. Karaoke in the next room, some babe belting out "Rude Boy." I was still trying to get somewhere with the information I had, but I hardly had any, and since the afternoon, except for a short stretch at the beginning of dinner when effects waned, I had been either high or drunk. That made the whole deductive effort a joke.

It was a straight shot along the quay to the hotel under a slice of moon and a dazzle of stars. Saw Lo Scoglio for the first time. Big fucking boulder. Eerie at night, not so comforting in the day either, but at night it rose up black and prehistoric. A small crowd of revelers teetered over a bridge to get to it. I could barely see a railing. It looked like a miracle, people walking on air. The wind was up, waves crashed against the boulder, throwing up a white spray. The people shrieked and retreated.

I stumbled on, got back to the room by three, and passed out on the cot. When I woke up the next morning, I wasn't sure the day before had happened.

Siracusa, Day 2

Taylor

I WAS A BIT put off by our guide. Gina had a hard quality—flat face, narrow aggressive black eyes, swarthy complexion, long straight stringy pitch-black hair she kept off her face with sunglasses perched on her head. I particularly noticed her sandals. The sturdy tough style turned out to be quite common here; black leather straps with silver studs crisscrossed her ankles. Her red pedi was peeling. She was packed into skinny white capris and a tank top with Mickey Mouse on her ample chest. (That also turned out to be common; many women wore cartoon characters, Mickey, Minnie, and Donald Duck being the most popular, although also occasionally in Siracusa I saw a Woody Woodpecker.) Hard, tough, cheap, that was my first impression.

Nevertheless it was a relief to have someone in charge, and we followed her like puppies. After that unpleasantness at dinner the night before, I was dying for a day off from Finn. He had been planning to go to the open-air market with Lizzie, but she had decided to sleep in. He would meet her later. In the meantime, he limped along with us, monopolizing Gina, quiz-zing her on everything. She had three sisters, and in her tourist business, she had two partners who were her girlfriends. What was the copper coin hanging on a leather thong around her neck? I forget the answer. She had studied classical singing for a year in Verona and did not play the mandolin—one of Finn's more ridiculous questions.

Barraged by him, she forgot her job. I was hoping these crum-bly streets might come alive. Instead we rolled on, one antiquity after another passing us by like billboards on Route 95. Finn never seems aware of the purpose of anything and could end up in Madrid on his way to Beijing just from prodding and poking at random irrelevant curiosities. What a relief when he took off in search of a spicy provolone, but with Finn finally gone, Gina revealed herself to be a robot. She must have memorized guide-books, telling us the most boring things in the most boring way. "The oldest part of Siracusa, they call Ortigia, is founded in the eighth century B.C. by the Greeks. Romans capture it in 212 B.C. during the Second Punic War." She spoke always in the present tense with no feeling or special emphasis. I'm sure she had no idea what a Punic War was. Even I didn't and I came prepared, al-though my profession is not Siracusan tour guide. She had none of Giorgio's fun Italian passion. She couldn't bring the past to life, yet another disappointment.

She did manage to navigate us to the Caravaggio located in the Church of Santa Lucia alla Badia.

Only about eighty of Caravaggio's paintings exist (also he seemed bipolar to me, reading between the lines), and one of them was right here. It had to be the most famous thing in Siracusa; still, the unassuming reddish brown metal sign, *Caravaggio*, screwed to the wall was easy to miss. One might not notice the church at all—a jumble of styles, mostly Baroque, and of modest architectural interest—except to avoid the blind accordion player sitting outside on a folding metal stool, serenading us with "Cielito Lindo." How odd, isn't that Spanish? He wore dark glasses and a navy plaid shirt. His backpack was the same navy plaid. I had never seen a person whose shirt matched his backpack, and it was especially peculiar because he was blind. I suppose he had a wife.

In front of him, on a wooden box, stood a fancy glass goblet. For a blind man to display such a desirable object was foolhardy. The base was navy (that amused me because it also matched his shirt), the thick round stem navy banded with gold, and the bowl gold.

I gave Snow a coin to drop into it and followed Gina into the church.

Snow and I had read about Caravaggio, and we had laughed because, in his self-portrait, his thick eyebrows arched all the way down to his ears. I was about to remind Snow of that when I was captivated by the floor tiles. I had never seen anything so whimsical: identical squares, each an intricate abstract mosaic of black and white squiggly lines, curlicues, and funny dots of royal blue. They had been inspired by the sea, I am certain, because, well, I'm sensitive to art and its influences. The mosaic background of tiny scallop-shaped pieces could be made today only somewhere like China where they probably have no child labor laws. I could imagine the teeny-weeny fingers necessary to make them.

I had to share the tiles with Snow.

I glanced toward the apse where the Caravaggio was hung but then, on an instinct, peeked back outside to find her with the blind man, her hand in the goblet.

"Snow?"

She took her hand out.

I had to laugh. "Are you testing to see if he's really blind?"

"Shush," she said.

Of course she was right. He could hear. I was so embarrassed. Later I wondered if perhaps my catching her doing something innocent and curious, but behind my back, prompted her subsequent behavior. Inadvertently I might have provoked her.

No one was allowed close to the Caravaggio, hung as a sacred object between two overwrought Corinthian columns, behind a velvet rope. Tiles aside, this church with its bright white walls and electronic candles for offerings did not seem the proper venue for *The Burial of Santa Lucia*, I was thinking, as Snow and I squeezed into the crowd and got our first glimpse of the large gloomy oil painting.

In the center of the composition were two half-naked gravediggers illuminated with golden light. I suppose Caravaggio intended to imply the light was celestial since this painting is about the burial of a saint, although the light didn't appear to come from the heavens the way it usually does in religious art. There were no diagonal streaks emanating from above, for instance, more like arbitrary spotlights here and there to highlight the men's nakedness. It seemed that Caravaggio was more interested in those gravediggers than anything. Their bodies were muscled, articulated, and gigantic. They could have been on steroids. The men, bending over, wielded shovels, about to dig. Between them on a pallet lay a young girl a little older than Snow, her skin waxy as if all the blood had been drained from her body.

She lay there in a cave as if it were exactly where she was killed, in disarray, her dress pulled down to expose a single bare shoulder. Is this an erotic painting? I was confused and anxious. Should I have brought Snow? Those gravediggers, so massive, wore only what looked like giant diapers made of white sheets.

I reached out to put my arm around Snow, but she edged sideways out of reach. I remember wondering if people noticed my daughter snubbing me.

Gina, hovering behind and reeking of a sickeningly sweet perfume (the kind that can give you a migraine), recited the story behind the painting as if it were a recipe for minestrone.

"Lucia refuse to marry a pagan. She want to be holy. A virgin. The pagans get angry. They say she has to have sex in a brothel."

"What is a brothel?" said Snow in quite a loud voice.

"A house of prostitution, kiddo," said a man to a rumble of amusement.

Please don't talk to my daughter, I wanted to say, but that's dangerous, isn't it? To have a contretemps with a stranger. We were trapped too. People pressed in from behind. Everyone was listening to Gina, who, like a top, once she began, kept on until she ran down.

"They try to take Lucia. Lucia, she is like, how do you say, in cement. They bring oxen. No one can move Lucia to brothel."

Snow, gazing up at this enormous male sexual fantasy, fiddled with the strap on her tank top, easing it off her shoulder.

"My daughter doesn't need to know everything to appreciate an oil painting," I told Gina, but she moved in between us.

"To punish Lucia, they take her eyes with a *forchetta*." Gina demonstrated, working her arm as if she were prying the eye out of a whale.

"*Forchetta?*" said Snow, her gaze on the painting.

"Fork," I snapped. I fear I did snap, which is not like me. How could Gina know the word *brothel* but not *fork*? There was something sick about that painting, something evil. Something evil about Gina too. I wanted to sweep Snow right out of the church.

"When that not kill her, they stab her in the neck," said Gina.

Snow sank to the floor.

"Get up," I said. "Are you crazy?" Everyone was looking at us now. I yanked Snow's arm. It was dead weight. A man leaned over her. I pushed him away. "Mind your own business."

She was faking. I don't know how I knew but I did. I slipped my arms under her, wrapped her waist, and pulled her up. She kept her legs limp. I pinched her hard. "Ouch," she said, finally standing. I led her away from the crowd and through the church. A woman chased us. "Is she all right? Does she need water?"

"What was that? What were you doing?" I said as soon as we were outside.

Snow straightened her skirt.

"Snow, answer me."

She looked around curiously as if the world were a fascination and I wasn't part of it.

"Lucia visit her," said Gina.

"Don't do that again. It's not funny."

Snow murmured.

I leaned in to hear.

What she said hurt me deeply.

"We won't need you anymore," I told Gina.

Somehow I got us to the hotel.

Looking back, things deteriorated very quickly after that.

Finn

LIZZIE AND I HOOKED UP late morning at the open market. Lizzie cranking on about exhaustion, showing no sign of it, nudged me this way and that under the blue-and-white-striped umbrellas, declaring it great before we barely had a glimpse. A friendly humble busy place with stands built of wooden boxes. We mingled with Sicilian women with bra straps hanging down their arms, admired piles of slimy octopus and calamari tossed onto sheets of ice, the vats of almonds and walnuts, aluminum tins of huge red peppers sliced open, gutted like fish and charred black around the rims, looking fresh from an autopsy.

Lizzie insisted we try every orange—twelve varieties, she counted. We sat on a bench, tasted them, fed them to each other, she tucked a few away for Michael—always about Michael, save some for Michael—then dragged me into a bakery where the cookies were so hard they might have been excavated from a quarry. Lizzie ranted about how much women used to hate it when men on the street said *Smile*, and how now they sign off with smiley faces and weeping emojis.

"That was never a Maine thing," I said.

"What?"

"Saying 'Smile' to a woman."

"Of course not. Nobody walks in Portland. They drive."

"They walk."

She smacked my arm. "I can't believe you're even having this conversation with me. I'm on a ramble. Saying 'Smile' and emojis have nothing to do with each other, but thank you for acting as if they do."

I broke off pieces of a cookie for her while we crossed a funky bridge out of Ortigia into the ugly part of the city. Streets were wider, spacious cracked sidewalks in front of plaster apartment buildings aka future rubble. Lots of imagination at work— air conditioners stuck through holes cut by someone obviously blindfolded at the time, bundles of electric wires scrolling up walls and into windows.

"I was talking about emojis," said Lizzie, "because I'm trying on ideas like dresses. I'm fishing stuff out of a trunk in my brain—like telling a woman to smile, I mean how outdated is that? Fifteen years? I have nothing to say but I'm hoping to find that I do have something to say, that there's a future in one of my sentences. A future in a sentence. A book. A measly article."

I can't always track Lizzie but I like listening to her jabber.

"Suppose I'm over?"

"Bullshit."

"I can't get work, Finn. Nobody's interested. I don't know most of the editors, what's left of them, what's left of magazines. I send out queries. I charm people at dinner." Lizzie covered her face. "Give me a second," she said from behind her hands. "Everyone's getting fired or offered early retirement. Kent Steinhardt, who was stupid enough to divorce his wife, marry someone thirty, and have a baby, got laid off at *The Atlantic*. I can't work at a website, not that they'd hire me, I'd be the same age as everyone's mother. What is this cookie? Almond? I'm halfway around the world—not really, but sort of—and all I can think about is myself. Pathetic. I am pathetic. And, by the way, don't kiss me again and don't act like you didn't."

"How was it?"

"I don't remember."

"Come work for me."

"Very funny."

"Ditch Michael, move to Portland."

"Taylor would love that. You would love how miserable it would make her. Seriously, suppose I'm brain dead?"

Brain dead and fucked besides. I didn't say that, didn't break the news, was wrestling with whether I should. She snuggled in like old times, wrapping her arm around me, tucking into my shoulder. There's always heat coming off Lizzie.

"Let's hijack one of those boats in the harbor," I said. "Let's do it, rent one, see what happens."

"From hijack to rent? Finn, what's happened to us?"

It was wry the way she said it—not moaning or wailing or laughing it off, could have gone those directions too now that I think about it, but it was her offhand coolness, the way she gutted the feeling that got to me. For real, it could have been different.

My mom said, "She's a merry one," when she met Lizzie.

"Finn, you know." Lizzie was seeing where my pea brain was heading. "There are some people who shouldn't marry. Some people are best single, and pity the ones who marry them. And you know what else?" She shoved me sideways against a lamppost and poked a finger in my face. "There are some people who dump all their misery into marriage, make wedded bliss their neurotic nest, and the best version of them lives outside that ugly place."

"Who are you talking about?"

Lizzie grinned.

"I've got a surprise," I told her.

By then I knew I wanted to keep my trap shut, but I wanted to make her happy. Like my pop giving Oscar a steak bone when we knew he was going to be put down the next day. Yeah, like that. Lizzie, poor innocent dog, about to be put down. Not by me. It was a matter of time. Michael's pussy was in Siracusa. Lizzie would find out. Michael set it up, brought her here. Vicious sick fuck.

Look, I'm bad. Once a woman followed me into the men's room, I locked the door, did the deed, and told myself it never happened, and worse pretended it hadn't a month later when the lady blew through town again, but in my rule book this was different. Bringing her to Siracusa—Michael had built a bomb and lit the fuse.

I steered Lizzie down the block and under a flapping awning into Voglia Matta. Gina had tipped me to it. "Best gelato in town. Best anywhere."

We sat outside at a tilting tin table and had gelato for lunch—brioches sliced open slathered with pistachio, coconut, and chocolate. Lizzie made happy noises. Finished the meal with Americanos, and as we walked away, she looked into the bag of cookies. "Only Nutella left. How does something this cloyingly sweet and as sticky as glue get popular? Maybe I can write about Nutella. Look at that sign. Van Gogh Video Games." Lizzie dug out her phone and snapped a photo of the shuttered store. "Van Gogh and video games, a perfect match. In Sicily no less."

That's kind of how I've got her framed now in my head. The way her face lit up when she found something ridiculous.

Dorothy said I avoided the hotel room. Two hundred fifty dollars an hour for that wisdom. She said avoiding my family is my MO and why I spent a good hour in what passed for a bar, a table with a plastic cloth, red wine and white, next to reception, hoping to catch Michael. Playing gumshoe. If I caught him, he might ship her out. I was running interference. Let Lizzie deal with heartbreak somewhere safer and kinder. But he didn't show, neither did Polish American Wonder Woman, and finally I let myself into the suite. Snow, dreamy at the mirror, didn't hear me or didn't care. I never knew what was up with her—was she preoccupied or just didn't give a shit that Daddy was home? Standing sideways peeking at her reflection with one of her smug smiles, she unbuttoned a bit of her shirt and pulled it down to expose a bony sweet shoulder. She licked it. Licked it and strained to watch while she did it. I considered walking in again, a do-over, it kind of stunned me. Then she faced the mirror square on, blinked rapidly, her eyes rolled back in her head—

"Snow."

She turned. I expected something. Fluster. Something. She only waited.

"Where's your mom?"

She thumbed toward the bedroom door. Inside I found Tay flat on her back, arm over her face. Tay never lies on the bedspread in a hotel room, and can do fifteen minutes on how disgusting hotel spreads are. I switched on the light.

"Turn it off." Her voice wobbled.

"What's wrong, babe?"

"Close the door." She let loose with sobs, smothered her face with the pillow.

"What the hell happened?"

Finally she pushed herself up. She was a mess, eye goop drooling around her red eyes and down her cheeks, neck stringy as a chicken, every tendon at attention while she struggled for composure.

"I should never have shown her the Caravaggio. It's provocative sexually. Too provocative for a girl as sensitive as Snow."

"It's not porn, babe."

"You didn't see it, Finn. You weren't with us."

My wife's a lot of sharp angles. That movie, *Edward Scissorhands*? He reminded me of Tay, a vulnerable type who might slice you up. I did my best to hug her without getting knifed by an elbow.

"I shouldn't have scolded Snow about the blind man. I

embarrassed her. It's entirely my fault. I upset her. And when she pretended to faint—"

"What?"

"In front of the painting. She dropped to the floor, like the saint in the painting."

I laughed.

"You don't get it, Finn. You never get anything."

I let her go. She can suffer if it makes her happy. Weird thing about Tay. Even when she's mean, she's a sad sort.

"What did Lizzie say about me?"

"Nothing."

"Snow said—" Tay wiped her eyes some more, shook her head.

"What?"

"Doesn't matter."

"What?"

"She said they laugh at me."

"Lizzie and Michael? No way. No one laughs, you're not funny. I'm sorry, I'm an asshole. Bad joke. I don't think anyone laughs. Just Dani. Dani, our lady of the reception desk, thinks you're a laugh riot."

"At me. Laughs *at* me. Like I'm silly or stupid. They think I'm ridiculous."

I looked at her in a crumple, lips twitching. "Snow didn't say that."

"I just told you she did," said Tay.

"If you're bawling, it's over Michael. Snow said, 'Michael

laughs at you.' It's Michael you care about. Michael you're preening at. Snow's no fool."

"I'm not going to dinner."

"I don't give a shit what you do."

I got the hell out of there. "Be nicer to your mother," I told Snow. "You're a lot like me, kiddo, secretly you're a handful."

Snow didn't look up from her iPad.

Michael

"I WANT A RING."

I'd dozed off. Opened my eyes to find her face a whisper away.

"My parents asked about a ring."

Had not wanted to sleep at all, irritated it happened. Any moment without all my faculties seemed risky. I scooted back against the headboard (the way a frightened person might escape a spider).

"Mikey?"

Stood up, pulled on my briefs, sank down again. Off balance. Woozy. Took a bottle of water off the floor and gulped most of it. Couldn't go from horizontal to vertical quickly. Could no longer spring up. My springing days were over. Julien could. Julien, my alter ego, could have left by the window and scaled four floors down. I got lost sorting out the ways I had aged out of the situation I was in.

"I could send a photo to my parents. I could post it. Do you want to rub that on me?"

"Not this second, thanks." *Not this second, thanks?* I'd forgotten what conversation I was supposed to be having. *Would you like to rub lotion on my breasts? Not this second, thanks.* "Post it?"

"A photo of my hand with the ring. On Instagram and Facebook—"

"Kath, no."

"I'd just, like, put *from mystery man.* Not *engaged.*"

"Kath. Katarina"—remember to use the endearments—"would you want to be with a man who . . . who was capable of . . . ?" She squinted, displeasure or confusion hard to tell. Beware of hypotheticals, keep it simple. "I can't do that to Lizzie. I told you. I am not that kind of man. I can't risk her finding out while we're here. It's cruel."

"I want a ring, Mikey."

Had to mollify, no choice. With K I had to proceed as if nothing had changed. Had rendezvoused with her as soon as Lizzie went off with Finn to the market to cavort, to collect tales of salami. The better to enchant me with. Such a tender thing, the responsibility she felt to keep her husband amused. Look where it got her.

"I won't post it."

Two more days in Siracusa. "If you count today, three," Kath had said, coveting the time left on the first adventure of her life.

She had a view of the centaur's ass from an attic room small and dismal enough to be in a college dorm. Felt idiotic having sex on a single bed. After sex we could study. Or the roommate would show up.

Keep her on the string. Do whatever it takes. "When we're back in New York—I swear, I'll buy you a ring as soon as we're back."

"Today, Mikey."

We'd pretended it had all gone well, that my cock hadn't failed in the line of duty. Quite perversely it had made it in and then gone limp. My conscience turned out to reside there.

"Are you sleeping with her too?" she said.

"No," I lied.

Couldn't get it up earlier with Lizzie either, but she said, "My luck, eat me," and spread her legs.

K wiggled naked on the bed, her magnificent breasts lolling this way and that. "Giovanni Di Battista," she said.

"Our primo artist"—Dani, K's collaborator, had told her about him, supplied a glossy brochure. "Artesa Jewels. Inspired by the sea." Sea horses with diamond scales. Octopus pins with ruby eyes. Gaudy stones. Attention getters. Rings for a Las Vegas moll. That's who I was—a high roller with a chippie when I strolled into Giovanni's shop with K hanging off my arm.

We had left the hotel separately. K had insisted I get the directions. "You're the man," she had said, a dubious assertion when she could tell me like a dog to sit. I was thinking about my credit card. Lizzie paid the bill. What did these rings cost? Should I take euros from an ATM? Either way she would notice.

I was screwed. Obsessing about that distracted me. When K, flattened against a building, popped out into my path, I gasped like a girl.

"Woo-hoo," she said.

Knew where the others were. Taylor with Snow at the Caravaggio. Finn and Lizzie at the market, although who knew where
their spirits might take them. Hopefully to bed. Wise to proceed
furtively, sneaking for K a turn-on—or as she said, "a fun thing"—
now that our days of secrecy were numbered. "I can't wait till we
go public," she said. She must have learned that expression from
the posse that got her here. Making a game of it, she'd peek
around a corner, wave back an all-clear. In between she bobbed
beside me, a skip in her step. When we paused to appreciate a
fountain—"really old," she called it—she stretched in the sun.
"Feel my arms," she said with happiness. "They're baking."

Siracusa had splendor hidden in the dross. The stunning
Piazza Duomo, the lesser but lovely Minerva where we'd dined
the first night, and now this pleasant modest square with its
really old fountain across from two stories of polished stone, the
interior visible only through a porthole window. Artesa Jewels.
K peered in. What she saw left her breathless, and she entered in
awe, gazing at the mosaic ceiling as into a starry night and then
into the welcoming smile of Giovanni. Ready to serve, advise,
and personally unveil his treasures.

"I am Giovanni. How may I help you?" he said, deducing
our native language, at which he was probably genius. Or was it
obvious?

K's grip on my arm tightened, a prompt. "We are shopping
for a ring," I said.

Everything was more beautiful in Italian, K was more beautiful in Italian, and Giovanni caressed her with the language
while gliding her from one display case to another. Beautiful,

bellissima. Seducente, enchanting—translating the prosaic English into the language of love. He sees where her eye falls. Before she knows what she wants, he knows.

Giovanni was younger, more suited to K, slim and sprightly with a mustache that curled at the ends. Considered trying to fashion a match. Betrayals all around, the more the merrier, anything to loosen the choke of obligation and guilt. To divert the storm. To avoid catastrophe. Although the situation was out of my hands, such speculation was conceit; I was a bystander now, flotsam caught in the current. The Sicilian, tanned to a coppery glow with a snarl of long hair (to match), could sing his syllables and be moved by his own art. When the first ring she tried fit, the Italian declared, "You are my woman. *Tu sei la mia donna.*"

For us to admire the ring, K held out her hand, plump and soft. "My fingers are fat," she said apologetically. Of her nails painted purple: "I'll change the color."

"Women do this." Giovanni confided his woe. "They think they are not beautiful enough for my creations. When is the opposite."

"It's ginormous," K giggled. The ring dwarfed her finger. "I could punch out your eye. What is it?"

"Morganite," he said of the glassy pink rock. He angled a light to catch its sparkle.

"Morganite?" said K.

"Cousin to the emerald."

Hopefully a distant cousin. A cousin once removed, surely a much cheaper cousin. Had to be cheaper than the gold sea urchin encrusted with diamonds lying to the left. I was about to ask the price when she whispered, "I want something I've heard of."

"Something?"

"A stone."

"What else do you have?" I asked, but now she was emboldened to make a selection of her own.

"Could I try that?" She pointed, as did Giovanni to the very same one, and they laughed. From there she tried many until onto her finger he slipped a ring you needed a pickaxe to scale: a pileup of gold wrapped around something smooth, large, bullet-shaped, and red.

K studied it closely. "Look." She pointed to the setting. "See all the tendrils."

How could I miss them when their tips were diamonds?

"This ring, *speciale*," said Giovanni. "One night I dream I am in a sea bed." He waved his arms, wiggled his fingers. He was seaweed. He was undulating. "When I wake up I skip the espresso and go to work. For a Sicilian to skip the espresso. A Sicilian man, he opens the window, he say hello to the day, he has espresso, and then . . ."

"What's the stone?" I said.

"Oxblood coral." Its rarity, its color, its *passione*—he waxed on, spinning a web of desire.

"Isn't the sea horse cute?" said K of the eighteen-karat creature curled around the stone.

Giovanni knew about sea horses too. So romantic. *Così romantico.* They mate for life.

"I love it, Mikey."

The jeweler wrote the price on a card and palmed it across the glass. Thirty-five hundred euros.

Giovanni's elbows rested on the display case. His hands were clasped, finally still. The deal was a done deal, K rosy with thrill. No other customers. No way to get lost, to escape. To feint, faint? I handed over my American Express.

"I want to wear it out," said K.

Afterward she was too enamored with her ring to engage in drama. As if she had finally had the orgasm of her dreams, she was calm, spent, satisfied, thank God, pliable. "I'm doing the town with Dani tonight," she said, letting me know she'd be out of my hair. Now she could afford to be generous, while I, at that moment, was too pussy-whipped to care. Frankly. If Lizzie turned up around the next corner, so be it.

Obliged her request: With her phone I snapped a photo of her hand. "I'll send it to my parents when I get home," she said. "A text from here costs too much. Or maybe I'll wait and change my color so it looks prettier. Dani will know where I can get a mani."

We stopped for Prosecco. Sat in plain sight. Toasted the future. "To us." I was done with elaborate phrases of love and seduction. Something about Giovanni made them seem ridiculous. To us. Good enough.

She lifted the glass to her mouth and the ring snagged her nostril. "I don't think I should sleep with it on," she said.

The next morning: Lizzie.

"Oh God, you won't believe who was at breakfast. Michael, you won't believe. That woman who works at Tino's, the hostess, but how weird. I had no idea who she was. And then, when she reminded me, all I could remember was her vision board. Remember, she told us once about her vision board. I said to her, 'Was this on your vision board?' She kind of whooped. You're looking blank, do you know who I'm talking about?"

"Vaguely."

"Her name is Kath. I never knew that. She was on her way to swim. 'To the rock,' she said. That's where they swim here. Lo Scoglio. She spoke Italian with so much excitement. Her entire face contorted. 'Lo Scoglio.'" Lizzie did an impression. "She was sweet. She said we should go there. Everyone swims there in the day. The bar delivers drinks. It sounds like the place all the locals go, looking to score. What an innocent. She'd never been to Europe and now she's partying on a Sicilian rock. Are you all right?"

"The usual. A headache. I drank too much."

"You can't sleep in, darling. Should I pet you? I can cure a headache. I've got some time. You have to hang with Finn and Snow today. On the boat. Taylor and I are going shopping. When we get back to New York, you should quit drinking. We should do it together. Like for a month."

Buried my face in the pillow, groaning. Had to rope in Finn. Lizzie had to cheat. Not to give me a way out, but for a way to stay. When she found out about Kath, I'd need to even the playing field. Even the playing field? What a ludicrous expression. Who the fuck am I?

"What time is the boat?" I said.

Siracusa, Day 3

Lizzie

THE DOLANS WERE SILENT, eating at a round corner table when I sailed into the breakfast room and buzzed the buffet. Limp slices of fruit swimming in a sugar sauce. A platter of overlapping squares of ham and white cheese. A bowl of shelled hazelnuts with a teaspoon standing up in it. A basket of hard rolls. A pitcher of orange juice. There were several cakes, half eaten, all one-story and dense, and single-serving plastic containers of yogurt on an aluminum tray.

In spite of ancient architecture, thick arching and intersecting stone walls, the sub-terra room seemed suited for a bingo game in a senior center. The walls and floors were a bit shiny, as if they'd been disinfected. The chairs with round backs and bottoms upholstered in a tweedy yellow brown were squishy, something depressing about that, and the frames stained walnut. "Of all the stains, walnut is the dreariest," said Taylor, despairing of her plight. Her skinny shredded clothes with unexpected tucks, surprising necklines, and uneven hems could not have been more out of place. No way to feel sexy in that room or around that food, and yet I did.

Sexy and unflappably cheerful. Basking in the joy of having Michael back.

At another table, a sturdy gray-haired couple who looked as if they'd walked their way to Sicily passed a phone back and forth, admiring photos.

What does it matter? The chairs? Who was there, the buffet, the room? My obtuseness matters. My being observant and clever about the wrong things. My delusional state. My smugness.

Although suppose you see the corner of a building at sunset and one side is beige and the other flamingo pink when both are in fact the same drab red brick? And a second later the vision is gone because the earth has moved infinitesimally. Was what you saw reality? Is there always more than one?

"What's the plan?" I set down my plate.

Snow locked eyes with her mother.

"Snow saved that place for Michael," said Taylor in a dull voice.

"Are you feeling okay?"

"Fine," she said without inflection.

"Michael's working this morning. I'm bringing him coffee. He's had a breakthrough, isn't that wonderful? On his book. Still, just in case he changes his mind—" I left the chair empty next to Snow.

They hate me. As soon as I thought that, I banished it. Why would they hate me? Didn't I make things more fun?

Finn bounced a roll on the table.

Taylor poked at a slice of semolina cake, tipping it over. She dug out a few candied cherries and corralled them. No guidebook. No reading aloud. No prepping Snow for the day.

Not me, I think now. They hated each other.

As for Snow, looking back, I marvel at how elusive she remained as she gained more and more power. Snow's passivity was an art form. What a perfect criminal she would make, I remember thinking: someone who could be present and invisible. Given her beauty, that was truly remarkable. What was she doing? Something methodical. Peeling the foil off her yogurt—turning the container as she did to tuck up the edge—examining the yogurt as if peering into a pond, then eating small spoonfuls. Now and then her eyes darted toward the door, checking for Michael.

When I was back at the buffet, pouring a glass of juice, Finn came up. "Would you go shopping with Tay today?"

"Do you think Italians invented hard rolls for breakfast to have something to do with their stale rolls?"

"Ask her, okay?"

"Aren't you going to the Greek ruins?"

"No." He took my juice and drank it as he went back to the table.

"Taylor, do you want to go shopping today? Finn just said you're not going to the Greek amphitheater."

"She fired Gina," said Snow.

"She wasn't good," said Tay.

"I'm taking Snow on the boat," said Finn.

"With Michael. I'll remind him when I go up. He promised to go too."

"That's why Snowy agreed to hang with her dad, right?" He poked her in the shoulder. "Because she gets to hang with Michael?"

Snow scraped the bottom of her yogurt and licked her spoon.

"Ms. Ross?"

She was barelegged in flip-flops, a man's blue-and-white-striped shirt dangling to her knees. "I'm the hostess at Tino's? Kath?"

I jumped up and hugged her. I had never hugged her at Tino's, an Italian place we ate at every couple of months, but when you're away, everyone you bump into from home is family. "I apologize. I didn't recognize you. Michael has exactly that shirt. You look gorgeous. Are you on vacation? This is so weird. This always happens."

"What?" said Finn.

"This. It happens to me all the time. Once on a subway I sat down next to my piano teacher from when I was ten."

Finn moved between us and extended his hand. She shook it, giggling for no reason, the Finn effect.

I introduced her. She supplied her last name, Bicks, and she sat right down in the seat saved for Michael, treating Snow like a little sister, oblivious to Snow's cool. She showed Snow paper packets of sugar she'd been collecting since she arrived, scooping a handful out of her bag. She told her about swimming, about the men. "Ooh la la," she said. "They dive off this big rock and they are always offering to show me around. Lo Scoglio."

She insisted Snow repeat it, and Snow did. *The Sicilian men will make mincemeat of her*, I thought. "Have you been pickpocketed?" I asked.

"Does that happen here?" Her blue eyes grew rounder.

"I'm sure. You should be careful."

That morning at breakfast was the only time we spoke. I almost wrote, "as I recall," but I would have recalled. I tend to speak of that time, particularly about her, as if I'm testifying on the stand.

She arranged the packets in rows on the table, moving one and another from here to there, an artistic display. "That's famous." She pointed to the image on a heart-shaped one. "God reaching out to touch Adam."

"Michelangelo," said Taylor. "Snow knows about that. Thank you for the offer, but I don't feel like shopping."

"Come on, please. It will be fun."

"Zoom, zoom." Kath pressed a finger on a packet and zipped it in Snow's direction. "They're all different. This one's crazy— what's *Italia Zuccheri*? Zucchini sugar? Oh, and isn't this a pretty yellow? Would you like to have one?"

Snow took the Michelangelo.

"But that's Kath's favorite," said Taylor.

"No, it's fine. Good choice," said Kath. "Do you want to come swimming with me, Snow? I'll take the best care of her, I promise."

"She's going on the tour boat with her dad."

"And with Michael," I said.

"What tour boat?" she asked.

"They're right near the bridge to Ortigia," said Tay.

Snow ripped open the sugar packet, severing God from Adam, and dumped the sugar on her plate.

"Whoa, Snowy," said Finn.

"It *is* sugar," said Taylor. "You're supposed to open it."

Kath took a second to react. We all waited. She laughed. She seemed a cheery positive type, the sort in high school that one might dupe and then feel guilty because she was so trusting and forgiving. "Where's Mr. Shapner now?" she asked.

"In the room. Writing."

"Tell him hi."

"Where are you from?" said Finn.

"Indiana. Bloomington. Well, New York City now. Well, not really. I live in New Jersey. Jersey City. But I'm moving to New York soon." She swept the rest of her sugar packets off the table into her bag. "Nice to meet you all. Snow, you're going to come swim with me sometime, aren't you? It's a date." She waved with a scrunch of her fingers and left.

It was a sweltering day. Taylor turned up in a hat with a wide brim that she kept clamped on her head with one hand. We'd never spent much time together alone, and ended up discussing deodorant. As I do when I am stumped for conversation and wondering how in the world to connect, I confessed something inappropriate, that I used clinical strength and sometimes rolled it halfway down my arms. Taylor didn't like greasy sunblock, she said, and didn't believe 30 was as effective as 60 even though some doctors say it's good enough. Finally we were rescued from pseudo intimacy by the shops on shiny and clean Corso

Matteotti, a wide street near the entrance to Ortigia before it spidered into a maze.

Taylor threw herself into shopping the way a camper might seek to prove she was a good sport. She flipped through racks of clothes, pulled out this and that, held it at arm's length, and then popped it back in again. "What do you think?" she would say, and often not wait for an answer. We both knew these fun, cheap stores were not her thing. She pretended to consider a white shirt with a transparent back. "Better for that woman. The one with the sugar."

"Definitely better for her. Well, she's younger for one thing. Wasn't she nice to Snow?"

I worried then. She *was* nice. Finn had moved right in on her. She was someone he would discover could juggle oranges and he would talk her into doing it on Lo Scoglio and the next thing you knew, she would have a serious crush, and he would, God knows what Finn might do. Better him than the Sicilian men. Maybe not.

"Did you see her ring?" said Taylor.

"Yes."

"Horrible."

We both laughed, our first unstrained moment.

"I wonder who bought it for her? A man. Older. Richer. She is sort of luscious. I never noticed at Tino's. Married. A married man, I bet."

"She's brainy," said Taylor.

"Not possible."

"She was reading *The Red and the Black*."

"Stendhal? Weird. Michael is basing his novel on it."

"Well, she's reading it. When I first met her, she was carrying it."

We were in a lingerie shop now. Taylor lifted leggings off a display, striped plum, peach, and white.

"Those would look cute on Snow."

She sank into a chair with the leggings in her lap.

"Is the signora all right?" asked the saleslady.

Taylor sniffled quietly, located a tissue in one of her zippered compartments, and mopped her eyes under her giant Prada sunglasses, which, when she raised them, tipped her hat at an angle.

I was holding six pairs of thong underwear, two for five euros, a great deal, and put them back on the rack. "Taylor, come on. Let's go."

She bobbled up, letting the leggings slide to the floor, where the saleswoman snatched them, and started to walk toward the dressing rooms. "This way." I pointed to the front door.

Even desolate, so upset she seemed not to know where she was going, she wasn't someone to comfort. From the distance she kept, from her rigid posture, always leading with her small proud breasts—it seemed that touch wasn't something she liked. Every so often I grasped her twiggy arm to keep her from walking into a light pole or tripping on the low metal chain strung like a garland along the sidewalk. That garland was odd. What was it doing there? Was it culturally significant, reflective of some demented Siracusa-think: Those crazy drivers, always taking shortcuts on the sidewalk, this will stop them.

Thank God a café turned up on the next block, although

unfortunately located on a little triangle where two streets inter-sected. Vespas and cars raced by on both sides. Taylor flinched at every rev of an engine.

The menu had pictures. I pointed to an orange drink in a tumbler that looked girly, refreshing, and lethal, and held up two fingers.

"Do you want to talk about it?"

"About what?" said Tay, which made me laugh.

"I'm sorry, I didn't mean to laugh. About why you're upset?"

What with all the eye-wiping, nose-blowing, and general mournfulness, she'd taken off her glasses and hat. She blinked into the sun without realizing she could do anything about it, like ask the waiter to adjust the umbrella, so I did. I noticed too that perhaps her stretchy top was on wrong. Her left arm might be coming out of the neck hole. She might be wearing it side-ways. The thing is, all the openings—neck, sleeves, and bottom—were cut ragged and loose. I wasn't sure.

"Snow," she said.

"Oh."

The tears welled again. She sniffled loudly, then sucked her drink through the straw. "This is good. What is it?"

"No idea. It tastes like orange and it has an orange slice in it. I'm guessing orange liqueur with something else. Wouldn't this drink be a lovely nail polish color?"

"Amber," she said. "I had the cutest amber cardigan but I left it somewhere." She waved her hand as if she were dismissing what she was about to say before she said it. "I upset her."

"Snow?"

She nodded.

"Did she upset you?"

"What?"

"I had this shrink once who said sometimes you switch things around. For instance, you say you upset her when she upset you."

"I don't like therapists."

"Why?"

"They're troublemakers."

"I went to one after my dad died. She helped me a lot. It was around the time I met Michael. Therapy smoothed the way."

She took the skinny straw out of the glass and drank the rest. "Michael is so charming."

"I know. He is. I feel, whatever else I did in life, I got that right."

"You're in sync. So devoted."

"Michael betrays me all the time. He falls in love with his novel, or play or whatever he's writing, and I have to seduce him back. I think if you have secrets from the rest of the world, you are married for life. That's how I keep Michael. I figured out his secrets. He adores you." I have no idea why I said that except I felt sorry for her.

"He does?"

"Absolutely."

"He doesn't think I'm stupid?"

"Hardly. Why would you say that?"

"I don't know." She poked at the ice. "He's much more sophisticated. I thought maybe he was polite, but then, you know, after, he laughed at me."

"Of course not. Besides, Michael loves an audience."

"I'm an audience?"

I had stepped in a minefield. Had I meant to give her a zap? "I mean, you're charming too and smart. He loves to talk to you."

"Should we have another?" She grinned as if she'd suggested something naughty.

"Definitely."

She turned to find the waiter hovering. She'd expected him to be there. Whatever she was insecure about, it wasn't attention from waiters. "Two more, please. Do I look awful?" she asked him, laughing, and, without waiting for a reaction, swiveled back to me. "Do I?"

"Not awful. A little sad."

"Snow fainted at the Caravaggio."

"What? Was she dehydrated?"

"I mean, she pretended to. Gina was going on and on about Saint Lucia and how she was sentenced to have sex in a brothel. 'They bring oxen. No one can move her to brothel.'" Taylor imitated Gina.

"She said that to Snow?"

"'They take her eyes out with a *forchetta*.'"

"Whose eyes?"

"Lucia's."

For some reason that struck me funny, and I laughed so hard I snorted. "That's so funny."

"It is?" Taylor started crying again. "I never think anyone thinks I'm funny." She pulled out one tissue after another. Once she'd used it, she pressed it flat, making a stack. "Snow dropped to the floor. She kind of melted."

"How scary."

"More embarrassing. We were in a crowd, everyone pressing in. I could smell people's sweat, that close. I knew she was faking. I know Snow. I hauled her up and out. That's why she said—"

"Said what?"

"It's not important."

"Snow probably wanted to embarrass you. She's getting older."

"I was up all night, wide awake, and I finally thought, yes, that's what I'll do."

"What?"

"I'm going to homeschool her."

"You're out of your mind." I realized I'd said it aloud when I meant only to think it.

"Excuse me?"

"I mean," I said, "who wants to learn that stuff all over again? Math—can you even do it? You'll have to if you teach her."

"She's vulnerable. She needs protecting. She could get led down the wrong path."

"Romano, Mussolini's youngest son, was obsessed with jazz. Snow's embarrassing you is nothing compared to Romano's. I'm sure he loved Benito as much as Snow loves you."

"Benito?"

"Mussolini. The dictator, the dad. Imagine this fascist ruler was at war with the U.S. while his son Romano was in his bedroom listening to jazz. Nothing is more American than jazz, nothing is groovier, actually. Excuse the word, I'm from Berkeley. You're lucky I haven't used *hemp* in a sentence. Nothing is less fascistic than jazz."

"How do you know he was in the bedroom?"

"I'm guessing."

"I don't like jazz."

"Neither do I, but I admire it."

She passed a flat hand across her face to reveal a hideous grimace and burst out laughing. "My mother always used to tell me not to make faces, and I would stand at the mirror and distort myself." She sucked up the last of her drink, the waiter materialized, and she nodded, another. "How do you know about Mussolini?"

"My dad loved jazz. And he was obsessed with this journalist Murray Kempton, who wrote about Romano giving a jazz concert in Siracusa after the war. To play with him, he invited Julius Farmer, a New Orleans jazz marvel. This trip is about my dad. About the things he loved. In Rome, *La Dolce Vita* and the poet Gregory Corso. I wanted to come here because my dad showed me pictures after he read me an essay Kempton wrote about Siracusa, Romano, and Julius Farmer."

She stiffened. "This is your trip?"

"Huh?"

"This trip is about your dad?"

"I miss him and do things with Michael that keep his memory alive."

"Why do you think they have scenes in movies that take place in men's rooms?"

I looked around to see if there was something to provoke this bizarre change of subject, but there wasn't. Except drink. "I suppose it's interesting to men. I've noticed that so much of movies are what's interesting to men. I almost never go."

"We see women on the toilet all the time too."

"Maybe women are turning into men."

"What do you mean?"

"Proving they are just as crude. Or maybe it's just, we all pee, get used to it." Might that be an article: Why do they always have movie and TV scenes of men peeing? "There are lots of things I don't understand about restrooms," I said. "Toilet flushing, for instance. It's gotten way too inventive. Half the time in a public restroom it takes me five minutes to figure out how to do it or else the toilet surprises me by doing it itself."

Taylor's mouth hung open. She gaped. I couldn't remember what we'd been talking about that ended up here. Probably neither could she.

"You gave Finn that toilet book," she said.

I had to think. "Oh, your wedding present. Just a joke."

I took out my phone to make a note about movies, TV, and toilets as a possible article.

"You talked Finn into coming here."

"A little, I guess." I was tapping and not paying attention.

"I hate this place. It's ugly and stupid."

I looked up then. She was standing and scribbling in the air for a check. Her arm was definitely coming out of the neck hole. She looked like a chic woman gone mad.

"You hate this?" Confused, I gestured around. "The drinks were delicious."

"Siracusa," she spat. "If you're so happy with Michael, why do you flirt with Finn?" She shouldered her bag, knocked her glass over, and didn't look back. As she was about to cross the street, a waiter caught her arm, saving her from being run over.

"Your top's on wrong," I shouted.

Michael

THE CAFÉ WAS HIDDEN. Or so I imagined. No sign. A *Herald Tribune*, the reason I went in. The paper caught my eye through a small dirty window, hung on a rack with a clothespin. Armchairs, for God's sake. Peace, sanity, respite.

Left Lizzie reading. Lame excuses, the usual, how could she continue to buy them, and yet she did. Brain on fire, catching magic in a bottle, juices flowing—an avalanche of clichés to justify flight. Like the blessings of a beautiful day, my excuses filled her with happiness. She beamed. "Of course, go, think, walk, make notes—I'm shopping with Taylor. At Finn's request. They are one of those couples that do that thing, ask other people to help their mates because they can't. Infantilize each other, yes, that's what it is." She struggled with her zipper. "Pasta. They divine each other's needs that they can't or won't fill and dump them on other people. Don't forget the boat," she called as she left.

Got dressed quickly, scurried past Dani the sentry, evaded Kath. According to Lizzie, who had encountered her at breakfast, Kath was off to sun and swim. The wife provided intelligence

on the mistress. Can't say that didn't amuse me. K, a nightmare,
going rogue, wanting to post selfies, demanding a ring, tripping
on her power. Never thought I would be exposed by something
as prosaic as a credit card charge. No way to hide that. I don't
pay the bills. Too talented. Geniuses don't pay bills. Lovely Lizzie took care of all that. Lovely Lizzie, who was not stupid, who
could be conned for only so long.

Also that wrinkle of K's using my miles. I was cooked.

Had two restorative hours of reading about Syria, the Sudan,
and the Palestinians, a long feature on why people like game
shows, another on steroid addiction. Outside a monk passed by,
trailed by two more, their hands tucked up the sleeves of their
brown cloaks, undoubtedly sweltering, but from where I sat,
lucky. Considered signing up. Was that what it was called?
Rather than continue on to inevitable catastrophe, could clang
the heavy iron knocker on the thick monastery door and ask for
sanctuary. Dani could mark the route and put a big X at the
destination.

Idea: Julien could have a breakdown and take refuge with
the monks. What could be further from the travails of New
York social climbing than a monastery? Not a bad idea. Inject
spiritualism or the more contemporary mindfulness. Made a
note about that, then checked the time.

Only Finn could save my marriage. How fucked was that?

The boat. It was my opportunity.

Four ducks in brown water. Snow and I leaned over the railing to watch them. White ducks in a circle swimming away from
one another, not sitting up and cruising as ducks do, enjoying the

sights, but their feathered bodies flat, their webbed feet paddling hard (fleeing toxic togetherness?). Dispersing north, south, east, west. Snow glued to my side, Finn left alone to amuse himself— Finn did that so well—as the last of the passengers received a helping hand onto the boat from Captain Emilio.

Heard her voice—was I having a minor psychotic break? No, it was she. Snow heard her too and straightened up, a distasteful look marring her studied impassivity. Crossed dockside to see K in a spirited canter across the bridge. "Wait for me," she shouted, her hand high, waving.

She was wearing my shirt. The striped one. I'd forgotten I gave it to her.

"That woman," said Snow. Was it my own horror at K's arrival, or did Snow's lack of inflection seem clinically lethal, a lepidopterist sticking a pin in a butterfly?

The ticket seller held the launch while K pawed through her bag, offered a handful of euros, and let the woman select what was needed. As soon as she had jumped on, Emilio, whose spindly legs spanned the boat and dock, unlashed the rope and shifted his weight on board.

"Hi," she said, breathless.

"Hello." I extended a hand to shake.

"I can't, Mr. Shapner, this ring will murder you." She sighed with mock exasperation and held out her hand to show Snow. "I got it yesterday at Artesa Jewels. Your mom would love that store."

"You're here," said Finn to K, turning away from the Serbians he had chatted up (in spite of having no languages in common).

"It sounded like fun." She giggled. "I'm drunk on sunshine. We didn't observe daylight saving in Indiana until I was twenty-one years old. You can Google that if you don't believe me. That's why I love sun."

The boat lurched into motion; K squealed. It backed away from the dock, its motor groaning.

"It could break down," said Finn with some pleasure.

"Really?" said K.

"The engine needs oil, the gears are grinding." He took a pause. "She lives in New Jersey. She's expecting to move to the city soon. She has a vision board, you're on it."

"I'm sure I'm not."

"A handsome man with a shaved head, right?"

K's cheek twitched. She smiled uncertainly. "No."

Snow took my hand and pulled me back to the railing. K followed along. I was trapped between them.

Weren't boats ideal for accidental deaths? Didn't people disappear off cruise ships, young women on honeymoons, at least one a year? Of course, unlike this motorboat, cruise ships were small cities and overnight trips provided opportunity, moonlit walks along the deck when who knew what might happen, still. I began to plan K's demise. For amusement. Call it a literary exercise. It would allow me to survive the hour, keep rage in check. What pretty flags, I noted, off the stern. K and I could loll there on that wooden love seat by those pretty triangles of blue rippling in the breeze, away from the stench of gas and the grind of the engine. K, the sunshine queen, would like that.

Although Snow. What would I do with Snow? Who clung like a jealous girlfriend.

The Serbian men, husky and hairy, who filled their shorts and polo shirts to capacity, clustered together under the rectangular awning at the opposite railing. The women, overdressed in pantsuits and gold chains, also under the awning, hogged the long bench, facing inward, uninterested in the sights. That love seat, merely a plank across the stern, was at the end of an exposed empty deck that no one wanted anything to do with, yet it was no more than fifteen feet from the sheltered area.

I'd never get away with it.

Although:

Years before, at a summer party on Block Island, the guests were gathered in the garden near the Jacuzzi when a toddler fell in, and no one saw or heard but her mother. Everyone had marveled—it had produced a giddy horror—how close they came to a child drowning in front of them, unnoticed amid cocktails and chatter. How easy this could be. Lolling with K in the stern, I could point to something in the water, a silver fish, suggest Giovanni might sculpt it in gold, and when she tilted to look, roll her off. Gently. I imagined the water. Sucking her down. Its surface bubbling, then peaceful again within seconds.

Although:

She could swim, not that I knew for sure, it had never come up, but most people can, and she could yell. No, I couldn't get away with it, I thought, when fate conspired: Italian pop music wailed over a loudspeaker.

"It's Jovanotti. Lorenzo Jovanotti. Isn't he fun? Isn't his voice hot, Snow?" K reached around me to poke her. "They played this song last night at Tinkitè. Dani told me about him. He's like as famous as Kanye."

Music. I could pitch her overboard and, if she shouted, no one would hear.

"If I were cleaning my apartment," said K, "I would want to play this song because it makes me so happy. Is that a ukulele? It sounds like a ukulele. You can never be sad if you listen to a ukulele." She swayed and bounced in time.

Snow focused on the sights. She pointed, lifting only an index finger, leaving me to hazard what might interest her, this relic or that. It was a game. A flirtation of sorts. She pointed, I invented. "A rest home for ancient parrots who can say only 'Ciao.'" "A seawall that dolphins jump onto at night to spin on their tails and entertain us." "Why is the sea slimy green here and nearly black there? Because a mermaid named Snow sleeps on a bed of seaweed and every morning she paints the water."

"Are you there too?" said Snow.

"At noon, I dive in."

"What are you two talking about, if you don't mind my asking, Mr. Shapner?" K said, and when I ignored her, a rebuke, pressed her leg against mine.

We circled the tip of Siracusa past a stone fortress, Castello Maniace, a spectacularly large and impressive turreted ruin. The Serbs alerted each other as if one could miss it. "A princess lives here," I told Snow. "She is ten years old, her hair spun of pure gold."

"Is it a brothel?" she asked in her whispery way.

"A brothel? No. Not a brothel."

She slipped her arm around me. I felt uneasy then, on edge, her arm around my waist, her hand pressing the flesh on my side. The odd provocative question. Brothels? What did she know about brothels?

"Look, Lo Scoglio," said K with a happy clap. The boat was farther out to sea on this side of Ortigia; sunbathers on the rock appeared as small as matchsticks.

"Yo, Lo Scoglio," K shouted. "That's the bridge." The short metal bridge that linked the coast to the boulder appeared no larger than a Lego. "I'll take you, Snow. So fun."

Would have to lose Snow, the child, to get rid of K, the half child. Too complicated. Impossible.

With that I abandoned the fantasy. Reluctantly.

Although:

I would have to ditch them both to get to Finn. Finn. I glimpsed him, then and not.

Under the awning near the bow, a rippled rusting metal partition separated out an area for a bar. The flimsy wall didn't quite reach the railing, allowing sneak peeks around it. We'd been watched. The jealous dad had been spying.

"Snow, hang with Kath a second. Kath, would you stay with this lovely creature?" I stepped back, nudged them close, and circled around the partition to Finn.

A teenage boy picking at his nails sat in a metal folding chair near an open cooler where bottles of beer and soft drinks poked out of the ice. Finn, looking out to sea, glanced back.

"Do you want a beer?" I asked.

Finn swiveled and leaned back against the railing, resting on his elbows. "A guy shows up at my joint once a week."

"Two Morettis, *per favore*."

"Stan Bajek. He brings his wife, they order steaks medium well, and every time they come, his girlfriend shows up too. She sits at the bar and watches them. At first I thought, she's stalking him. Then I figured it out. Foreplay."

I spoke quietly. "I didn't expect her."

Finn spoke quietly too. "Get her the fuck out, back to Jersey, you sick fuck, or I'm telling Lizzie."

"Lizzie's in love with you." I offered a beer. Finn ignored it. I set the bottle down near him as if Finn were a pit bull I was trying to befriend. "I want her to be happy."

Finn took a minute with that. He leaned a bit farther back over the water and looked down the railing in the direction of K and Snow. "She's nice," he said finally.

"Nice? Lizzie's a force."

"I'm talking about—" He thumbed in the direction of K. "Throw her back, the way you would a fish too small to eat."

How had he found out? Did Taylor know too? I was surprised. Blindsided.

It was like being pickpocketed. That had happened once. Discovered it at the end of a day when I'd been on subways, battled crowds on Broadway and Sixth Avenue—did I remember a jostle on the train, what about while waiting to be seated at the Monkey Bar, always a jam there at one? Where had I been violated? In this case I could ask, give my pestering brain relief, get a clearer sense of the humiliation. Had Finn seen K and me fucking in an alley or skulking out of Giovanni's? But asking was weakness, a wound to the ego. *The man who understood edge so well he could teach a master class in it was losing his edge.* "If you want to soften the blow," I said silkily, playing the serpent, "make love to her."

"You're pimping out Lizzie?"

"I'm asking you to give her someplace to go when she's done with me. Somewhere she'd rather be. Where you'd rather be. Go back in time. Make it right this time."

Finn appeared to consider it.

It's what you want, the serpent hissed.

A scream.

Finn sprinted, knocking me out of the way.

The man astonished himself, made him wonder forever about his own humanity, ugliness he would never confess especially given what happened later, as if it might point the finger at him, but he paused. He took another swig of beer before following.

Arrived to see Snow throw herself at Daddy. Finn lifted her up and she wrapped her legs around him.

The Serbs jammed the railing. Had one thrown K overboard? No, there she was, bent so far over I thought she was puking.

Again the man held back a beat to suggest mere curiosity, as if he didn't really know her, she was not his to comfort.

"What happened?"

"It's gone, Mikey."

"Shush."

"Oops, I'm sorry, I mean Mr.—"

"Michael is fine."

She turned her heartbroken face to mine. "It was the most beautiful thing I've ever had and it's gone. I let her try it. It was loose on her finger."

"You shouldn't have come on the boat."

"It fell off her finger."

I looked back at Snow, too old and tall for Daddy's lap, but there she sat, woeful and chastened, imitating some sculpture or other she'd seen on the trip, Finn wallowing in his moment of usefulness, petting her head.

"Bella," the captain said of Snow, before coming over to shrug and apologize.

"I told her," said K.

"What?"

"She said she was a good secret-keeper so I told her."

"You told Snow about us?"

"She asked. She said, 'Do you love Michael?' It's not your fault," she called to Snow. "It's okay, I'm not mad." K started sobbing.

"Drink this. Not the beer." I gave her the flask.

She put her head back and drank it all.

"I'm very sorry." We heard Snow's soft voice behind us. "Please forgive me."

K held out her arms and Snow fell into them.

There was a collective *ahhh* from the crowd. "I'll take you for ice cream, a gelato, would you like that?" asked Kath.

Later:

When they left the boat, they walked together, K holding

Snow's hand. Finn, who had rediscovered fatherhood, having been of some use to his daughter for a short while, limped alongside, and I lagged. Every so often K threw a look back at me— I've tried to remember—was it longing, beseeching, needing reassurance? Luscious. She was always luscious, especially now, wilted, vulnerable, and only wanting not to cause pain to a ten-year-old girl.

Whenever K looked back, Snow looked back too.

Last I saw of them was when I stopped at a wine store to see if they sold anything stronger.

Finn

THE BOAT WAS A PIECE OF SHIT. Shredding deck, peeling sides, a cheesy orange aluminum awning, engine groaning, gears grinding. A stink too from the gasoline. Decomposing like the rest of Siracusa, which we viewed in its decrepit glory as we circled, light skating off the water, a gentle hump to the waves, views of seawalls twenty feet tall. We were four: Snow, me, Michael, and, turning up at the last minute, what a surprise, Kathy, his frisky, innocent-as-a-puppy lover. Kathy was her real name, she'd told me when we'd shared the elevator at the hotel. Was Kathy too ordinary a name for Michael? Most likely he'd shortened it. He had to turn her into something more, he turned everything into something more. On the boat she continued to play the Indiana card: midwestern rube, not calculating bitch starring in a famous author's sex romp.

Was that scripted too? Was she in on it? Did Miss Kathy Bicks know it was making Michael's cock hard to up the stakes? Maybe, to get hard, he needed to up them. Their affair might have grown dull. Rote. He needed more help than he used to. Bring her to Siracusa where we're on top of each other, where keeping Lizzie in the dark will take a viper's skill. Danger is more erotic than sex.

I'm guessing.

On that scenic tour, Snow was their beard. I spied on them from a lookout near the liquor where a kid too young to drink, who kept a soccer ball trapped between his feet, sold beer and Coke from a cooler. I was Lizzie's protector. It would kill her to find out, especially here far from home where nothing was certain but our friendship and that this place that had survived multiple invasions from fuck-all could survive the toppling of one marriage, maybe two.

"I didn't expect her," Michael told me.

Asshole. Save those lies for Lizzie. "Do you ever tell the truth? I'm serious."

"Lizzie's in love with you." He never answered a question he didn't want to, only unleashed a smile that showcased every single one of his big white teeth and rumbled on in that low seductive voice. "Sleep with her. Give her somewhere to go. Soften the blow."

I've been trying. I didn't say that.

I stuck by the rail, looking toward the stern, watching Kathy make friends with Snow. When I was a kid, I traveled in a herd. Not Snow. Too bright, too beautiful, too fragile. This idiot Michael imported was kind to her. I had noticed that at breakfast. She could babysit, I thought, if she weren't screwing Michael.

As his foolish lover confided in Snow, I ached for my daughter, for something so common in the life of a girl to be so rare in hers. Confidences, secrets. What did Kathy whisper after making Snow promise—*cross your heart and hope to die?*

The scream, high-pitched like a wounded animal, scared the shit out of me. Snow. Snow overboard.

Thank God not. It was Kathy's yelp. Snow had dropped her ring while trying it on. Into the water. Gone.

Snow threw herself at me, poor Snowy sobbing with horror. For the first time in her life she'd done something careless she couldn't take back.

I was pissed. I wanted to kill Kathy for letting Snow try it on, Michael for bringing Kathy here. Now there was another victim besides Lizzie. Snow.

A vulgar ring, Taylor told Snow later, much later, even made a joke about her doing Kathy a favor by dropping it into the deep, but Kathy thought it was beautiful. She loved it. She must have spent her life savings on it. Taylor shops, buys, wears, discards, buys more—meaningless gratification. This ring was something that made Miss Kathy Bicks think she'd landed.

Why did that birdbrain let Snow try it on? Snow would never have asked.

Then, classy kid, as soon as she had calmed down she apologized, took responsibility, and melted Kathy's heart.

They went off for a gelato at Café Minerva. "It's so cute there," said Kathy. I didn't give it a second thought. Let them go larking. Good for Snow, something normal. It wasn't that I wanted a smoke. Okay, I lit up the second their fannies twitched off down the street, craving that first drag that fogs the lungs and clears the head, and for the sexy little stick between my fingers. Still, it was the right call. I stand by it. Fuck Tay and fuck Dorothy.

I went to sample some Sicilian wines.

Lizzie

IT WAS AN INNOCENT REMARK buried in an otherwise rambling and ultimately hostile conversation.

I wasn't aware I'd noticed it.

On the way back to the hotel I'd obsessed about Taylor. What a bitch. Self-centered. Controlling. I relished the thought of her parading around in a sideways top. Thank God we were leaving the next morning, going our separate ways. All I was thinking, or all I thought I was thinking, was that meant them to Ravello, us home.

I was lightheaded from three sweet killer drinks on a hot day, but that didn't stop my raging. There would be no dinner together that night, our last night. Taylor and I couldn't stand each other's company.

I couldn't bear Snow another night either. I got all twisted up about that. Is detesting a child a failure of character? Of empathy or understanding? A failure of adulthood? I relished it. Found it daring, like breaking a taboo.

Consciously I had no idea what was driving me to move

quickly, but I was too impatient for the elevator and took the stairs two at a clip. As soon as I entered our cramped, dim hotel room, I tugged Michael's suitcase from under the bed. He'd dumped his dirty clothes in it. I felt around and found the book.

She's brainy. She was reading *The Red and the Black.*

I flipped through to find what I knew was there—Michael's scribbles in the margins. Not a book he'd found in a pile in the back of a bookstore. His copy from home.

How remarkable that you found that book.

That conversation plagues me still. When I'm buying a turkey sandwich at the twenty-four-hour market—that's mostly where I buy my meals now, I've gone basic, given up worshipping food, it was so much a part of our life together—or getting cash at the ATM or dropping off dry cleaning, I replay my most foolish moment, my collaboration with his lies.

Not that you needed another copy, but good luck to find it here in Sicily. What are the odds?

I always collaborated with his lies, which is why, well, I had to do what I did. Ultimately.

I ripped off the cover. Shredded the pages.

Then I bolted. Out of the room, skittering down three flights, down the hall and out the doors of the hotel. I crossed the lot, the street, and, gulping breaths, thumped along the narrow sidewalk along the balustrade. The sea was churning, crashing against the rocks, sending up great sprays. As the path headed uphill, I was getting more and more winded, and then it zigzagged and went down again. I was raggedy now, almost tripping over my feet. Vespas buzzed by. I stepped off the sidewalk to pass a bike locked onto the railing and screamed when a horn tooted, missing me by a breath. The walk leveled off and I passed a stone plateau, actually the flat stone top of a fort with a low parapet. It jutted out, and in the sea just beyond loomed Lo Scoglio. Being late in the afternoon it was shady on this side of Ortigia, all the swimmers and sunbathers leaving. I remember turning around, confused to find myself in a crowd, looking out at the stone island. People gingerly negotiated its uneven surface, crossed a short bridge to another outcropping of rocks, and, lugging towels and totes, filed along a slim metal bridge attached to the seawall, its floor a metal grate through which the trekker could see the water slosh and the bleached rocks turn black and hairy with seaweed. Michael would have hated that bridge, heights freaked him, I thought, for a second forgetting that I no longer lived in the world where his quirks mattered or were endearing. Once off the metal bridge, people bunched up and spilled around me and into the street. They were mellow, sun-stoned, toasted, some shiny with oil. A boy offered to sell me water and it frightened me, his grin, the plastic bottle in my face.

I used my hands to carve a way forward. The wind ruffled my hair. I remember because it was like a rap on the shoulder. Stop. And I did. Ahead of me, separated only by two women, one bending to fasten her sandal, Snow and Kath crossed my path. They were holding hands. I heard Kath's loud American enthusiastic, *"Scusi, scusi,"* as they made their way to Lo Scoglio through the stream of bathers clearing off.

It might be interesting to be married to a woman who wears baggy clothes because then you're the only one who knows the body underneath.

I burst out of the crowd and crossed the road, heading away from the sea. Before hurrying into the maze of spidery streets, I looked back. Snow was ahead now, pulling Kath along the metal bridge. Kath's long striped shirt billowed behind her.

Michael has the same shirt, I'd told her.

That was the last I saw of them.

Taylor

I WAS VERY HAPPY to be packing after spending the day
shopping with Lizzie. I had gotten tipsy and my negative feelings about Siracusa had shown through. Given my maternal dis-
tress, I forgave myself for my outburst. Lizzie was cruel to shout
that my top was on wrong. I comforted myself that at least I
hadn't been strolling around Portland. What did it matter who
had seen me? We were leaving tomorrow. I never again intended
to step a foot in this petrified place.

Finn could go to dinner without me. He could take Snow.
He could amuse himself with Lizzie on this last night since
obviously that's what this whole entire trip was about, not Lizzie's father. Does she think I'm stupid? Her New York superiority makes me nauseous. I grew up there. I'm as sophisticated as
she is. I was sorry not to be seeing Michael again, and I liked to
think, him, me. But as long as Snow had a final dinner with
Michael, that was all that mattered. It was important for her to
spend as much time as she could with such an impressive man.

After going to the room long enough to use the bathroom

and fix my top, I went back downstairs to the hotel's lone computer, located in an alcove off the lobby, and after wiping the mouse and keys with Purell, I confided all in a long e-mail to April and felt much better. The computer had a European keyboard and it kept making capitals. I could not figure out how to stop it. "April," I wrote, "this keyboard has a mind of its own." Then I Googled Maine's requirements for homeschooling and they didn't seem daunting, filing forms, of course, and yearly tests Snow would have to take. There were even curriculums available. I had just gotten up from the desk when Lizzie ran by. Ran. How inappropriate to streak through a hotel, even one as puny as this. Thank God, I didn't get up from the computer a moment sooner or I would have bumped into her.

I recoiled at the thought. It was then I realized how much I had grown to dislike her.

Back I went to the room. It amazes me to recall how peaceful I was just then, which proves you never know what's coming. Now that we were leaving, knowing we would be out of Siracusa in less than twenty-four hours, I had to concede the room had a nice view, early for a sunset, maybe four in the afternoon, but the sky was dark and glamorously threatening. A wind was up, I could see because the ocean was all afroth and atumble, smashing against the rocks.

Even the room had its charms: the wall, a blue-gray halfway up, then a little strip of stenciling, and cream above. The window was tall with a satisfactory drape of striped cotton. As you can tell, I was in a forgiving mood.

I started packing, a serious activity, since we had dirty clothes now, and I had packed in anticipation of visiting four cities. I needed to rotate things to the top of the suitcase and relegate the dirty clothes to the bottom. I designate certain compartments for each.

I was rolling Finn's cranberry crewneck—sweaters are best rolled, not folded—when I realized my hands were a bit gritty. I examined my palms. Specks of dirt. How funny, there is no dirt in Siracusa. I went into the bathroom. I was about to rinse my hands when I thought, *That's right, there is no dirt in Siracusa. It's wall-to-wall stone.* What I mean is, if you found yourself with dirt on your hands in a cell block, you'd have to assume some-one was digging a tunnel. You'd figure, *Hey, something fishy is going on.* Those brown bits looked familiar. I smelled them. Tobacco.

I rifled the pockets of Finn's cargo shorts. Then his Dockers. I pulled the pockets inside out and did the same with his sports jacket. Flecks were everywhere.

He'd promised. He'd sworn, I think he'd sworn. He did. With Snow in my arms, he'd sworn on the grave of his father that he would never smoke again. His dad had died from it or would have if he hadn't had a heart attack. Doesn't smoking cause heart attacks? I believe so. He did die from it.

I expected to be crying but I wasn't. I felt hard and angry and so unlike myself. Should I confront Finn the minute he gets here, in front of Snow? That would upset Snow. I try never to argue in front of her. Finn and I sometimes go days without speaking, but raise our voices? That's a no-no. The smell in the taxi to Siracusa must have been him. Perhaps not. Perhaps the driver. As you can tell, I was questioning everything. One time I told Finn never to let his brother in the car because he had stunk it up with his Camels. I bet it wasn't his brother, but Finn.

Now I understood his friendship with Jessa. They were smoking buddies. That woman smoked while she breast-fed, and I don't mean during the time she was breast-feeding, I mean at the very moment I'm guessing but I wouldn't put it past her. She's the only lobsterman, excuse me, lobsterperson who reeks of cigarettes. That is not easy to accomplish—to spend all day in the brine and smell of tobacco.

Did Lizzie know Finn smoked? Did all of Portland know? Had it been going on for years?

Most important, he didn't care enough about his daughter to stop.

Where were they? Why weren't they back yet?

I went down to the balustrade overlooking the sea to phone my mother and wait for Snow and Finn. Since it was windy and Siracusa is in a perpetual state of disintegration, specks of plaster and dust swirled in the air. Waves crashed with a roar. I had my phone out, about to press call, when I thought, *Don't. With the wind and those waves, you won't be able to hear a thing. Besides, Finn's smoking will make Mother happy. Proof I shouldn't have married him.* April always points out that Penelope makes me feel worse. "Has your mother ever made you feel better? Ever? In your entire life?" she asked.

Just then, as I was about to cross back to the hotel, Michael came around the corner. I started to wave, but he took a quick look in both directions, furtive looks, it seemed. I might have imagined it. Waving felt wrong, an intrusion, but then he saw me and strolled over.

"Just trying my mother," I said, turning off my phone. You'd think I'd have been comfortable with him after these days together, but if anything, I was shyer. "How was the boat ride?"

"Oh, fine," he said.

"Have you seen Finn and Snow?"

"Not since."

"He's smoking."

"Ah."

"I don't know what to do." It surprised me I told him.

"Cigarettes?"

"Yes."

"Do you smoke?" he asked.

"At Vassar, I used to do it now and then, but it didn't take. I must not be an addictive type even though my roommate, MaryPat, she was southern from the same town Harper Lee was from, and . . ." I realized I'd started a story I didn't know the end of. "Finn's so—"

"What?"

"Immature."

"Yeah, he is a little." His eyes were twinkling and he had a flirty grin. I think he was attracted to me. At that moment, I felt a definite charge. "Don't tell Finn you know."

"Why not?"

"Ammunition," he said.

"Ammunition?"

"You've got something on him, something he thinks you don't know but you do. It gives you power. Like having an ace up your sleeve or a gun in your boot. The only kind of power worth having is secret power. When you lose it, you're screwed."

I was so self-conscious that I was thinking, *He's talking to me*, while he was talking to me, you know, aware that I was having this intimate fun conversation with Michael and wishing my mother could see. I was standing awkwardly, my hand up to keep debris out of my eyes. Certainly I wasn't my most graceful. Still, secret power? I didn't know what he was talking about.

It stumped April too. How can you have power if no one knows about it?

"Smoking's a vile habit," I said. "It can kill you. It smells. He's a father. He has responsibilities."

"Why I'm not one. I'm going up to the room." He looked grim now. "Last night here, thank God."

"Do you hate Siracusa too?"

Michael burst out laughing. I joined in although I didn't know why. He gave me a kiss on the cheek. "See you at dinner."

"I'm not coming," I started to say, but, as he walked away, I realized the hotel was in shadow. This was the east side of Siracusa, I should explain, which meant that the sun in the west had sunk out of sight below the height of the buildings. Where were Finn and Snow? What in the world could they be doing? Snow had no patience for her dad. He would have driven her crazy by now. She would want to be with me. I checked for a text. When I looked up, Michael was gone.

I followed him to the lobby, at least I assumed that was where he went. "Any messages?" I asked Dani.

"No."

"Did my husband and daughter come in while I was outside?" She shook her head.

For all I knew they had hopped a bus to Mount Etna. Finn might jump on whatever passed by. I went back outside to wait for them but instead of crossing to the water, turned left and peered around the nearest corner. Most tourist destinations— restaurants, Piazza Duomo, the churches—were this way.

I ventured down the street hoping to encounter them but kept looking back in case they pulled up in a taxi. There was a cat sitting in front of a door. An elegant cat. Way too elegant for Siracusa. *This cat wants to move to Rome,* I thought, which amused me. Slender, with a snow-white face and chest and a slate-gray back, it looked unexpectedly chic against a cocoa-colored door that, while peeling and in need of repair, still provided a lovely contrast. This cat was female, it simply had to be, with its delicate face and pointed ears, sitting with its head tilted just so as if a photographer might have positioned it. Her large gray eyes— nearly colorless—were rimmed in a thin line of black as if precisely drawn. I do my own eyes like that but prefer a smudgy look. Seeing that cat was like encountering someone from my family. I mean the Seddley side: elegant, opaque, and standoffish. I slipped my hand under its belly and lifted it to my chest. In a sudden motion, its paw shot out.

I screamed and dropped it. The cat ran off.

Very gingerly, I patted my cheek. The tips of my fingers came away dotted with blood.

I pulled out my phone for the mirror. There were three long scratches across my cheek, and here and there, as if stitched with a needle, pinpoints of blood. My face. My poor beautiful face.

I rushed back to the hotel, colliding with Finn coming in. "What the hell happened to you?" he said.

"Where's Snow?"

"She went for a gelato with Kathy. What happened, babe?"

I started crying. "A cat scratched me."

He patted my shoulder in an awkward way. "You should put something on that. Witch hazel."

"Witch hazel! The only person who uses that is your mother. What are you thinking? Who's Kathy?"

"That woman Lizzie knows. The one at breakfast."

"But they're not back yet. When did they go?"

"Around three. When we got off the boat."

"But they're not back, is she back?" I asked Dani. "You know, the young blond American woman. Always going swimming."

"Signorina Bicks?" said Dani. "No, I haven't seen her. I will get you some ice."

"It's six thirty. Snow isn't here."

"I'm sure she's fine," said Finn. He followed me into the restroom.

"Oh my God, my face." I dabbed at it with a towel and water. "I picked up a cat. It clawed me. This is awful. Where were you?"

"I went to Montavi Brothers."

"What's that?"

"Gina knows the owner. Mario Montavi, a face like a growl, sets out a glass and a bottle, a plate of tasties, crosses his arms, plants them on the table, and leans over like he's giving them shade."

"But I fired Gina."

"She set me up with a wine tasting." He stuck out his tongue, cherry red. "Fichera, a red liqueur. How to make ice cream lethal."

"You left Snow with a stranger?"

"Michael and Lizzie know this woman."

"They don't know her. She works at a restaurant they go to."

We stopped back at the desk to pick up the ice. Dani spread out a cloth napkin, plopped on some ice cubes, folded up the corners, and tied them together.

"*Êtes-vous une infirmière?*" said Finn.

Dani smiled.

I gave him a look.

"What, Penelope?"

We got in the elevator, where the mirror was huge and unavoidable. Along my right cheek, the scratches were blossoming into bright pink welts. I started to cry again.

"Use the ice."

"I can't feel anything through the napkin. It's too thick. 'Are you a nurse?' Is that what you said? How ridiculous. And stop acting as if Penelope is the worst thing you can call me. Why are you friendly to a hotel employee when something awful is happening?"

"You got scratched, babe. It'll heal."

"Snow is missing."

"She's having fun. She's not missing."

An hour later, he had to admit I might be right.

Michael

PACKING, THE MAN ASSUMED. How she found it. Found him out. A quick thumb through Stendhal, perhaps the book engaged her and then, reading, she found his margin notes.

That sort of thing interested him, the how of it. He tried to cast this catastrophe as a plot problem, and Lizzie, an unwieldy character that he hadn't properly writ.

I lingered over the fantasy, a perverse amusement. Lizzie settling into the comfy chair, one leg slung over the arm. She flipped through *The Red and the Black* while tugging at a curl. She was a book lover, the sort to fall into or get caught up in an unlikely read.

Although what the fuck was she doing in my suitcase?

As a rule she didn't pack for me and, as for herself, left it until the last minute. She was hunting either for the book or for evidence. What made her suspicious? Was it something I said? Or she saw? Was it something about the encounter with K at breakfast that tipped her? Had K sent another note, one Lizzie intercepted? That I doubted. Had Finn told Taylor, and Taylor told her? Or had Finn told Lizzie? No. Finn would never hurt Lizzie.

But I would. I'm her husband.

Betrayal of this magnitude is the exclusive province of married couples.

Perhaps Lizzie had phoned home or checked e-mail and found a message from American Express. "Alert. Unusual activity. Call."

Why would she assume that a charge from Artesa Jewels wasn't a present for her?

I'd entered the room relieved not to have encountered K in the hotel. Relieved it was my last evening in this stone city in the company of the Dolans. I was near to being back in New York and thus able to resolve the mess where we lived, where we were entrenched, and everything would seem less unhinged and manageable. Where I had a chance of holding on to Lizzie. We weren't rich enough for a decent divorce, were worth more as two and not just socially. Neither could continue his or her life on half the money.

Had Snow told Lizzie about K, whispering, hesitant, her eyes darting nervously? All Lizzie would want to do, all anyone ever wanted, was to ease this vulnerable girl's anxiety. "I can't hear you," Lizzie would say sweetly, leaning down.

In that soft poisonous voice, what would Snow say? She specialized in nuggets. Queen of the short and cruel.

Of everyone who had victimized him on this trip, the man decided, she had been the cleverest. The most seductive. It was strange that in thinking of the collision of Lizzie and Kath, this Italian romp gone south, he now blamed Snow for all of it.

Although it made no sense to do so.

But he was a writer. He trusted his subconscious. He was used to letting unlikely truths float to the surface and then figuring out why they had.

How could I get rid of Kath? Get rid of her and not lose Lizzie? Eventually Lizzie would return to the room. Her clothes were here. Her passport.

When I'd walked in, the door swinging back had caused several pages to fly up off the tiles. They were scattered everywhere, some whole, some in shreds. Like a dead body, the hardcover lay there flat now, disemboweled.

Finn

MICHAEL HAD OFFERED LIZZIE like she was a plate of sardines.

I can't say I didn't ruminate on that on my way over to Mario's. Gina had set me up with him, a sad-eyed Sicilian with a feast of a shop not far from the dock. She'd talked him into letting me sample his wines. He knew the best. I fell hard for the Planeta vineyard and, with Gina translating, arranged for export. Gina was fun. Second night in Siracusa, after Tay had fired her, I'd spotted Gina while on my night prowl. She was with her friend Carina. They squeezed over. I squeezed in.

"I am *un restaurateur*," I told Gina, with a pretentious little wave of the hand. "I am looking for some cheap Sicilians to import. Wines, not waiters." It was late enough that only the desperate or drugged were still out, Gina a little of both, and even a joke that bad got a laugh.

What haunts me—Snow's hand in Kathy's as they sashayed off down the street. I remember wondering if Kathy was Catholic.

How she came by that forgiving nature. Thinking, if I could stand Michael, I'd ask.

"You let her go with a stranger?" said Taylor, so rigid she was vibrating.

"She's not a stranger."

"When did you last see them?"

"At three or so."

She burst into tears.

"Babe, stop it. It's what—not even seven. That's noon Sicilian time. Maybe they're with Michael."

She was shaking her head, her nose running and she didn't even know.

"Hey, she's okay."

"Not with Michael. I saw him."

She sank down on a chair and clasped her hands. "God, bring her back. God, please."

First time she'd ever mentioned God. I noticed that. Tay doesn't pray. On Christmas Eve we go to church and she sits with her arms folded, head swiveling, taking in the architecture, never opening a Bible even to sing. Snow's being missing—soon I was freaking too—split me in two, part of me right there scared shitless and knowing it was all on me, the other part making dumb observations, disconnected like I'm on the other side of the world because that was where I wanted to be.

"Where were you?" she asked.

"I told you. Tasting wine, salami, green olives, ricotta, every sea critter or veggie that could be marinated."

"How come you're not drunk?"

"Who said I'm not? Want me to get some more ice for your cheek?"

"That cat. I was going down the street thinking that you and Snow might be coming from . . ." She shook her head. "Shut up. Please just shut up. I probably need a plastic surgeon."

"Do you want to go to a hospital?"

"In Sicily?" Scorn.

"Nothing's happened to Snow. Kathy's nice. Good-hearted. A little flaky maybe."

"Flaky?"

"Enthusiastic."

"You let your daughter go off in a foreign city with someone flaky?"

"She might not realize the time is all. When Snow dropped her ring in the water—"

"What?"

"That monster she was waving around at breakfast. She let Snowy try it and it fell off her finger. Gone."

"Gone?"

"Some octopus is wearing it."

"Poor Snow."

"Yeah. It ripped her up. In a flash, done, over, no way to take it back. She was sobbing her little heart out. You would have been proud of Snow. She apologized. Took responsibility."

"You are the stupidest man I have ever met." Contempt. I didn't recognize it till I rehashed it with Dorothy. Contempt, that's Dorothy's word. The nostrils on Tay's skinny nose flared, her eyes narrowed, her lip curled. I felt like something dirty she'd forgotten to wash off.

Tay threw herself into packing.

I watched that sick enterprise—the compulsively neat way she folded things. One uneven crease and she begins again. "Motive," she said.

"Motive?"

"I don't believe for one single second she forgave her."

"She did." But I was thinking, Did she? "Motive for what?"

"Make them call the police."

I phoned Michael first. "Is Snow with you?"

"No. Have you seen Lizzie?"

"My daughter didn't come back from being with your girl-friend." I hung up.

"Girlfriend?" said Tay.

"He's fucking her."

"I'm sure he's not."

"Fine. He's not."

At the desk, the second I said *police*, Carlo, the slump-shouldered night receptionist, summoned the manager, who bustled down the hall straightening her jacket. "Marianna Bianchi," she said, shaking our hands. She was a stout woman, no idea how old. She had a firm handshake and a sensible brown suit. Her short yellow hair was a bit of a bird's nest. Tay referred to it later as an unfortunate perm. "May I help you? Is there a problem?"

"Signor Dolan's daughter didn't return," said Carlo.

"She's ten. She's missing," said Tay. "Our daughter went off with Kath—"

"Kath?" said Marianna.

"Signorina Bicks," said Carlo.

"Your daughter's name?" said Marianna.

"Snow."

Marianna spun a pad on the counter her way to take notes. "Where did they go?"

"We don't know," said Tay. "If we knew—"

"My wife's upset."

"Of course I'm upset." She started crying again.

"I'm sorry," I said to Marianna.

"Why are you apologizing to her?" said Tay. "Signorina Bicks is one of your hotel guests. Call the police right now."

"I'm sure they'll turn up," said Marianna, with a practiced smile. "It often happens. Siracusa is very stimulating. Many men, as you say, flirt. The girls stop in a café, they make friends. 'Can I buy you a Prosecco?' the boy asks. *E così*, it's three hours later."

"It's over four hours. She's not a mother," said Tay in my ear.

The lobby was happening now, guests on their way to dinner crowded into the small sitting room where wine was open on the table along with water and a tub of ice. A boy sat on a chair with a bounce, jumped up, and bounced back down again. His little sister hid her face in her mother's skirt while the mom had her change purse out examining her coins, trying to see what was what. A man with three cameras slung around his neck was discussing a trip to the Papyrus Museum. Taylor put her hands over her ears, strode outside and back in. "You don't want to call the police," she said loudly, "because the last thing you want is the police in your hotel. It's bad for business."

"I assure you, Signora, it is not true," said Marianna.

"Tell her 'bullshit,' Finn."

"My wife needs you to call them right now."

"Fight." Taylor jabbed me.

"I am."

"No, you're not." To Marianna she said, "I am head of the tourist bureau in Portland, Maine, and I am well aware of how little any hotel wants to have police on the premises." With that she burst into loud sobs, and Marianna gestured that we should go down the hall. She directed us to a small office and waited for us to settle in the two white metal chairs before sitting at her desk—a pine plank with a phone, a laptop, and a stack of papers that she picked up and placed on the floor.

"We have small crimes. Pickpockets—*borseggiatori*—but nothing dangerous." She dialed.

While she waited for an answer, her eyes landed on Tay's face and got stuck there.

"My wife was scratched by a cat."

She nodded. The bitch didn't believe me.

We listened to her torrent of Italian on the phone. "They are coming," she said, hanging up.

"We'll wait in the lobby," said Tay.

"May I provide you some refreshments? A cocktail? Bruschette?"

"No," said Taylor.

We sat silently on the couch near reception. I put my arm around Tay. She slid away. "I want a divorce," she said.

I went outside. The moon floated in a strip of sky between heavy clouds. My skin was prickly with fear. I was praying. "Mother Mary, full of grace—"

I ducked around the corner, took a few drags, popped a Tic Tac, and returned.

"I mean it," said Tay, her tone bloodless, her face too except for those cat scratches brighter and uglier.

"Snow's missing," I told Michael when he exited the elevator and saw us.

"What do you mean?"

"Is she reliable?" Tay started to cry again.

He sat down and put his arm around her. "Is who reliable?"

"Kathy," I said.

"I barely know her. What do you mean, she's missing?"

"They went for ice cream after the boat trip," I said, "and didn't come back."

"I wouldn't worry," he said.

"What?" squeaked Taylor. "Why not?"

"I don't know her, just an impression from the restaurant, but she seems sweet, excitable but not reckless." He shut up then. I figured he was reconsidering that, the asshole. "What happened to your face?" he said.

"I picked up a cat."

Michael threw a look my way. Couldn't read it. Was it, *She's protecting you*, like I was some animal who'd clawed her, or sympathy 'cause Tay and I were in the soup?

"Maybe Snow's with Lizzie?" he said.

"They don't like each other."

After I said it I heard it 'cause of the silence. I hadn't known I knew that. No one disagreed.

A bright blue car with a white stripe and the word *POLIZIA* pulled up. Tay rushed outside and sank to the ground.

An officer grasped her elbow, raised her up, and held on until she was steady on her feet.

"Our daughter is missing," I said, and heard Marianna behind me translate. "She went for ice cream and didn't return."

I was in another dimension still, jumpy with terror yet aware that I should have comforted Tay, should have leapt to help when she dropped. It must have looked odd to the cops that I didn't, but if I'd tried, she would have yanked away. *Don't*, she would have sneered.

I was afraid of her, that was what Dorothy said. Who knows, maybe I still am. It's a way of life.

I was sure they were going to slap the cuffs on and arrest me. Guilt, said Dorothy. Tay thought I was a lousy father and she'd turned out to be right. I'd let my kid prance off with a stranger, and God help me, she was gone, and after the deli I'd spent a couple of hours hanging with Gina, smoking, lying on a chaise on her tacky terrace, and feeling an unfamiliar calm looking over tile roofs into an empty sky, same light blue as Agente Penzo's polo shirt.

There were two, Agente Penzo and Detective Carrudo—

Penzo fair, Carrudo dark with blazing black eyes and a mole on his cheek. I thought I'd spotted Carrudo singing karaoke on one of my night prowls. I remembered the mole.

We crammed into Marianna's office. Penzo spun her chair around and straddled it. Carrudo loped a leg over the corner of the desk, crossed his arms, and stared down at us seated before him like misbehaving pupils. Marianna, beside him, crossed her arms, hoisting her breasts, and viewed us sternly as if she'd joined the force. Michael squeezed into a corner.

"She has extreme shyness syndrome," said Tay again and again, keening.

They didn't seem to understand that—fuck, who would, and fuck knows what the translation was—but Carrudo, after taking our names, made a show of noting that on a pad he'd pulled from his back pocket.

"My wife is saying that Snow is very shy, she's nervous alone, nervous with strangers."

"Nervous crossing a street," said Tay, while she continued to rock and moan.

"She's vulnerable and innocent," said Michael. Tay threw him a grateful look.

That caught their attention. "Name?" they asked him.

"Michael Shapner. My wife and I are traveling with them."

"He's a famous American writer," said Tay.

"Hardly," said Michael.

"He is," said Tay.

"Where's your wife?"

"On a wander."

That drew a blank from Marianna. "Sightseeing," said Michael.

There were pauses while we waited for Marianna to tell us what they said and to tell them what we said, and the pauses were freaky—places for our words to hang out and start to sound funny. Innocent answers grew horns.

The cops conferred with each other and with Marianna. Carrudo's hands danced, illustrating whatever the hell he was talking about, tapping his cheek, his fingers swimming here and there.

"They want to know about your face, signora," said Marianna.

"A cat scratched her," I said.

"Around the corner, do you know the cat?" Tay pleaded with Marianna. "Gray and white. I picked her up."

They all conferred again.

"There are strays all over Siracusa," Marianna finally said. "Everywhere. Even in cafés. Did you not notice?"

"We're not looking for a cat," said Michael. "We're looking for a ten-year-old girl."

Tay gave him a weak smile. Again Carrudo took note, not an actual note, but he scratched his nose while shifting his gaze among us.

I showed him a photo, they passed my phone between them, and I told them what Snow was wearing. It was surreal. Snow last seen wearing . . .

"*Bella,*" said Carrudo, viewing the photo and giving Tay a nod of credit.

My phone pinged.

"Oh God," said Taylor.

Carrudo handed it back and waited for me to check the text. From Lizzie. *I need you.*

"Who is it?" said Taylor.

"Nothing. The restaurant. I own a restaurant in the U.S. I'll call them back."

"My daughter was with an American staying here," said Taylor. "The woman hasn't come back either."

"She is with a friend?" said Carrudo.

"He knows her." Taylor nodded to Michael.

"I don't know her. She works near where we live."

They asked for a description and Tay blubbered it out. "Blond, straight hair to her shoulders, sometimes pulled back, tan, blue eyes, her nails painted purple. This morning she was wearing a man's striped shirt, long, to her knees, kind of like his." She pointed to Michael. "Silver flip-flops. Big orange tote bag. Perforated. You know, with little holes. Looks like leather but plastic."

The cops huddled with Marianna, then stood formally for her to deliver the verdict. "They will put out the information to all police cars," she said. "He would like that photo of your child," said Marianna.

After about fifty fumbles trying to type in his e-mail, I sent it.

"They want you to know the police take kidnapping very seriously," said Marianna.

Kidnapping. Jesus. Tay burst into loud sobs. What did we think, but whatever it was, it wasn't that. Just gone, missing, lost, but not a big scary word like that.

Carrudo offered a card with his number and they left, escorted by Marianna. We all fell dumb.

"I'm sorry," said Michael after a bit.

"Snow's probably all right," I said.

"Idiot," said Taylor.

Marianna popped her head back in, beaming. "Your daughter is here."

We knocked into each other running.

Snow. Just inside. The glass doors framed her like the arch of a church. Snow so still, for a second I wasn't sure she was flesh and blood. Dressed differently too. A pair of loose white pants, worn low, hung off her hips, belly button exposed and a bit of bony hip. A flimsy white tank barely covered her on top. Pink on her lips. The red sunglasses.

"It is all, all right," said Marianna with a clap.

Tay took off Snow's glasses, kissed every inch of her face, then pulled back to look at her. They were beautiful together. I could tell Carrudo admired that.

"Where are your clothes? What happened?" said Tay.

"Where were you, Snow?" I said.

Snow's eyes shifted toward the police and she shuddered against her mother.

"What happened, sweetheart, tell me," said Tay.

"Where were you, Snowy?" I said.

Snow clucked.

"She clucks when she's upset," said Tay. "No, sometimes she just clucks. I think it's a way to connect, to let us know she's okay or she doesn't want to talk, or—I'm not sure. She's very bright."

"Clucks?" Marianna did not know how to translate.

"That noise you make—your tongue against the roof of your mouth," I said. "A cluck."

Carrudo spoke to Marianna.

"Does she need a doctor?" said Marianna. "The police would like to know. Also they would like to interview her."

Tay hugged Snowy again, who allowed it but I guess that's all you could call it. I could see my kid was strange, taking in but giving back nothing, and everyone else noticed too. Her beauty got in their way, though, that's my sense of it, given how gaga they were. It made it hard for them to assess anything.

Then Snow saw Michael and smiled.

"Hi, Snow," said Michael. "I'm glad you're back."

"Are you hurt?" said Tay. "Tell me."

Snow clucked again.

"No, that means no," said Tay. "Did Kath buy you those clothes?"

Snow's eyes shifted.

"Yes," Tay told the cops. "The woman bought them for her. I recognize her lipstick too. Her bright pink color."

"Did anyone hurt you, Snow, and tell you not to tell us or they would hurt us or you, because they won't," said Tay.

Again my kid fucking clucked. I caught myself about to smile. She was messing with the police. With us. She was stonewalling. I know my Snow. Piece of work. Dolan for sure.

"She needs to be with me, that's all," said Tay.

"We're leaving Sicily tomorrow," I told Carrudo. I figured in the end all these cops wanted to know was whether this was still their problem. If we were going to be gone, ciao and good riddance. "We're fine," I said. "Our daughter's fine. We're sorry to have bothered you. Thank you for coming."

They left in high spirits as if they'd solved a crime. Penzo stopped at the desk to ask Carlo where Dani was, at least that was my impression.

"You okay, beautiful?" said Michael.

Snow lifted her eyes to him. "What?" He leaned down. She whispered in his ear.

Michael jerked away. "What are you talking about? Who?"

"Mommy, I have to go to the bathroom," said Snow to Tay.

Michael grabbed Snow's shoulders.

"Let her go," I said.

He shook her. "What the fuck—"

I hauled him off, twisted his arm to swing him around, and punched his face. He staggered backward and I slugged him in the gut. The guy crumpled, blocking the doorway. We had to edge around.

Guests cowered as if I were a madman planning to take them all out. I propelled Taylor and Snow past and ushered my family to the elevator.

Tay pushed in Snow ahead of her, swiveled around, and put up a flat hand at my chest. "We don't need you now."

The door slid shut.

I texted Lizzie.

Lizzie

HOW STUPID WAS I? Plotting his seduction, wooing him with dead poets, imagining my competition was a novel. What a pretentious notion.

All those times she'd greeted us at Tino's, escorted us to the table in the corner. "The scampi is delicious tonight." How that must have turned him on.

Games we played at other people's dinners now played on me. Did he feel her up on the way to the men's room?

"How is everything?" She'd checked on us often. Now and then I asked her about herself. To be polite I was curious. At Christmas she went back to Bloomington to see her parents. "They don't approve of New York," she'd said. Was he fucking her then? What did he give her for Christmas? Once she'd confessed to a vision board. It had amused me. I often asked about it. "How's your vision board?"

Last month she told me it was coming true.

Is he in love with her?

My brain rattled, every moment reconsidered, thoughts ping-ponging around as I stumbled down one spindly street after another. I didn't encounter another soul. Except for the noise in my head, the silence was unearthly. Houses were mostly shuttered, doorways covered with rusted iron gratings; some were partial shells with exposed second floors as if bombed in the war. I mean, like in World War II, those photos of Dunkirk. Maybe they were. In one, a man popped like a jack-in-the-box into the empty frame of a window. He rushed out, babbling in Italian. I burst into tears and ran.

Finally a house, formerly grand, larger than others, a chalky yellow, with clothes drying off the balconies, had an open arched entrance. Under the arch were several inner doors secured with iron padlocks and two large green trash bins. It was cool, dark, and rank. I sat on the ground, my back against the wall, too tired now to rerun the marriage tape. I think I might have dozed for a while. When I woke I texted Finn.

By the time I heard back I had wandered on and found a café, a funky patio surrounded by pots of bushy green things and miniature spiny palms, slatted wooden picnic tables with plastic sunflower placemats, and, off to the side the sort of portable bar you might find by a pool. I sat at a table and ordered a Coke.

"Will you have dinner?" the waiter asked, a charmer, not more than twenty, the short sleeves of his tight T-shirt rolled up to his shoulders. While he told me the specials and presented a menu, he kept up a running conversation with two hotties at the bar. I asked him where I was, showed him the map, and texted

Finn the information. He showed up quite a while after the par-migiana I'd ordered to be able to stay.

Finn scouted the bread basket, selected a mini pizza square topped with pesto, and stuffed it in his mouth. "They make pesto with pistachio and parsley in Siracusa. What happened?"

. I couldn't get words out.

He jammed his chair around next to mine. I put my head on his shoulder. He patted me like a kid who doesn't quite know what comfort is or how to provide it.

"Michael's been cheating on me. With that woman. The woman you met at breakfast. He brought her here." I burrowed into his shoulder and waited until I could hold back the dam. "How could he do that?"

"What?"

"All of it."

Finn propped me upright. "Let me get settled." He took out rolling papers, sprinkled on tobacco, spun and sealed it.

"You're rolling your own cigarettes? When did this start?"

"Want one?"

"No. I don't know what to do."

He glanced at the menu and ordered a bottle of white. "How'd you find out?"

"Did you know?"

"How would I know?" said Finn.

"I don't know. I just now got this feeling that maybe you knew. What am I going to do? How can I get out of here? Get home?"

We stopped talking while the waiter uncorked the wine. "Drink this. Drink a lot of it. *Très bien*," he told the waiter. "It's the way you like it, Lizzie, not too dry."

"I don't want to drink. I need to think."

"No, you don't."

"I'm a dope. A dupe. Do you think he's in love with her?"

"It's a game."

"He makes it all up, you know. His life's a fiction. I could blow him out of the water."

"I'll drink to that." Finn clinked my glass. "She took Snow somewhere and returned her looking like a hooker."

"What? What are you talking about?"

"Take three big gulps."

I downed the glass. He poured another, and ordered after asking several questions about the fish. "After the boat ride, the two of them, Snow and Kathy, went off for ice cream. Hours later, they weren't back. Taylor was bananas. Me too. I told the manager, you better fucking call the police or else, and these two cops showed up, and then suddenly Snow walked in." He started laughing.

"What's funny?"

"Nothing. It was the scariest shit ever, the end of life."

"I'm sorry." I rubbed his arm. "Do you want me to kiss your eyes? It makes you feel better."

"No, that's okay, I'll pass on that, but Snow . . ."

"Is she okay?"

He brightened, grinned. "She stonewalled the cops. Reminded me of myself when I was a kid. Wily as hell."

"But didn't—" I couldn't say her name. "Did she say what happened, where they'd been?"

"Kathy didn't come back. Just Snow. Kathy's still out partying."

"After all that, you came to see me. That is so nice of you, Finn. And thank Taylor for not minding. Don't tell Taylor about Michael. But that was nice of her, really nice, to release you. She must still be around the bend."

"Yeah, she is, but better for Snow if Taylor calms her down. Not that Snowy needed calming. Better if she's just with her mom, though. I'm hopeless."

"I saw Snow and her."

"Get out."

"I did. I saw them walking toward that big rock where everyone suns and swims. Snow was—you're right—different. Teenage. I was so crazy, I mean upset, startled to see"—forced myself to say it—"Michael's lover. She was so close I could touch her, I almost didn't notice Snow, I didn't think. He brought her here on our vacation. He's a monster. I married a monster."

"The parmigiana is okay, signora?"

"Oh, it's delicious. I'm just not hungry."

"She eats like a bird," said Finn.

"The Italians always ask that, if you leave anything, have you noticed? They expect you to clean your plate. No, they want you to be happy. A tragedy not to enjoy a meal. I'd kill for that to be my tragedy. What do I do?"

"Spend the night somewhere else. Go back in time to pack and get on the plane."

"What do I do with my life?"

Finn emptied the rest of the wine in my glass. "We need somewhere to spend the night." He went over, chatted up the bartender and the two young women, and returned with a card. "This way. Down this street."

I stood up, drunk and dizzy, sat down, and started over very slowly. Finn wrapped his arm around me. He smelled sexy, of tobacco, sweat, and garlic.

"Come on," he said, "let's get you a room."

Taylor

I BLAMED FINN.

He'd let his daughter, too shy to ask directions, waltz off in this stone city with no stop signs or stoplights, where streets while not identical to each other were as indistinguishable as one natural pearl from another. I have a pearl necklace that belonged to my great-aunt, Bunny Seddley, three strands, and while each is different, the differences are minuscule. These houses and streets aren't pearls, of course, nevertheless. He didn't take her cell number either. Can you imagine? Later he pointed out that most likely she couldn't afford data roaming. "Bet she didn't have data roaming," he said. "Costs a bundle." I pretended not to hear. He'd trusted his gut. I think he said that while we were waiting for the police. Maybe I only think he said that because it's the kind of thing Finn would say.

My gut tells me this person is reliable. I'll entrust my daughter to her. My only daughter, not that I mean it would be any different if we had two but we don't.

I knew, sitting in that lobby with his uselessness next to me, that Snow and I would be better off without him.

As for the police, I barely recall anything, following them down the hall, my legs wobbly, the manager's office, rocking in the chair. "You were making animal noises," Finn told me. I said to April, "Why would he say that? Why would he tell me I humiliated myself?" On the floor under the manager's desk were a bunch of wires held together with a rubber band. Wasn't that a silly thing to notice? I thought, *She needs a snap-collar cable like the one I have.*

I remember biting down on my fist not to scream, and Michael interceding, being so grateful for his intelligence and assuredness. They had to think, if he was with us, that we were important Americans.

When I saw Snow, it was as if my life was given back to me.

Grief overwhelmed, but then, what in the world—Snow was made up as if she'd gone wild at a makeup counter. Her clothes were trampy, that's the only word I can think of—no, slutty. Snow was suddenly sixteen. Yes, sixteen and jailbait.

I wanted to throw a blanket over her.

I had to keep my wits, a challenge with the police trying to dig in and get some information. Snow was too vulnerable to be submitted to a third degree. Being a mother has made me a warrior, that's what I told April.

I suppose we were all overwrought and I should forgive Michael. So rattled was he that he actually shook Snow for something she said to him. Shook her?! I ultimately concluded that his reaction was a perverse expression of relief, but Finn let him have it.

I kicked Finn out, took Snow to the room, and ran a bath.

"Are you hungry? Do you need something to eat?"

I didn't hear her answer and went back into the room where Snow was lazily circling, letting her hand dance along the bed and across the bureau.

"We ate," she said. It thrilled me, the ordinariness of simply hearing my daughter's voice.

"Oh, that's nice. You had a gelato, shopped, and then ate what?"

"Pizza."

"Where?"

Snow stopped at the mirror and picked up the brush. She leaned in to see her face close-up.

"Snow?"

Her eyes caught mine in the mirror.

"Where did you eat?"

"A café. With boys." She brushed slowly, arcing the brush to let her glorious hair fan out and settle.

"Where did you go after that?"

"Nowhere."

"Did anything happen? I know I asked you downstairs. You might not have wanted to say then. This is just between us."

"This is just between us," said Snow.

She sounded exactly like me, which mixed me up. I lost my train of thought.

I wanted those clothes she was wearing. I wanted to stuff them in the wastebasket, but I thought, no, I'll do what I do with Finn's awful clothes, misplace them later.

Snow fluttered toward me and then around me. I spun to follow. It crossed my mind that she was hyper, although she is not hyper, she has always been the opposite of hyper and I hate labels. Still, she did seem overly excited. "I'm glad we're going to Ravello tomorrow. Snow, if you don't take a bath, you should wash off the makeup."

She tugged the string on her pants and let them drop to the floor.

"My goodness, she bought you a thong."

I don't know why I even say this, it is obvious, but Snow and I have no modesty. Yet I was embarrassed to talk to her standing in the middle of the suite, naked except for that little triangle patch over, well, barely over her fuzz of sprouting pubic hair.

"Put on your pajamas." Conveniently they were out on the chair because I had left out everything we would need for the trip tomorrow. I thrust them at her. "Where is that woman now?"

"She went with them. I got lost. It's hard to find your way here."

"What an irresponsible dolt she is. Leaving you to find your way back. How awful for you. Were you frightened?"

She only blinked. Rapid blinking for five seconds or so, a long time to blink. I recognized it as one of her turtle moves. She walked into the bathroom and brushed her teeth. Nothing strange about how she did that. She's a vigorous brusher and afterward she always bares her teeth, examining them in the mirror, and, with her tongue, swipes them across the top. I found it comforting to see, business as usual. From that alone I knew nothing bad had happened.

I decided not to make a fuss about her washing off the makeup.

"What did you say to Michael?" I asked as she slipped into bed and drew the covers up to her chin. "What did you whisper to him, Snow?"

She flipped over on her tummy and closed her eyes. She was done. Too exhausted to answer, I'm sure. Too traumatized. Better forgotten. A night we would delete from our mental hard drives.

Watching my daughter drift into slumberland, letting my hand rest lightly on the small of her back, feeling the rise and fall of her breath was pure joy.

Lizzie

WE KISSED ON THE STREET. Finn slid his hands up my jersey. My breasts were nearly exposed, yearning to be. I lifted my top and pressed against him as we stumbled on, half walking, half making out. We peeked through the glass into Hotel Zero. A man was asleep at the desk, his head back, snoring loudly.

Finn knocked. The old man shuddered awake and unlocked the door. I stood behind in disarray while Finn paid in cash.

He nuzzled me up the stairs to number five at the top. When we opened the door, the dim yellow bulb in the hall cast a sickly pall over the dark spread on the bed with its two flat pillows. The only room light was overhead. Finn switched it on, throwing glare on our undone flushed selves, and as quickly switched it back off. Better not to see.

I was so drunk, so emotionally at sea, I could have done unmentionable things with a stranger, and yet it rumbled through my consciousness that I had been fifteen pounds lighter when I slept with Finn last.

In this small, airless cube with a slanted ceiling I felt a wave of nausea, which I swallowed back before we fell on the bed, which sagged under our weight, and wiggled out of our clothes.

The sex was familiar, the way the taste of something stays locked in your unconscious. (Proustian, a madeleine, Michael would have invoked that cliché.) We lay pressed together on our sides, Finn slid his hand up my leg, and then he got down to business. He always flips on top, practical, no deviations off his route, no detours exploring the landscape or sudden bursts of inspiration. He likes to fuck and he knows what he needs to do, so I'm happy too.

I kept my eyes closed.

I had to put a man between me and Michael.

Finn left an hour later, rustling me awake.

"Why did we break up?" he said.

"Oh, God, not now."

He mussed my hair.

"Because you drove me crazy. All our dreams were different. I wanted to go to New York. It was the end of summer."

"I love you," he said.

"I love you too."

Later I thought it was not love but loyalty we were expressing, the way two devoted friends might end a conversation or a telephone call. Loyalty: a more honorable pledge than love. Did that make Finn's betrayal greater than Michael's?

When I woke up and craned my head at the window, the swallows were swirling and whining in the slip of colorless dawn between this roof and the one opposite, an uninhabited wreck.

The bathroom, with a plastic accordion door and nearly too

small to turn around in, had a dirty mirror over a miniature bowl of a sink with one spout, cold, a toilet with no seat. A metal shower spray poked out of the wall, greenish around the edges. There was a drain under my feet. I soaked myself with icy water, then realized there was no towel. I rolled around on the bed to dry off. It was disgusting.

The anesthetic of sex and alcohol had worn off and I was beginning to feel jumpy. My hangover was like nothing I'd ever experienced, a vise across my forehead and over my head to the base of my neck. My arms and legs felt barely attached or under my control. My eyes had deep dark circles, my skin sallow. I looked discarded. I had been.

But I had Finn. I had always known I had Finn, even though I didn't know what I wanted to do with Finn. But I had him, and Taylor didn't, and that was a comfort.

Trembling at the thought of seeing Michael, scared of him, I realized, scared of his seductive games, worrying about how he might confuse me, and frightened at how much I wanted to kill him, I gave myself orders. Spoke them aloud: Go to the hotel, pack, ignore, take a taxi solo to the Catania airport, and find your own way back. To Berkeley.

I would visit my mother. When we pulled into the driveway, I would cry as I always did at the sight of my dad's bicycle still chained to the front porch, rusted into art, and I would blame him for Michael.

Digging through my purse, I located a stray lozenge that I rinsed off and sucked. It was 6:42 a.m. according to my phone.

A little girl in pajamas pawed a scooter in and out of the front door of whatever this was, a vacation flophouse. As I was trying to figure out which direction to walk, a cheerful woman bustled out of the back, waving a dishtowel. She shooed the little girl outside, walked me to the end of the block, and pointed me right. I could see the sea and sky but not the horizon, the ash blue of one disappeared into the other. "At the water, *a sinistra*." She signaled left.

I walked unsteadily to the water, and when I got there realized I was standing nearly at the tip of Siracusa by a stupendous fort. There wasn't even a wisp of wind and over the seawall, looking down, water lapped the rocks in a friendly inviting way. I thought about diving in, about crashing headfirst into the clear shallow sea, my head splintering. I also thought about the time between diving and landing when I imagine all people changed their minds. For me it was only a flirtation, not serious, merely an acknowledgment of how much I was dreading the next hours. It cheered me that I could have that fantasy.

Sticking to the route along the seawall, I figured I was a half hour from the hotel. As people passed—a few joggers, some barechested men in trunks with towels slung over their shoulders—I clung to the balustrade railing for balance and calm. Eventually the path zigged sharply and I could see Lo Scoglio. I quickened, wondering about the crowd gathering at the entrance, the patrol cars, the cops waving traffic to pass farther from the sea side and closer to the buildings. A boy climbed the nearby parapet angling for a better view.

When I walked into the room, Michael was asleep in bed as if nothing in his life were remotely askew. I shook his shoulder.

"Lizzie, Jesus, Lizzie," he shot up.

"I was just at Lo Scoglio."

"Where? Thank God you're back."

"The police were in wetsuits. There's a narrow canyon formed by spiky rocks beneath that behemoth, that boulder, Lo Scoglio. Do you know where I mean?"

"Were you with Finn?"

"Fuck you, Michael. Do you know where I mean?"

"No."

"I don't believe you. I don't believe you ever. Beneath that narrow metal bridge suspended between that sheer wall and Lo Scoglio, there's a treacherous jumble of rocks."

"I've never been."

"I'm going to break your heart if you have one. She was found there. Your girlfriend. She's dead."

Michael got up, staggered around for a bit, and slumped down again. He clasped his hands and slammed them into his forehead.

"So you know who I'm talking about? Say her name, please. She deserves that at least."

"Kathy Bicks," he said dully, as if viewing the body.

"Her hair was matted with stuff, sea stuff and kind of green. She passed by on a stretcher. The police have these stretchers in mesh, it's weird, like a strainer, they can rescue a dead body and leave the water behind. In less than a night, sea creatures had feasted on her face, eaten her eyes. Her beautiful blue eyes. But it was her. I recognized her shirt too. Your shirt."

"Are you sure?"

"I was close when they passed by with her body. What's with your face? You have a black eye. Why's your cheek red and swollen? Did you have a fight with her?"

"What are you thinking?"

"That she killed herself or you killed her. I hate you. I hate that I could think evil of you. You make me sick. I never imagined you could do any of the things you've done already. Although that seems like my stupidity. What do you feel? Do you feel anything?"

"I don't know."

"My God, I saw her with Snow. I hope Snow's all right." I ran out, nearly tumbled down a flight of stairs, and pounded on Finn and Taylor's door.

Snow opened it—Snow, her hair tangled from sleep, in screaming-pink shortie pajamas decorated with zebras. "We're leaving today," she said in a flat voice.

Finn turned up behind. Rumpled. Barely focusing. In boxers and a T-shirt. I could see the cot he slept in, opened near the couch.

"I'm so glad you're fine, Snow." My legs nearly buckled. I sagged against the wall. Finn came out, pulling the door closed.

"I was worried about Snow," I said. "I was worried something happened to her. On my way back I saw—"

"Hi, Michael," said Finn, looking over my shoulder.

"We should talk. All of us," said Michael. "Not with your daughter."

Siracusa, Day 4

Michael

"*WHAT ARE YOU THINKING?*"

"*That she killed herself or you killed her.*"

Woke to the news. Lizzie shook me awake to deliver it. Kath dead. Frankly, we are being frank, I couldn't imagine it was true or that Lizzie could believe I had anything to do with it.

Not possible she was dead. I wasn't superstitious. Didn't believe in fate. As a romantic concept, found it idiotic. As powerful as I felt, I knew my fantasizing couldn't make it happen. Besides, wanting something and getting it were different things. My passion for K had proved that.

Still, didn't believe she was dead. Pounded on K's door, expecting her to open it. Lizzie watched silently.

Even as I walked to the bench to meet the other couple, I thought, *She's alive,* although the passing ambulance was silent, creeping along like all the cars here in case, on these narrow streets, something was coming from the other direction. Why wail a siren when you're on your way to the morgue? Why did I cling to a shred of hope when there had been that chilling moment with Snow the night before?

Lizzie had left her suitcase at reception, asked for a second taxi for an earlier departure time, an hour hence, then had followed me to the rendezvous, a bench not far from the hotel. My idea. Always on the lookout for places to hide, I had noticed it at the back end of the market. Outside was better. Discretion imperative.

It was ugly here, not far from a Dumpster and some trucks. Yet this area had an incongruously knockout view, the open sea in one direction. In the other, a small cove, haven for sailboats and small yachts. Lizzie sat half turned away at the end of the bench. As a favor, sensing her repulsion, I stood. I watched her ignore me.

We waited.

"You can't leave her here," said Lizzie. "That poor woman dying miles from home. You have to stay."

I didn't answer. The situation was much more complicated.

Lizzie was trembling. I offered the flask and, in return, got a look of disgust.

"What you did to me is unforgivable," she said.

"Nothing is unforgivable," I said. "It depends on your capacity for forgiveness."

"Is that remark a consequence of this trip?" said Lizzie. "From seeing so many Christs bleeding on crosses? Has it made you think about forgiveness?" She fell silent then. Hearing the cleverness, I guessed. Unwilling to be us.

"I didn't bring her here."

"Liar. You're as guilty as if you shoved her off."

Saw the Dolans advance, Taylor in a bright, quick stride, Finn, gimpy, a pace behind.

"Do you want to sit down?" I asked Taylor.

"I'm fine." She checked her watch. "I want Snow to have something to eat before we leave. I'm sure the food at the Catania airport is awful, and we're flying to Naples, and then there's the drive to Ravello—the Amalfi coast can be sheer terror in a car but quite stunning. I would like her to be able to enjoy it."

"I wanted to tell you what Snow said to me. Last night. Awkward, I realize. But if the police question me—"

"Why would they question you?" said Taylor. "What about?"

"About the drowning. I knew the woman. Snow was with her."

"They'd gone for pizza," said Taylor, "and shopped."

"Your daughter told me—" I stopped, struck by Taylor's lack of curiosity, her cheerfulness. Finn snuck glances at Lizzie, who kept her eyes low. "Snow whispered to me, you remember I'm sure, when we were all weak with relief and the handsome *agenti*—"

"Spit it out, Michael," said Lizzie. "Don't make it a story."

I remembered every lousy detail—the smell in the lobby from the olives and salami that had been laid out as snacks, the faint musk of wine, Snow reveling in the attention. I had leaned down to hear her breathy secretive voice. She was an efficient child, she didn't waste words: "'She won't be bothering you anymore.'

"That's what Snow whispered," I told them.

Finn closed in behind Taylor, an instinct like a mobster's. Family first.

"How did she know that?" I said. "How did she know Kath wouldn't be bothering me anymore?"

"You're full of shit," said Finn.

"Why would I lie about that?"

"Why do you lie about everything? You do it. Your whole life's a fable. Lizzie told me."

Lizzie nodded, acknowledging her tit-for-tat.

"I'm only telling you that if the police interview me, I will tell them what your daughter said."

"You want to get involved with the *polizia*? You want a date with the Italian justice system?" Finn snorted. "You'll spend the rest of your life in a Sicilian jail."

"He *is* involved," said Lizzie. "He has a moral commitment. He brought her here."

"I didn't bring her."

"Fuck you," said Lizzie.

That stopped me for a second. Taylor gaped.

"'She won't be bothering you anymore.' That is what your daughter told me," I said. "I'm sure it's hard to imagine."

"You can't imagine," said Taylor. "You don't have children."

"Who scratched your face, Taylor? Did Snow do that?" said Lizzie.

"How dare you?" said Taylor.

"Are you accusing Snowy?" said Finn.

"I'm telling you what she said."

"I saw them at Lo Scoglio," said Lizzie. "Kath and Snow together."

"They weren't there," said Taylor.

Finn shoved me. "You're accusing my daughter? You're crazy."

"I saw them at the rock. I told you last night, Finn," said Lizzie.

"You were freaked out from this asshole. Drunk as a skunk. You told me you couldn't think. You sure couldn't walk."

Lizzie flinched as if he'd hit her.

"My daughter always tells me the truth," said Taylor to Lizzie. "She wasn't there."

A moment of spontaneous understanding—we could be overheard. We lowered our voices.

"When did you see Lizzie?" Taylor asked Finn.

"While you were taking care of Snow," said Finn. "Lizzie was distraught. I met her at a restaurant. As I said, she was loaded. You were out of it, Lizzie. Like you'd remember anything."

"I remember last night," said Lizzie.

I heard the betrayal.

"Kath and Snow shopped," said Taylor. "They bought inappropriate clothes. Snow had pizza with her and came back alone."

Foolish Kath. Befriending Snow. Turning a scorpion into a playmate. No doubt in my mind how it happened. Them sitting together, legs dangling over the edge of the boulder, laughing, maybe Kath reading Snow's palm, she loved to do that. Told me she did it with girlfriends in high school. Snow scooting back, standing up, giving her a push. Wouldn't have taken much of a push. Kath mellow and happy, a little sunstroked, maybe even buzzed with her new favorite, Prosecco. *She won't be bothering you anymore.*

Lizzie was crying now, sniveling, wiping her nose with the back of her hand.

I would give you an alibi for anything. I would swear to the police, "No way, she did not do it, she was with me the whole time. Release this beauty." I recalled our dinner, Lizzie's question. *I'd alibi you for anything, Snow. I'd say, "Release this beauty."* Had she believed that? Had she taken my theatrics seriously? Were Snow and I conspirators?

"Lizzie was at Lo Scoglio," said Finn. "She told me. She saw Miss Indiana. She didn't say there was anyone else with Miss Indiana. I'll swear to that. Lizzie knew you were doing her. Maybe you wanted out of the marriage or maybe you didn't and she put the screws to you. You're the one with the motive. You and—"

"And me," said Lizzie to Finn. "She was sleeping with my husband."

Finn ignored her. Spoke only to me. "That's what I'll tell the *polizia*, that Lizzie was at the rock. If they ask me. She killed herself," he said.

No one disagreed.

"They don't know who she is," I said. "Not yet."

"They won't for a few days," said Finn. "Not until she doesn't check out and the hotel notifies the cops and gives them her passport number."

I took out the flask and passed it to him. He took a swig and passed it back.

"We're leaving her?" said Lizzie.

I knelt, looking up into her face. "We don't know her. She's barely an acquaintance. Fortunately we're getting the hell out of Italy today." I looked at Finn. "You should too."

"Fuck Ravello," said Finn to Taylor.

"I'll call Gloria," said Taylor. "I don't mind missing Ravello, although I'm sorry about Venice. It's early. I'll have to wake her, but no problem. I have all Gloria's numbers. She won't mind. This is a good spot for cell reception." She pulled out her phone. "I hope Snow won't be too disappointed."

"So we agree," said Finn.

Lizzie hoisted her purse and dug around in it. "Take my picture," she said, handing me her phone. "If I ever think of having anything to do with you, I want to remember this moment. Go on, Michael, do it."

I snapped her photo and went back to the hotel to pack.

Portland, October

Taylor

IT's FOUR MONTHS LATER and I am deep in plans for a harvest festival. There are pretty displays of pumpkins on Monument and Longfellow squares and near the historic society on Commerce Street. The air smells piney; the holidays are not far off. This is the last month for tourists. Everything will slow down in November, well, it has already, the turning of the leaves came early this year. The Lil' Whale Bakery is making pumpkin everything—bread, muffins, cookies, and pies. I have given my notice, however, to a very dismayed Mayor Beemer because it's become clear that I can't do my job and homeschool Snow.

The sixth-grade curriculum is daunting, but there are subjects of great interest to me, like early Greek civilization. Even the science is exciting: electricity, the metric system (it's about time I learned that), and best of all, the ecology of the Maine coast. Perhaps next year, after studying Greece, we'll all go to Athens. When a subject is more than I want to handle, I can buy tutorials for Snow to watch on her iPad. I have made contact with other homeschooling mothers on Facebook, and they have advised me to start each day at the same time, with the hardest subjects first. We've created a nook in our sunny den where Snow and I can work side by side.

Snow, so smart and focused, will probably set a record and be in the seventh grade by March. I have enrolled her in some dance and theater classes where she can interact with kids her own age in a supervised environment. Now that she is nearly eleven—her birthday is next month—and still painfully shy, I am very aware and wary of the mean-girl syndrome. In spite of all attempts by that poor dead woman to turn her into a harlot, she remains pure.

About six weeks after returning from Italy, Snow and I visited New York City to see Penelope, who is having physical therapy, which she hates—especially the ankle lifts with the elastic straps—and to squeeze in some fun mother-daughter shopping. Who did we encounter as we exited the revolving doors of Bergdorf Goodman? Lizzie. She looked like a truck had run over her. She had dark circles under her eyes, sallow cheeks, messy hair. I doubt if she'd washed it in weeks. It had that oily sheen. No makeup of course, but she never did wear much makeup. Her rumpled shirt looked as if it had been plucked from the dirty laundry. The whites of her eyes were red; I noted that especially because it was almost ghoulish.

Given her wreck of an appearance, I would say her insides were out.

I will never forgive her for the blame she attempted to heap on my daughter. Truly I believe she is evil or at the very least twisted. Still I was polite. With a Seddley, being polite is a way of life.

"Hello, what a surprise," I said. "We're visiting Penelope. She might have to have another surgery. She may walk with a limp forever."

Lizzie made no remark to that, can you imagine? Not a word of greeting. She merely stared at Snow, who shrank backward. Best to remove my daughter as quickly as possible from what was clearly a hostile situation.

Later I wondered, had Lizzie been on some sort of medication?

In spite of everything, I have fond feelings for Michael. He's a troubled man.

Siracusa ceased to exist the minute we left. We fell back into our old life. The trauma of Snow's disappearing, the fear it aroused in me, however, has only grown—a bond between Finn and me as he feels it too.

I often think of that dinner in Rome, Lizzie attempting to perk up our conversation with her hostessy question: Why does your marriage work? Because, I told her, Finn and I both know, Snow comes first.

Snow is rarely out of my sight. Nevertheless, sometimes when she is in the back or front yard and I glance out the window and don't see her, I break out in a sweat. My heart races. Often I dream, nightmares where I can't find her, and wake up screaming. I keep some Valium and a bottle of water near the bed and take a half when that happens.

I have never brought up Finn's smoking. I like knowing something about him that he doesn't know I know. I like finding the bits of tobacco in his pockets or a cigarette or two in the glove compartment. Sometimes I mess with him by throwing them out. Michael was right. The only power worth having is secret power—how did he put it?—like having an ace up your sleeve or a gun in your boot.

I bought a beautiful pair of Prada boots, by the way. Navy suede. They help keep that fantasy alive.

Finn

DID SIRACUSA CHANGE MY LIFE? Dorothy asked me at my first session when I couldn't shut up about it.

Found some good cheap reds. Finally got some respect from Taylor. Maybe it turned me into a dad. Gave me PTSD for sure. Tay says being worried about my kid all the time isn't PTSD, it's fatherhood and I'd resisted it.

Jessa, who caught an eight-pound lobster while we were in Siracusa, wears her dad's fraternity ring around her neck. He died a couple of years ago, and when she talks, she holds the ring and swings it. I think of Kathy when she does it—how she bounced onto that tour boat and waggled her finger with the forty-pound ring. The flashbacks cooled me on Jessa. You never know what's going to turn off the heat.

Sometimes late at night, after I close up my joint, I stop at St. Joseph's and light a candle for her.

Now and then I send Lizzie texts, a photo of a flounder, my big toe, something that will make her laugh, but she doesn't answer. Eventually she will. I'll wear her down.

New York City, October

Michael

LIZZIE WAS GONE. *The man didn't admit to anyone that it bothered him. Turned up at his usual haunts except Tino's; hit the Waverly Inn, the Monkey Bar at lunch. Enjoyed the speculation, how had the perfect couple broken up? No one knew about events in Siracusa. That was the advantage of traveling with people who were—how to describe them?—not you.*

Lizzie's riding off to the Catania airport in a taxi was my last sighting. Her friend Rachel came over with a mover for her belongings, and said only, "You're a pig."

Fuck Lizzie. I changed her life. Her talent was modest. Being with me gave her cachet. Bluntly, it got her hired.

She was never comfortable living in my shadow. Envy was in the subtext of her praise and worship and even her sexual heat. She returned to Berkeley with her tail between her legs, I heard, but is apparently back. Joel Fried spotted her recently having lunch at Pain Quotidien. Alone with her laptop. Eating avocado toast, Joel reported. She'll probably write about that. She was always mining the ludicrous for ideas.

In retrospect, Kath was as much the stalker as I. We were to each other both stalker and prey. When I returned and opened my office door, it was as if Kath had peed all over it. Two computer files were open, one to my passwords, another to CheapOair. Armchair pulled up next to desk chair—she and her friends plotted her trip like girls at a slumber party, my office, my sacred writing space now a teenager's bedroom. She left a bottle of purple nail polish on the floor and a sponge hanging from a knob in the shower.

As for Snow, she seems a part of Siracusa, phantom and real, enchantment and horror. Could not have happened and yet it did, and every day I find it harder to remember or believe.

Eventually, I'll take Lizzie back. She will turn up, no question. Broke.

Although the man knew he was fine without her. For single, charming, talented men in their early fifties, the city was ripe with women waiting to be picked.

New York City

Lizzie

TRUTH or CONSEQUENCES

by Lizzie Ross

Published November 5 in *New York* magazine

We met at a literary party, those 6pm–8pm wine and cheese events that rarely happen anymore to celebrate the publication of a book about the Gulf War. Spring 2002. Wikipedia was a fledgling, born the year before, which meant the web was still figuring out how to track our lives, and, up to that time, we could still to some degree shape and alter our histories. He was somebody. I was not.

He slipped his arm around me as I passed and pulled me into his conversation. "This is—"

"Lizzie Ross," I said. I knew all about him. He'd won a Pulitzer for his first play, *Dealing*. Written at twenty-one. Now he was thirty-seven.

Michael Shapner came blessed by my father. I had been raised in Berkeley, California, paradise for people who wanted to live in the past. "Lizzie, get out," my dad said often. He had died the year before I met Michael. He'd fallen off the red Schwinn he rode all over the hills of Berkeley. A professor of political science (specialty civil liberties), he remained to his death lonely for New York City. He'd subscribed to the *New York Review of Books* ("and I read it," he joked) and to the *New York Times* (always arriving a day late when I was a kid). He took me for Chinese dumplings and to foreign films. My bedtime stories were the poems of beat poet Gregory Corso, and my dad's god was the dazzling essayist Murray Kempton, who wrote for the *New York Review of Books* as well as a column in the *New York Post*, to which my dad also subscribed. Kempton had written about Michael's play and compared it to a jazz riff. As I said, Michael Shapner came blessed by my dad.

Our life together began that night.

I had been married before for a short time to a carpenter, living someone else's country life, avoiding becoming anything much less the writer my dad had hoped for. I had a wild post-breakup affair on a detour to Maine with a charmer who was a Republican. My dad would never have approved of him. Finally, about to turn thirty, I made my way to New York City.

Michael had read my journalism and had clipped one of my articles.

When he told me that, I fell in love.

"Divine the insecurity and compliment it," I heard him say not long after he'd used the trick on me. I heard him say many of the things he said many times. That one never varied. Most of them were improvisations. He never told a story the same way twice. Jazz riffs? Someone else would call them lies.

I loved his stories. I loved the way he commanded the room, his resonant deep voice. His stories were dramatic. His boot out of Yale for dealing drugs, which became the basis for his first play; his dusty, weary trek with lonely bus stop holidays in search of the dad who had abandoned his mother and him when he was five. This became the memoir *Bastard*. He was a raconteur who told stories as if he were writing a never-completed fiction. He kept revising it.

I loved that. I especially loved it because I knew the truth. There was no Yale, but a year at CCNY. The now dead father had turned up faithfully each weekend to take his son to the movies or Coney Island. Cleverly he did not begin telling the Yale tales until a few years after his play so they were never in print, but became lore, and even—although this is pretentious and he was—part of his myth. In the case of *Bastard*, his father was dead by then, his mother loyal. By that time he was addicted to lying. He told me the truth very late one night and very drunk. It sealed our love.

We lied together and eventually about everything, even the ice cream we hadn't eaten that afternoon. It became a game to have something over the person you were talking to even though the person wouldn't know and wouldn't care if he did. We were social liars, amusing ourselves at dinner parties. Making it even more wicked and fun, this was the New York world of literati—people both brilliant and smug. We goofed on all of them. Our lies were power, we imagined, although why I'm not sure.

We were giddy with lies. Every tiresome event became an adventure.

Eventually he lied to me because eventually a liar lies to everyone, that's the truth. I had imagined I was exempt, especially since I knew his truth, but lying that way all the time for no reason is compulsion. Then, on a vacation with friends in Siracusa, a wreck of a city in Sicily, I discovered that he had, on the side, someone younger, sexier, more adoring, although as far as that last is concerned, how could it be possible? Siracusa, crumbling but sturdy, had survived invasions from Greeks, Romans, and Spaniards. The destruction of our marriage wouldn't leave a mark, but it was there that games played on other people became a game played on me.

When this happened, Michael and I had been together thirteen years, eight of them married. We didn't have kids. Our lies were our children. Perhaps not our children but certainly our dog. We and our lies were a family.

It turns out there are all sorts of foundations for marriage. Lying is one of them.

When this happened, I was no longer getting journalism assignments, and Michael had never lived up to his early promise. He was years behind finishing a book he wasn't writing. I was desperate for work, desperate not to be discarded, imagining my every thought might somehow morph into the idea that would save me. Then I realized Michael was my ticket back.

I outed him in print, what you are reading right now. This literary god (to some) is a serial fabricator.

I am sitting in Starbucks reading the article. It looks great in print. The photo of me in Siracusa "looking haunted," my editor said, sets the tone. My cell phone is on the table, and I'm expecting to hear from my agent. She submitted my book proposal to publishers last Friday with an early copy of the article. My agent is sure I'll get an offer by noon, most likely several.

What I write will not be just an exposé of him but of us, a memoir of how I got sucked into his pathology, why it thrilled me, how our pas de deux became a madness. I felt uncertain and unworthy before Michael, trying to please a father I idolized. My agent feels that other women will relate to that.

I saved the bombshell for the book, poor Kath's accidental death—that's how I'll tell it.

Michael and I were worth more married, I always thought. It turns out, I am worth more divorced.

People will say what they will.

From the time I left Siracusa, I have never spoken to Michael except through lawyers.

On a sweltering day in late July, a week after my return to New York, while floundering down a dismal stretch of 58th Street, I found myself face-to-face with Snow and Taylor. They'd been shopping at Bergdorf's. I was about to scream, "Murderer," but the fawn shied back against her mother. Poor frightened little thing, I thought instead. Can you imagine? My gut instinct was to protect her. I was astonished at myself. By the time I had recovered my voice and venom, Taylor had hustled her into an Uber.

Michael will be hated with glee and land on his feet. He still gets royalties from his hit play, and even his second, more modest success produces a little. He won't have to finish his novel. I'm sure his publisher would prefer a mea culpa. I'm sure he's fabricating right now the insecurity that led to his downfall.

He can always move to Los Angeles, the land of reinvention. Or he might meet a woman here who can support him. He's brilliant and witty. He likes sex.

I walk, that's what I do mostly, walk a lot, trying to wear myself out, dull my brain, escape my guilt about leaving Kathy Bicks in Siracusa, never telling the police what I saw, acting entirely in my own self-interest. There would be no justice for her, no peace for her family. If you had asked me if I was capable of that . . . if I had thrown out that question: Suppose you had information about a murder but in telling it you might implicate yourself, what would you do? A fun after-dinner hypothetical posited while everyone was tipsy and splitting a tiramisu. Would I keep my mouth shut? Was I capable of that? I would have sworn no.

The hardest thing to accept is not that it happened, but the person I turned out to be.

Acknowledgments

This is not a true story. All characters and circumstances are fictional. The Italian cities—Rome and Siracusa—are real, of course—the sites are real, but details about them are sometimes altered by my imagination and memory. Many locations like hotels and restaurants and cafés, although not all, are invented but faithful to the place as I experienced it.

I had the great good fortune to meet Aleksandra Jaeschke in Siracusa. During the years I wrote this book, she guided and advised me, engaged in endless conversations, and explained things I didn't understand and could never have figured out. She is brilliant and amazing and I cannot thank her enough. My deep gratitude to Giorgio Martorana and Marcella Mignosa, who welcomed me on all my visits. They were generous with their time and knowledge and friendship. The wonderful Paola Sarno, the translator at the Siracusa police department, was patient with all my questions, kind, and fantastically smart. Marcello Baglioni guided me through Sicilian food and wine and advised me so helpfully about my trip. The generosity of these friends I made in Siracusa was magical. Everyone opened their hearts.

To Don Lee, my boundless thanks for your crazy brain. And for taking me through all things restaurant, food, wine, and

Irish. Anna Harari, my beloved niece, thank you for accompanying me. Thank God you survived snorkeling in a nearly deserted cove and a bus to Mount Etna. To my dear friend Julia Gregson, who went back to Siracusa on my final trip when my life was difficult, for pushing me through, for the joy of nearly missing our plane while having kir royals in the Rome airport. Dr. William Fisher, I so appreciate your insights in grounding my characters. Deena Goldstone—I can't write books without you. Joy Horowitz, thank you for your wise counsel and clarity. To Lawrence Conley, my appreciation for sharing your Sicilian memories. Noah Reibel, thank you for all your advice and for introducing me to Aleks. To Jeremy Steinke, and Julia Wick, whose research helped launch my story, and to Hillary Weaver, who fact-checked it, my thanks. And to Alan Rader and Nick Pileggi, thank you for advising me.

Blue Rider Press has been my writing home. To Sarah Hochman, my editor, my deep appreciation for your talent, sureness, patience, insight, care, and friendship. Brian Ulicky, my gratitude for guiding this and all my books into the world. David Rosenthal, the publisher, thank you for creating a safe place and believing that writers have a compass. Jason Booher, immense gratitude for your brilliant design gifts. Lynn Nesbit, my agent, I could thank you forever and it wouldn't be enough. You are like having a warrior by my side. And Dorothy Vincent, as always, my deep gratitude.

To my husband, Jerry Kass, my love and devotion. Your spirit and belief in me made all things possible.

DELIA EPHRON is a bestselling author and screenwriter. She has written novels, including *The Lion Is In* and *Hanging Up*; nonfiction, including *Sister Mother Husband Dog (etc.)*; and humor books for all ages including *How to Eat Like a Child* and *Do I Have to Say Hello?* Her films include *You've Got Mail*, *The Sisterhood of the Traveling Pants*, *Hanging Up* (based on her novel), and *Michael*. Her journalism has appeared in *The New York Times*, *O: The Oprah Magazine*, *Vogue*, and *Vanity Fair*. Her hit play *Love, Loss, and What I Wore* (cowritten with Nora Ephron) ran for more than two years off-Broadway and has been performed all over the world. She lives in New York City.